LADIES IN BOXES
GELETT BURGESS

LADIES IN BOXES
GELETT BURGESS

COACHWHIP PUBLICATIONS
Greenville, Ohio

Ladies in Boxes, by Gelett Burgess
© 2021 Coachwhip Publications edition
Cover: Doll © Anonymous

First published 1942
Gelett Burgess, 1866-1951
CoachwhipBooks.com

ISBN 1-61646-517-4
ISBN-13 978-1-61646-517-9

CHARACTERS

Characters Concerned with the "Beauty Murders"
(All of whom are imaginary)

Hale Gilbert, a Novelist, who tells the story, and who lives at the Hotel Imperial, New York City.

Bob Catfield, called "The Bobcat," a Police Detective.

Karl Van Diegen, a German photographer, famous for his portraits of celebrities and society women. He has a studio on East 49th Street.

Señor Corrijo, a wealthy Argentine wool broker, living in Riverdale.

Hugo Vlack, a window-draper, in love with Berta.

Pierre, Señor Corrijo's chauffeur.

Major Godwil, an English ex-army officer, living on Park Avenue.

Alfred Gross, District Attorney.

Captain Joseph Little, Head of Homicide Squad, New York Police.

Sergeant Dan Leary, Detective investigating the Magister murder.

Sergeant Pearson, Detective investigating the Viray murder.

Sam Jones, a Negro, husband of Mme. Viray's cook, Delia.

Berta Conley, a fashion reporter and stylist, living at the Imperial.

Mrs. "Biddy" Rumsey, a woman living at the Imperial.

Maude Magister, an Englishwoman, ex-actress, living at an apartment on East 46th Street.

Madame Hélène Viray, a Frenchwoman, divorced, formerly a singer, living in a small house on East 58th Street near the river.

Marcella Northey, Spanish-American night club dancer.

Dolores Tallia, Secretary to Señor Corrijo.

Mrs. Ball, slightly deranged housekeeper for Miss Magister.

Delia Jones, Negress, cook and housekeeper for Mme. Viray.

Fraulein Frische, Secretary to Karl Van Diegen.

1

DOLLS IN BOXES

My name is Hale Gilbert, and I am a writer; a novelist I might call myself, if you like a more conceited term. And this is the story of the most exciting week of my life. It was the week, a year ago, when the New York papers were full of the accounts of what they called "The Beauty Murders." All three of the victims were exceptionally beautiful women.

Now I have had the luck of seeing many beautiful women in my day. I have often been to the Ziegfeld Follies, of course. I have seen several of the Beauty Parades at Atlantic City, when half-nude maidens, chosen by popular vote, or selected by Chambers of Commerce from every state in the Union, exhibit their pulchritude in a march along the Boardwalk. I have met many of the glamour girls of Hollywood, only to find that the dictionary definition of "glamour" was correct—"a fictitious glory or beauty; a deceptive or alluring charm."

There are two kinds of feminine beauty—women's choice, and men's. If you are a man, your wife or sister may acclaim as a beauty a damsel who leaves you cold and uninterested. And your wife or sister may wonder why you are so magnetically attracted to Miss Somebody whom they consider no one at all to get worked up about. And so these three women I am going to tell about were beautiful, you must understand, from my point of view. A man's point of view. But, all the same, whenever any one of them was present I always noticed that not only men's but women's eyes rested upon her in fascinated fixity; the men's openly admiring, the women's reluctantly, in a kind of resentful envy.

It is common enough, too, you know, to hear of a woman that her photograph doesn't do her justice, and when you meet her she's really much more attractive than you had expected. They say that of the Duchess of Windsor, for example. But the saying involves something deeper than mere looks.

The fact undoubtedly is that no woman can be considered truly beautiful, no matter how good-looking, unless she has personality. You see innumerable women in life, on the stage, on the screen, whose faces seem perfect in form and proportions but who fail to impress you with any charm or even interest. A deadpan expression, or lack of expression, puts most of these females into the wax-work class.

On the other hand many women who, to most people, have no great claim to beauty, are considered beautiful by artists and discerning minds, because they have personality. They have faces through which shines a soul. They don't have to be celebrated in paints like the Mona Lisa; you may find them sometimes, behind the counter of a cafeteria. And this quality we call personality is other than mere animation or egoism; it is more compelling than sex allure; it is something distinctive and unique which attracts you and interests you and holds you and makes you remember. It is something that satisfies some psychic longing like a secret hunger in you. It's like a special flavor or perfume.

But whatever it is, a pleasing personality is always associated with intelligence. A stupid woman may be photogenic, but she is never really beautiful.

Each one of these three beautiful women I met that eventful week, had, in the highest degree, that gift of personality. Each one had a separate kind of charm. They were as different as vanilla, chocolate and sarsaparilla.

And so, this is how I happened to meet them.

I left the doll show that lovely late June afternoon right after the award of prizes, and took away my three exhibits. They were exquisite hand-made dolls; each one was a masterpiece. In one box I had a French doll, in another an English doll—these I had brought from abroad—and in a third box was an American doll. It was made by Lili Dexter, the miniaturist. I was going to send them to my little niece in California.

On my way home I found myself near Karl Van Diegen's studio, on East 54th St.; and as he appreciated beautiful things I decided to run up and show him the dolls.

Karl Van Diegen was known as one of the more distinguished portrait photographers in New York. He was a stocky and round-spectacled German with reddish hair and beard. About forty years old, I suppose he was. I didn't overly like him, but I admired him. He had a cool, detached manner, and a considerable culture and stiff dignity. He had, besides, a consummate self-possession. I couldn't imagine Van Diegen losing his temper, but I felt somehow that, with his cold blue eyes, and thick coarse lips, if he ever did he would be capable of the most studied and subtle cruelty. This was merely a vague impression, though. It was probably accented by the precise, deliberate way he moved and the slow manner in which he enunciated his words.

I took the little automatic elevator in the old house where Van Diegen had his studio, up to the fourth floor. As I went down the short hall towards his door, I was sensible of someone coming down the stairs behind me. Those narrow stairs led up to the penthouse where Van lived.

I turned and saw a woman in black and white go to the elevator and press the bell button. Her back was towards me so I didn't see her face, but from what I did glimpse there were suggestions of rare beauty. A fluid grace in her movements delighted me and I wondered who she was. The implications of her presence there made me smile, too. She had been upstairs in his living rooms. Van Diegen, I knew, had a peculiar success with women.

Van's door was opened by a hard, blonde German girl in goggles, a Fräulein Frisch, and I passed through a small waiting room into Van's picturesque studio. It was more like an ample living room and it hadn't the slightest professional look, except for the portly camera in the corner.

When Van took his pictures he usually offered his subject tea or cocktails, and while they talked and smoked he would keep rolling his big camera about as if he didn't exactly know where best to put it; and the sitter would frequently inquire impatiently, "Aren't you ever going to begin?" and Van would say that he'd already taken a dozen poses. There wasn't a notable actress, society beauty or popular author who hadn't gone to him. He had the talent of making the most unprepossessing woman look interesting without ever condescending to prettify her.

I stood looking at a large illuminated tank let into the wall, containing beautifully colored, feathery tropical fishes, when Van Diegen came in and greeted me with his usual heavy and elaborate courtesy which always kept one at a distance.

After he had looked at my dolls critically, he remarked that sometime I'd have to see the collection of historic dolls a friend of his had, a wealthy Argentino. Then he chuckled thickly and said,

"But I imagine from your novels, my dear Gilbert, that you're more interested in live dolls," and he went over to a table and brought back the photographs of three women and spread them out before me. "Venus, Minerva and Diana," he named them, in his dry, precise, humorous way.

They were indubitably the most beautiful women I have ever seen in my life, and I couldn't decide which of them was the most striking personality. The one he called Venus was so delicious, so alluringly feminized as to be almost sensual. Minerva, as you might guess, was more intellectual and aristocratic, with finely chiseled English features. Diana, it seemed to me vaguely, I had seen before, but at the moment, I couldn't quite place her. She was a distinctly American type and her head was poised with spirit; she had a frank, sincere look and lovely tangled hair. She attracted me the most of the three.

I asked Van who they were.

"Would you like to meet them, Gilbert?" he asked. And then he told me that if I were free on Thursday evening he would take me to a dinner to be given by the wealthy Argentino he had just mentioned. The three lovely ladies had been invited and he had been asked, he said, to get another man to balance the party of six.

"What our host actually said was 'get a gentleman,' my dear fellow," and Van Diegen chuckled and patted my shoulder. "But I think you may do," he said.

Well, as you may imagine, I didn't refuse that invitation.

And that is how I happened to meet, less than twenty-four hours before they were murdered, the three ladies whose death was to make all New York talk, and mystify the police.

Now curiously enough, Fate began to entangle me in the lives of those ladies even before that memorable dinner. One of them, you may recall, I had already seen that afternoon coming down from Van Diegen's penthouse.

I went into the lobby of my hotel, the Imperial, late that afternoon with the doll boxes under my arm and ran into a silly woman named Mrs. Rumsey—everybody called her Biddy. One of those hotel denizens, you know, who hang around lobbies and grin and talk to everybody who will stand for her. She was a short, plump, sweetish forty, with a mechanically perfect henna-blonde coiffure; and I had always hated that silly yellow straight fringe low on her forehead. That afternoon, however, I made no attempt to evade her because she happened to be sitting with a most attractive bright-eyed girl of about twenty or so, with lovely light brown hair.

The girl was in a red suit with a fine black figure in it and she wore a very smart red hat and red wedges and red patent leather bag. The costume, I thought, was rather original and effective.

Biddy grinned at me and called me over and presented me to Miss Berta Conley. As she, too, lived in the hotel, Biddy said she was "a fellow Imperialist," and she said to her, "Bertie, be properly impressed, my dear. Mr. Hale Gilbert is a famous author, you know."

We stood awhile there in the lobby gossiping and laughing. Biddy did most of the talking, though. She said with giggles that she used to live in the rooms Bertie now occupied, and that made them sort of sisters, didn't it? As she lived now on the floor only a few steps below, perhaps they were step-sisters, she said, and she laughed and laughed. Miss Conley laughed, too, politely; but she gave me a glance I understood. I hardly knew what Biddy was saying, though, because I was looking at Miss Conley all the time. Something about her puzzled me a bit. And it wasn't until Biddy had left, warning me not to fall in love, for Bertie was a terrible flirt, that it suddenly came to me that Miss Conley must be the original, by jove, of one of those three ladies whose photographs Van Diegen had just shown me—the one he had called Diana. She was the one I had liked most of all.

Miss Conley's fine hazel eyes had a suppressed touch of mischief in them when she said she had heard of me and had even read some of my books. She lingered, evidently quite willing to prolong the interview, so we sat down on a huge carved oak settee that had once been elegant, and as we chatted about the wonders of the old hotel as it used to be in the gay '90's, I opened the three boxes.

"Oh, how lovely!" she said. "But—why, they aren't dolls, Mr. Gilbert," she laughed. "They're really little ladies, aren't they? And look, this one has hair just the color of mine." She held it up side of her pretty face. "What's her name?"

I smiled, and she seemed so friendly that I ventured to say that it was Berta; and she laughed a vigorous young laugh and she said,

"Oh thank you, Mr. Gilbert, that's cute of you. Do let me name the others, then." She took the one with the black hair out of the box, looked at it for a moment, and then said her name should be Hélène. "And that lovely golden blonde," she said, "her name is Maude. Oh, I'm sure it's Maude."

We laughed, and I put the dolls back into their boxes, and we kept on talking about this and that; and finally we walked towards the elevators. I thought it best to say nothing about the dinner on Thursday. It would be fun, I thought, to surprise her by my appearance there.

Miss Conley was a sort of freelance designer and fashion reporter, she said, and what they call a stylist. As we waited, she told me she had been "stealing fashions" that day, and she took a notebook from her red bag and showed me several very clever sketches of hats and costumes she had made on the street and even in shops, on the sly. She would study them, she said, and commit all the details to memory, and then hurry down to the women's rest room and quickly get the sketch into her book.

We soon discovered that we both lived in the Annex of the Hotel, and we walked through the famous Red Room of Stanford White's with its heavy orotundities of stucco wreaths, garlands and cornices, to the 31st St. entrance. And when the elevator stopped for us at the 7th floor Miss Conley asked me if I wouldn't come into her rooms for a little chat.

The Annex of the Imperial was originally a smart and spacious apartment house. It was taken over by the hotel when the Imperial was in its glory as the largest and finest hostelry in New York, patronized by Lillian Russell, Diamond Jim Brady and the theatrical aristocracy of that gay period. The eight and ten room apartments of the Annex had been divided into smaller suites. Mine was No. 761; I had three rooms, with a big one on the corner of Broadway and 31st St., full of great wide windows. And I found to my amusement that Miss Conley's was No. 768, right next door. She had a two-room suite with a sitting room looking out on Broadway. She had been in the hotel only ten days, she said.

Outside her door there was a case of bottled spring water. She said she'd call one of the elevator boys to take it in, but I insisted on carrying it through her bedroom and setting it in under the wash bowl in her bathroom. She already had a partly filled bottle on a table in her living room.

"I'm a cold water fiend, Mr. Gilbert," she said, "and I always drink six or seven glasses every day. Water and walking, and a raw carrot and a lemon a day beat any make-up ever made." She pulled off her hat and hung it on the top of an easel standing there and then I took the glass she offered me and then she poured herself a glass. We laughed and drank to each other as if it were champagne. I liked her. I liked her a lot.

We were sitting there, chatting about the hotel and the styles and the war when her telephone bell rang. She took up the receiver with a little impatience; then her face grew strained.

"No," she said. "No, I can't. No, I'm sorry, Hugo, it's absolutely impossible. I'm awfully sorry. Please don't call again." Then she gave a little forced laugh. "Oh, no, I'm *not!*" and after a second, "No, I can't, Hugo, really. No, I can't see you at all! Good-bye."

Then she turned to me, a bit confused, evidently.

"I'll really have to apologize, Mr. Gilbert," she said. "It was a man whom I don't want to see at all. I can't understand how he ever found out that I'm here, and it's most annoying." She gave me a look. "In fact, it's dangerous, in a way. I'm afraid I may have to leave the hotel."

I reached for an ash tray on the table. "Really dangerous?" I asked. I thought she was fooling, or romancing perhaps.

She sat a moment quiet, evidently thinking of Hugo, while I smoked and watched her. It was very easy to watch Berta Conley. Finally she looked up at me and smiled. "Well, I guess—I'll have to tell you," she said. "I can't seem to get him out of my mind." She got up uneasily and went and looked out of the window, onto Broadway, and then came back to me.

"Why, you see, Mr. Gilbert," she said, "I trotted around quite a little with this man last year, but he really got to be so absurdly jealous that I couldn't stand it any longer. He has a terrible temper, you know, and he's kind of queer and intense, and—well, I'm afraid he might do something reckless."

Then she abruptly changed the subject, and we went on talking about the war, and would we fight. But I could see she was pretty nervous. So I asked her about her work and she braced up and after a while she told me how she wanted to paint; and she got up and was about to show me a drawing when the telephone rang again.

"Oh, no, no, no, Biddy," she said impatiently, "really, I'm awfully busy just now." And Berta smiled at me archly. "I can't see anybody, Biddy, I just can't! I'm so sorry. . . . All right, after dinner, perhaps."

And then she told me that Biddy Rumsey was an awful bore. Biddy, she said, came up to her room all the time and borrowed things, and helped herself to perfume and everything; she was a perfect pest.

I was having a pretty good time. I told Miss Conley that I could forgive Biddy a good deal for having introduced her to me. She smiled roguishly and shook her finger at me. I asked her what the dictaphone on a stand by the window was for, and she told me she wrote fashion articles for a string of Western papers and she was trying it to see if she could save time that way.

She jumped up again and went into her bedroom and brought back some very clever little grotesque animals and figures she had made out of that striped blue-and-white insulated wire electricians use, which she said could be modeled better than the fuzzy pipe cleaners often used.

The figures were cleverly done, I thought—little dancing girls, and little men on horseback, and little toreadors and baseball pitchers. And then she showed me a crayon sketch she had just made.

It was the caricature of a Spanish-looking gentleman, dark and handsome. He was a friend of hers, she said, from Argentina. Could it be Van Diegen's friend? I wondered. She had pictured him attitudinizing with one hand on his heart and the other raised in a passionate gesture. We laughed and laughed over it. It was full of obvious ridicule, but remarkably well drawn.

I said, "I hate to think what you'd do to me in a caricature like that, Miss Conley. I know you'd betray my most secret fault."

"Probably," she said, "you'd hate me for ever after—but all your friends would scream at it. Caricatures and imitations of people are dangerous amusements. I'm afraid I've made a lot of enemies doing these caricatures," she said, "and I'm almost afraid to make any more."

I couldn't take my eyes off her. The way she threw her hair around when she turned her head fascinated me. I wondered if it wasn't the sort of fascinating awkwardness in her gestures—they were all extraverted gestures, she flung her arms outward a good deal—that made her seem so honest. Aren't we inclined, I thought, to distrust people who are too graceful? And then her phone rang again.

After she had said "Yes," and "No," and "All right" a few times she put down the receiver and told me that a friend of hers, an English girl, she said, a Maude Magister, was coming up and they were going to dine at Schrafft's together. As she didn't ask me to wait and see Miss Magister, I left immediately.

The next day was Wednesday. It was the day before the dinner to be given by Van Diegen's Argentine friend, and to which, as you may imagine, I was now looking forward with a new interest and curiosity.

Well, I had worked hard for several hours, that forenoon in my study, and I got up to stretch my legs and think out a fiction problem that had been puzzling me. I was standing at a window in my front room, I remember, watching a fire engine screaming up the street, when I happened to notice a man standing on the opposite side of Broadway. He was looking up at the hotel. When I went back to the window, after a while, to see if he were still there, darned if the fellow wasn't using opera glasses; and he appeared to be looking up at my windows, too, or those beside mine, which would be Miss Conley's, I couldn't be sure which. A tall, thin man, he was, almost gaunt. I wondered what the devil he was up to.

I got out my binoculars and hid behind a curtain. He looked something like William Powell, the movie star, his moustache did anyway, and he was dark. He stayed there on the sidewalk half an hour or so, it seemed to me, using his opera glasses occasionally.

The queer way he acted, so persistent, and all, made me pretty sure he must be the man Miss Conley had talked to on the phone, the night before. He was watching for her to come out, I suspected. Of course it was none of my business, but I didn't just like his hanging around like that; and I was relieved when I saw him walking off down Broadway. Well, I thought that perhaps my imagination had run away with me, and I went back to work and forgot all about it.

That afternoon I caught sight of the third of the trio of ladies whom I was to meet at that fateful dinner on Thursday evening.

I was walking up Fifth Avenue looking into windows, here and there, and I noticed Karl Van Diegen ahead of me, striding along in his tall, round-shouldered, abstracted way just ahead of me. He was always taking a walk on Fifth Avenue; looking for models, perhaps. I hurried to overtake him.

While I was still a little way behind him I saw him stop and greet a lady who had just come hurrying out of Arnold Constable's. She was rather tall and she was very simply but smartly dressed in a tweed coat and a plain felt sport hat. A bit mannish, she looked; or perhaps only a little too British. I lingered in a doorway and watched the pair; and when she turned so that I could see her blonde hair and fine, sharply chiseled features I was pretty sure that she was the lady whose photograph Van Diegen had shown me the day before—the one he had called Minerva. She had an aristocratic, intellectual look, and she was strikingly beautiful. By the expressive way she used her hands, and the way she moved, I judged that she might have been an actress.

Van Diegen walked with her, still talking with animation, to the curb where a taxi was standing. They stood there some little time. They seemed to be having some sort of discussion, a disagreement evidently, for she was gesticulating with emphasis, as if denying some charge. He merely nodded his head up and down occasionally, slowly; but I knew with what firmness he could press an accusation or repel an argument.

Karl Van Diegen needed no gestures to make his words carry home. Well, after a while she got into the taxi, still gesticulating, and drove off.

I thought it best not to speak to Van Diegen just then; there seemed to be a little situation there, but I did want to arrange with him more explicitly about going to the dinner he had invited me to Thursday night, and so towards five o'clock I went over again to his place on East 49th St.

In the little square vestibule I pressed the button and stood a moment, waiting for the automatic elevator. When it came down and the door opened, a young girl came out. She was a small slim creature about eighteen years old perhaps. She had on a plaid dress and a cocky little green felt hat with a quill, and she was crying. At least she was holding her handkerchief to her eyes. She had dark hair and an olive complexion, and she was rather pretty, but of course not in any way comparable to the compelling beauty of the three lovely ladies of Van Diegen's photographs. She didn't look at me at all, but went right out to the street rapidly.

Van Diegen's studio is on the fourth floor. There are rooms and offices on the second and third floors, I knew; and it was possible, of course, that the girl had come from one of those other places. But I had an impression, perhaps because Van Diegen knew so many pretty women professionally and socially, that she had come from his studio. And long after I had finished my talk with Van (of course I didn't ask him about her), I kept thinking about that young girl and wondering who she was, and why she had been crying.

But she soon passed out of my mind. It was those three lovely ladies who haunted me all the rest of that day. I decided to ask Van Diegen for copies of those photographs. For, when I went to bed that night, it occurred to me that they would be splendid characters for a novel—those three ladies, rivals, perhaps—and as I fell asleep I was trying to work out a fitting story.

I didn't know that Fate was writing that plot; and that the drama I was soon to see unfold and tie those ladies into a complicated tragedy, was far more thrilling than any my brain might concoct.

2

LADIES AT DINNER

The next day, Thursday, I called for Karl Van Diegen in my car at about 6 P.M. Van was ready in his studio in evening attire, but he said he couldn't leave for the dinner until his assistant, that disagreeable Miss Frisch, had come back. And while we waited there he told me, with his slightly guttural accent, rather slowly and heavily, with every word pronounced precisely, that we were going to dine that evening with the Señor Alberto Alvarez Corrijo, in Riverdale.

"The Señor," Van said, "is possessed of what the newspapers term 'fabulous wealth.' He has millions, anyway," he said, "and he loves to spend them." And Van told me with a satirical inflection, that besides collecting dolls, the noble Señor had other hobbies. One of them was rings. Van said that the Señor had a truly wonderful collection of rings, historic, priceless. Rings out of ancient tombs, he said, seal rings of emperors, poison rings and puzzle rings, and cabalistic charms; and for all Van knew he had rings that made one invisible or conjured up genii.

All this was intriguing enough, but what I was interested in most, I said, were the three ladies I was to meet; and I asked Van who they were.

"The one I call Diana," he said, "is Miss Berta Conley. She lives at the Hotel Imperial, so perhaps you know her." He gave me a shrewd glance. "You said nothing about her, however, when you saw her photograph. Discreet, perhaps?"

I protested that I hadn't known her then, but that I had met her since.

Van shrugged and smiled and went on. "Minerva," he said, "is a friend of Miss Conley's—an English girl named Maude Magister. Very good family, I understand; but I presume that Magister is her stage name, as she is somewhat of an actress, I believe, or has been. She is rather intelligent," he said. "Look out for her, my dear fellow. She may try to discuss phlogistics or the theories of mutation."

He handed me another photograph. "And the third one, here," he said, "the Venus of the trio, is Mme. Hélène Viray, a French woman, divorcée. She has a modest income, I believe, enough to make her want more. She hasn't been in New York very long, and I know nothing of her history. She has sung in concerts, but I trust the Señor won't ask her to sing. I don't like to encourage women who think they can sing."

I laughed and asked him if the three ladies were particular friends of his as well as beautiful clients.

"All my clients are my friends, I hope," he said dryly, "but they are friends rather of Señor Corrijo. Perhaps very good friends indeed. Whether or not he is *their* friend, and how fond a friend, perhaps you may be able to surmise this evening. Each of the three ladies, I think, would like to marry him—and his millions. They seem to be running, so to speak, neck and neck. We should have an amusing time tonight."

While he went upstairs to his penthouse apartment to get something he needed, I strolled over to a corner and on a small table I noticed a pile of curly photographic prints, silver prints they were. I picked them up and found that they were all studies of the three ladies we had been talking about, taken from various angles.

I was looking at them when his assistant, Fraulein Frisch, came in. I had never liked Fraulein Frisch. She seemed hard and dry. And I detest hair in braids wound up tightly about a woman's head like a sort of skullcap, and especially when it's yellow hair. I don't think she liked me very much, either, for she rather abruptly took the photographs from my hand and said she wished to put them away.

I said, "They're not at all like Van's usual work, are they? So sharply focused, you know, and literal, like a commercial photographer's. And taken from all points of the compass, too, they are, aren't they? Like the photographs of criminals, almost—full face, three-quarters, profile, all the way round, and there's even a back view of each of them."

The Fraulein seemed annoyed. She stared at me without expression. "Those studies were made for Señor Corrijo," she said tightly. "He knows what he wants, I suppose, and he pays very well for what he wants. They aren't meant to be shown." And she marched out of the room.

I looked at the fish with feathery tails, in the wall aquarium. I looked at several framed photographs of famous actresses.

Van Diegen came back soon and blew his nose rather snortily and remarked that I'd probably see some beautiful gowns tonight at Señor Corrijo's—all by the smartest *couturier* in New York. Each of the ladies, Van said, had been presented by the Señor with a costume to be photographed in. "It should be diverting," he said, "to see the three together—three goddesses." And Van chuckled. "Perhaps the Señor will award the golden apple tonight," he said.

"It sounds promising," I said. And then I asked him, "You mean he'll choose his bride?"

Van drew on his coat and adjusted a top hat to a careless angle. "That's what they're all of them expecting, I
imagine. He is a very wealthy man, you know. A great
catch for the lucky girl."

As we drove up Fifth Avenue through the traffic Berta
Conley's face came back to me—the joyous, frank girl I
had talked to at my hotel. And I felt a shock of disappointment to think of her participating in such a merce-
nary contest. Still, the natural goal of beauty is money, I
thought. What's the use of good looks if a girl can't realize
on them and advance herself socially? Berta, I knew, was
intelligent and ambitious. And money means influence
and power.

Van Diegen told me to drive out to Riverdale Avenue,
and then he would direct me to where the house was; and
he smoked cigarettes in a long white holder as we sped out
Riverside Drive in a thin, warm rain.

We talked about women's vanity. Van Diegen held that
vanity was the animating motive for everything women
did, whether in dress, education, business, art, sport, love,
charity or crime. Vanity, with women, corresponded, he
said, to what in men was called ambition. *"Vanitas, vani-
tatem,"* he quoted, ironically, and lighted another cigarette.

He had never had a woman customer, Van Diegen asserted, no matter how ugly, who didn't secretly think that
she was beautiful and could be flattered inordinately.
Women were all egoists, he said, self-centered, and ruthless and bloodthirsty, even—and yet, he said, they were
so amazingly credulous. Did any woman ever consult a
psychic or mystic, he asked me, and not expect and always
come away with some marvelous divination or prophecy?

Van Diegen's business was, largely, the flattering of
women's vanity, and naturally it had increased his innate
cynicism; but he had a dry, ponderous kind of humor that
rather amused me. I did my best to defend the fair sex;

not so much from chivalry, perhaps, as to keep him going. I care as little as anyone for generalities, but I said that women were self-sacrificing and more thorough and loyal and conscientious than men.

Van smiled and nodded sagely. If I didn't believe women were vicious, he said, I had only to ask them. Women were their own worst enemies, he asserted; and did I know a single one who wasn't ready to expose any other woman's tricks? Or one who honestly preferred women to men? Weren't they, in fact, always giving each other away, and selling their sex short?

I laughed; he was funny. And I told Van I didn't know why it was men enjoyed running women down like that; but making fun of women certainly was one of men's oldest games, apparently. They get the same fun out of it as they do in watching monkeys or laughing at babies. Even when they don't mean it, men together will joke cruelly about women and then go home and love, honor and obey their wives, even consider them angels.

"And every man's angel," Van chuckled, "will call every other man's angel a devil."

It was the old inbred rivalry and intrigue of the harem, he said—women's machinations for the favor of man, who alone could confer value. Women couldn't help it, poor souls, he said, it was in their blood. They weren't yet civilized, because they had never learned to co-operate. They were individualists because they had had for ages to stay at home alone in caves and boil the pot and sew the skins and tend the brat while their men were off hunting and fighting and learning the rules of playing the game together, one for all, and all for one. In short, constructing society.

"Then you don't consider women mysterious?" I asked him as we sped on, with the rain coming down a little harder, and I quoted Chaucer:

"'When the rain raineth,
  And the goose winketh,
  Little wots the gander
  What the goose thinketh.'"

"I think this, Gilbert," said Van Diegen, "educated
or ignorant, women are all actuated by only the simplest
primitive emotions, principally erotic passion and the
love of decoration. Their reactions are direct, and predict-
able. When they want a thing, they go for it in a straight
line, without regard or compunction, difficulty or consequences. That's why women murderers are more easily
caught than men. They leave a trail of fire."

We had crossed the viaduct and I was driving at an easy
pace in the rain. After we had got out on Riverdale Avenue a few miles, Van told me to slow down and in a few
moments he showed me where to turn in through a rather
pretentious stone gateway into a small park of chestnut
trees and formal gardens. The Corrijo residence appeared
as a large, handsome white Colonial mansion, and we drew
up at a wide portico with marble pillars. It was fronted by
a semicircular lawn with statues and a fountain.

Van had told me that the Argentine had dozens of servants and lived in truly princely style, and I found the
inside of the house, as I had expected, luxurious and elegant, almost palatial.

The minute Señor Corrijo appeared, smiling, in evening attire and wearing several foreign decorations, and
welcomed us with a sweeping flourish, I recognized him as
the unmistakable prototype of the caricature Berta Conley
had shown me that day in her room at the Imperial. He
even gestured with his cigarette in his hand, just as she
had portrayed him. He was fairly tall, but with a stocky
well-fed figure, and, with his heavy black hair and black
moustache and goatee, and even with his heavy John L.

Lewis eyebrows, he was undeniably handsome, in a swar-
thy Spanish way.

In spite of Berta's clever exaggeration of his rather
theatrical Latin manner, I liked him at once. The Señor
was indubitably a personage. He had a certain command-
ing pose and manner, as one used to money and power;
but he had a high-bred graciousness, too, that put you at
your ease; and a cultivated, deep, sympathetic voice, with
only the slightest trace of accent. I felt that, if I were an
ambitious woman, he was the kind of man I might like to
marry. Whatever he might be, underneath all that charm
and courtesy, he would at least be a personable, authorita-
tive, distinguished husband.

That doesn't mean, however, that I, as a man, would
altogether trust him. You can never judge a person, I've
found, until you have seen him, or her, angered. And I am
always a little suspicious of a person who smiles as much
as did the Señor.

We had been ushered by two tall liveried servants into
a handsome gold-walled reception room, and there we had
a cocktail or two and cigarettes with the Señor before the
ladies appeared. There was a slim, tall, Spanish-looking
girl in black satin with a red rose in her hair. Her black
hair was parted in the center and drawn tightly back. She
was fluttering about and smiling a lot, too, waiting to
receive the guests and take them upstairs. Señor Corrijo
spoke of her as his secretary.

Mme. Viray, the first of the ladies to arrive, drove out
alone that night in her smart little green sedan. She came in
with grace and immediately filled the room with her exquisite femininity. I recognized her from her movements and
her walk as the lady whom I had caught a glimpse of coming
down the stairs from Van Diegen's penthouse on Tuesday.

She was the one Van had called Venus. Her eyes were
a deep brown and with her dark hair elaborately coiffed,

and a carelessly curly little bang, and her white teeth, she was, in that blazing Chinese red gown with sequins oddly scattered down one side, easily the most sensationally beautiful creature I have ever seen. And if I sound a bit perfervid, I'll have to confess that I haven't even yet described what, in Hélène Viray, charmed me most.

There is, in some women's faces—but only one in thousands has it—a peculiar and subtle modeling of the cheekbones just below the eyes that I have always called, to myself, the "locus of beauty." And it gives to a woman's face, even to one otherwise plain, sometimes, a spiritual, almost, one might say, an angelic quality. In Hélène Viray's face, it lent her countenance a singular and delicate purity.

"Oh, my dear Señor," she almost sang; her contralto voice had a piquant French accent, and she held out her hand to kiss. "What time it is, your dinner? Perhaps I am too late, is that so? I am confused." She gave a playful, deep curtsy and said, "It seems, my dear Señor, I have not seen you this vairee long time ago. And I invited you so much to come and see me! You are a vairee bad, bad gentleman."

She turned to greet Van Diegen, and he too bent low and kissed her perfect hand. I was presented and we shook hands merely. Then she suddenly whirled around and postured and asked us all how we liked her gown, and she laughed and showed her perfect white teeth. I looked at her entranced. After a moment or two of persiflage she sat down on a settee covered with golden damask, and she beckoned to me and said,

"Oh, Mr. Gilbert, you are an author! How wonderful! I have always wanted to write a book, Mr. Gilbert, and some day I shall write a book so big as that! All about *Me!* My own self! Vairee interesting and vairee wicked, won't that be a good thing?" And she laughed with her eyes half closed.

Hélène Viray had lovely dark eyes; but truly lovely lips are much rarer, and it was her sensitive mouth with its delicate nuances of emotion and humor that I found myself watching.

She asked me where I lived, and when I told her she made a pretty little *moue* (because I hadn't a smart East Side address, I took it), then she shrugged and said,

"Oh, I from time to time go there. It is a not so bad place, the Impériale. I have a friend who live there, too." Then she rose and looked towards the door. "Oh, what you think! There she is now! Miss Conley!"

Berta Conley and Miss Magister had arrived together. They had been driven out in one of the Señor's cars and then there was a lot of feminine chatter. Pretty, lively Berta Conley, with her brisk, familiar manner was the very antithesis of the graceful ultra-feminine Mme. Viray. Berta swung in like a breeze and gave a jolly laugh and cried out in a light, prankish tone,

"Hello, everybody! Are we late? And if not, why not, and what the hell, anyway! Evening, my lord Señor!" and she waved a high hand. "Hello, Van!" She seized Van Diegen's forefinger and shook it joyously. And then she caught sight of me and she stopped in amazement.

"Well, the idea!" she exclaimed. "Think of seeing *you,* Mr. Gilbert! Why didn't you tell me you were coming? Why, you complete monster! Do you realize that you deprived a sweet young girl of twenty-four hours of blissful anticipation?" and her fresh young laughter ran up the scale and down again, and she looked at me in a way that was delightfully flattering.

Mme. Viray smiled at me with half closed eyes and said to Berta, "I think that man is vairee dangerous, Bertie dear. He is clevaire!"

Berta Conley, with her light brown hair so carelessly done, in that beautiful lemon yellow satin gown, very low-necked, looked maddeningly ravishing. You wanted to grab her and kiss her to death. But, beside the graceful, all but exotic dark Mme. Viray, she seemed a bit—well, if I must be snobbish —American. I mean merely that she was so careless and jaunty and—I don't know—healthy, with a sort of lovable *gaminerie,* that she didn't quite know how to wear that exquisite gown. She carried it as if it were a gingham play suit. But she was so frank and mirthful and such a good fellow that you forgave her slight lack of grace and dignity.

Just then, outside in the vaulted, white marble corridor I heard another woman's musical laughter and a clear-cut voice with a lifted aristocratic English accent and inflection. She was talking, evidently, to the Señor's chauffeur. And when she made her appearance—like a lady at court, I thought—dignified, but easy, oh, so easy and experienced in her manner, I saw that she was the same lady I had seen on Wednesday on Fifth Avenue, at Arnold Constable's talking with Karl Van Diegen. She was the one he had called Minerva.

Miss Maude Magister was the tallest of the three ladies, and she was a blue-eyed authentic blonde. Perhaps twenty-two or three, I took her to be. Her golden hair was quite short and she wore it in a complicated mass of little curls. It gave her head—she had a small head—a statuesque Grecian look. She had on a silk gown of a strange smoky blue, and there was no doubt of *her* being able to carry it off with superb style.

Maude Magister was, in fact, a highly finished civilized product. She seemed a bit cold and detached until she smiled; and then you found yourself waiting and hoping for that smile and trying to evoke it; but it came rarely. I can understand how a certain kind of man would rather enjoy pursuing and savagely conquering a self-controlled intellectual woman like her, and reducing her to a more human and passionate level.

I watched her with an amused interest when she greeted Van Diegen and I got the idea that she didn't exactly like his ironic manner, for she turned quickly to me and she said, with animation,

"I feel almost as if we were old friends, really, Mr. Gilbert. Miss Conley grew fairly lyric about you, coming out here, although she didn't tell me that you were going to make a personal appearance tonight." Then she smiled at Miss Conley. "It's a new pose of yours, isn't it, Berta? Fancy your being sly!"

"I'm not sly!" said Berta, laughing. "I'm candid. Everybody with hazel eyes is candid. Mr. Gilbert didn't tell me he was going to be here, that's all. *He's* the one who's sly."

"Oh," said Mme. Viray merrily, "nevaire be sly! If you're sly you'll be caught. It isn't clevaire to be sly, it's clevaire only to be clevaire, then you're nevaire caught—are you, Mr. Gilbert?"

I said in the same frivolous tone, "When you're entrancingly beautiful, Mme. Viray, you don't need to be clever or sly or anything but your own beautiful self." And we all laughed. And we all had more cocktails.

Miss Magister turned again to her host and said in her crisp, high-bred English way,

"Really, my dear Señor, you'll have to look out for that chauffeur of yours. We narrowly escaped an accident, didn't we, Berta? He bent a fender rather badly, you know, scraping into a telegraph pole, and we were frightened no end, really." Then she laughed. "Oh, but of course he's so horribly good-looking you could forgive that man almost anything, couldn't you?"

Señor Corrijo had never known Pierre to be careless, he said; he had always been most trustworthy. He couldn't understand it.

Berta Conley said that a man oughtn't to smoke while he was driving, anyway. The smoke gets in your eyes, she said.

Then Maude Magister dismissed the subject with a wave of her sparkling evening bag and she said, in her staccato way,

"Six is the ideal number for a dinner party, isn't it? It's really the most you can have in a single conversational group, you know, without any breaking up into exclusive tetê-á-têtes. We can all talk, and all listen, can't we? It ought to be no end jolly." Then she looked about, and said, with a touch of whimsicality, "It *is* a rather interesting party, here tonight, you know, really, isn't it? Fair women and brave men and all that. I must say, Señor, you do know how to do it well, don't you? It's quite too bad there's no motion picture camera here to record this notable occasion, isn't it?"

"There will be," said the Señor quietly.

"Really?" cried the lovely dark Mme. Viray. *"Quelle joie!"* and she clapped her hands. "Oh, I shall be ever so much happy to at last be in a cinema! Soon we shall be all Hollywood stars, *n'est ce pas?"*

Miss Magister turned to me. She was like a cold Greek statue against the gold of that salon wall. "You never quite know what the Señor is going to do, Mr. Gilbert, except that it will be something delightful and amazing."

Mme. Viray said dreamily, "You never know what *I'm* going to do, either, Mr. Gilbert—I hope." And we all laughed at the way she said it. "I would be *desolée* if I thought no longer I could give you a surprise."

"Oh, please do something wonderful," said Berta, she had a touch of mischief in her voice, "tonight! Please do surprise us, Hélène!"

Mme. Viray made an amusing melodramatic gesture, and she said in a deep voice, "I might murder somebody.

Would that be a nice surprise?" and she laughed and half closed her eyes.

Maude Magister put out her hand. "Oh, no—no murdering, please, Hélène; not till after dinner, anyway. Better begin with a little mild crime like robbery, you know, and work up to a climax towards midnight."

And Van Diegen said: "Please don't murder *me,* Hélène. I always hate to be murdered. It bores me."

After a lot more of that sort of thing, Señor Corrijo asked me if I were married and apologized for not inviting my wife, if I had one. I said I didn't, and ventured to ask him if he were married.

He smiled inscrutably. "I shall be, soon," he said. The three ladies' heads turned to him as if pulled by wires.

I said, "Then you're engaged, Señor, I suppose?"

The three ladies watched him, and in the sudden hush I think he enjoyed their curiosity—their anxiety, perhaps. Anyway, he took his time in answering.

"No," he said, smiling down at his cigar. "I have not yet chosen my bride."

It was a rather ticklish situation and it amused me. I felt sort of hellish, and I ventured to take advantage of everybody's sudden interest, so I said, "Well, you ought to be able to get any woman you wish, Señor Corrijo, with your masterful personality."

Van Diegen chuckled and said, *"And* your money."

Berta laughed and said, "And your looks."

Mme. Viray said in her colorful foreign contralto, "And your charm, Señor!" And how she smiled!

Maude Magister had the last word. She gave him a little mock salute. *"And* your experience, Señor!"

We were joking like that when dinner was announced. We passed into a magnificent dining room paneled in rosewood and lighted entirely by hundreds, it seemed to me, of red candles. At a wide, round-topped, mullioned window, the silk curtains were not drawn and outside there was a little patch of lawn and flower bed dim in the twilight.

Before taking seats the ladies stood at that window a moment or two, looking out. The weather had cleared, and they spoke of how the rain had brought out the scent of the roses, and about the stars; and they told one another how nice they looked. Van Diegen, watching them, nudged me, and grinned.

That dinner, as you may imagine, was diverting. It was easy enough to believe, when I saw them together, that the three women were rivals for Corrijo's favor—and his fortune. Not that there was any overt competition, of course; they were too civilized for that; but to my mind each was trying her best to surpass the others in animation and allure.

The urbane Señor, if he had arranged the affair for a purpose (and I suspected just that) certainly got his money's worth that evening. And it was a part of my enjoyment, and Van Diegen's too, I knew, to watch the clever way the Señor distributed his elegant attentions amongst the three ladies.

But not quite equally, I thought. It seemed to me that Berta Conley attracted him most, and I imagined that Mme. Viray noticed it too. She broke into their conversation often and seemed to be putting forth a little more effort to be gay every time that Berta made him laugh. Trust a Frenchwoman for that!

Maude Magister noticed it too, I thought, but she seemed merely amused, and she devoted herself mainly to Van Diegen and me. But don't think that keen, fine young lady didn't keep an eye on the Señor, meanwhile.

I don't think, though, I've ever been at a dinner where the conversation was better balanced. Everyone talked and everyone listened; and no one told long stories and no one tactlessly interrupted. And all the time we heard a faint,

wildish music from outside, somewhere, rising and falling
in fascinating rhythms. We talked of everything but the
war—that subject being by tacit consent *tabu,* the news
at that time was disheartening—and we were all laughing
most of the time. That is, at first.

Well, that gorgeous butler was opening bottles and pouring wine all the time, and the almost as gorgeous waiters
were going and coming and bringing things and taking away
things, and my plate was being changed, but I don't really
know what the marvelous dishes were that were served that
night—terrapin, I imagine, and little spicy game birds and
things under glass, and tropical strange fruits—I hardly
tasted the food. I do know we all drank, though, and that
the wines were plentiful and rare and stimulating.

We all drank, that is, but Berta Conley. She said she
never took anything but water.

Señor Corrijo made a ridiculous face. "Not that awful
stuff?" he asked. "Surely not that vile liquid in the old
corroded pipes of your old hotel?"

"Oh no," Berta laughed, "I always keep a lot of spring
water on hand. It doesn't take wine to intoxicate *me,* you
know." And she smiled dangerously on our host.

Mme. Viray quickly looked at her. Then she, too, got
in a smile at him that was devastating.

Then, for a moment, queerly, no one spoke. You know
those sudden silences that come, sometimes, in a general
conversation, as if by some concerted action? When I was a
boy we used to have a saying, and a belief, too, that those
lulls in the talk always occur at twenty minutes after or
before the hour. It sounds silly, but we always used to look
at the clock and very often it was proved true. I sometimes
find myself, even now, looking at my watch, at such times.

Well, during this momentary hush, I heard, and perhaps we all heard, I don't know, but I know Corrijo did, a
sound outside, and a voice some distance away.

It sounded like a heavy crate being set down on a concrete path or floor, and it reminded me of how cases of arms and ammunition used to sound, in the first World War, when they were being unloaded. The voice, faint though it was, was surely the voice of the Señor's secretary, for I had particularly noted an odd little whine in it. She had called out, in Spanish,

"No, not here! Over there, you fool! And be quiet!"

I was looking at Señor Corrijo. He seemed annoyed, even a little alarmed, I thought; and he half rose from his chair. But the music happened to grow louder just then, and Berta laughed aloud, too, in the silence, and we began to talk again. The Señor seemed relieved.

After another course of something delicious, the Señor, as suave as ever, now, called in the picture men. We were all still in a laughing mood.

Electric flood lights were set up and a camera brought in and Miss Magister and Mme. Viray went to work on their faces, although they protested that they would look ghastly without special movie make-up. Berta Conley didn't seem to bother about her looks.

"And now, Mr. Gilbert," the Señor said, "since you are a writer, suppose you tell us a story to amuse us—so that our expressions, you know, will be natural. I don't want the pictures to be stiff."

Well, I was flabbergasted. I had no idea what to say; I couldn't think of a darned thing. But I was in for it; I had to make good, somehow, as an author, so I smiled rather sillily, I expect. And then, having not the slightest notion of how I'd ever come out, I began.

You see, I had happened, luckily, just in time, to remember something a very clever chap I used to know once said He said that it would be a swell idea to concoct a little fable that you could get off on any occasion when you didn't know what to say. It would be so cryptic, he suggested, that people would think it must be clever, and they'd have to pretend to understand it. In that way it would apply to virtually anything. And he always said it might begin in the classic way, "There was once a fox." And so I assumed an air of wisdom and said,

"Well, there was once a fox."

And there I stuck. Everyone looked at me eagerly. I was sweating. I fully expected to have to stop ignominiously and confess my impotency. But as I looked at the Señor, to my relief, I suddenly got an idea.

"And this fox," I said, "was an inveterate thief; and he took steady toll from the hen roosts of a farmer." I shook my finger at Corrijo.

"I am *not* a fox," laughed the Señor. "I think I must be the goat."

"Now that farmer's hens," I went on, "were lovely hens. Perfectly lovely."

"Don't tell us we are going to be hens!" said Berta. She had caught on quickly.

I went on. "But there were so many fine hens—beg pardon, ladies, I mean chickens, of course—in the farmer's roosts that the fox couldn't make up his mind which he liked best."

Van Diegen chuckled and said, "And so he took them all?"

"No. He couldn't take but one at a time," I said.

"Why not?" asked the Señor, laughing.

"I don't know," I said.

"Perhaps," said Karl Van Diegen in his heavy way, "he thought the hens would fight amongst themselves," and he chuckled again and wiped his moist brow.

The ladies had laughed, but had made no comments so far, and they now looked a bit self-conscious. I couldn't tell whether it was because of the obvious application of my fable, or from the fact that a photographer had mounted a table with his tripod and had begun to turn the crank of his camera.

The three ladies were sitting round the table in characteristic attitudes. Berta had both elbows on the table and held a cigarette carelessly in one hand. She seemed, though, to be unconcerned at the fact that she was being photographed. But then, Berta was always a little different from other women, in whatever she did. I suppose it was because she was more artless and natural.

Maude Magister held herself, as usual, erect and elegant with her hands in her lap and her head lifted proudly, almost scornfully, occasionally sipping her champagne.

Mme. Viray, with that apparently careless, but artfully managed nonchalance of the French, was overtly posing for the camera. She tilted her head and leaned gracefully back in her chair laughing, and displaying to the best advantage her shapely arms.

"Mr. Fox," I went on, "fancied especially three of these beautiful chickens. A brown one (I smiled at Berta), a white one (I turned to Maude Magister) and a pretty little black pullet." I waved my hand to Mme. Viray, and she blew me back a graceful kiss.

I'm afraid I had already taken a little too much wine, but they were all staring at me so that I paused and took another glass, wondering how the devil to finish my tale. The cameras were still grinding away and we had to have some action, so I went right ahead blindly.

"Alas," I said, "while this Mr. Fox was trying to decide which chicken to steal, lo, approaching in the darkness was an elderly colored gentleman with a beard. His name was—let's see—Mortimer. Mortimer sneaked into that henhouse, ladies and gentlemen, and he nabbed all three of those lovely, lovely chickens, and he—let's see, he put them—yes, he put them into some boxes," I said, "and he carried them all away before poor Mr. Fox could make up his mind. The End," I said.

"Bravo!" cried Señor Corrijo. "Quite equal to Aesop."

Van Diegen said my fable was more like La Fontaine.

Mme. Viray turned her lovely dark eyes on me and said, "I am afraid you are a vairee dangerous man, Mr. Gilbert. That was very clevaire symbolism, that Mortimer."

Berta looked at her and then at me and wanted to know why. She gave me a little wink.

Maude Magister, who had missed it, said, "Have you forgotten your French, Berta?" and added, a bit patronizingly, *"Mort* means death, you know, doesn't it?"

"Oh, does it?" But Berta affected playfully to be still baffled. "Well," she said, "then I suppose the boxes mean something too, don't they?" Trust *that* girl to get the point, I thought.

Miss Magister said, airily, "Oh, we shall all have to be put into boxes sooner or later, shan't we?—hens and women too." She smiled and crossed her hands demurely over her breast, and bent her head, as if she were in her coffin. Then she looked up gaily at Señor Corrijo. "And we know just *how* we'll look, thanks to you, don't we, Señor?"

I didn't know what they were talking about, and I wondered if they did when Mme. Viray said, half-singing it, as if it were a poem,

"We won't look vairee preettee, we won't look vairee preettee, in our boxes, any more!"

And then Berta Conley made an impatient gesture. "Oh, wasn't it ghastly!" she said. "The skeleton was bad enough, but that gradual rotting away in the coffin—*ugh!*"

And then, seeing my puzzlement she told me that they were referring to some macabre entertainment they had witnessed at a party the Señor had given a few weeks ago. Then, evidently to change the subject, she abruptly asked

Señor Corrijo if the music the orchestra was playing outside wasn't a Hungarian *czarda*.

Mme. Viray asked eagerly, "Oh, are they really *tziganes*, your musicians, Señor?" and her face lighted and she said she hoped that amongst them there might be a fortune teller. And she clasped her beautiful jeweled hands and she begged that he might be brought in to read our palms.

Señor Corrijo gave an order to the gorgeous butler, who disappeared and in a moment brought back a crooked, piratical looking fellow in a gaudy green and gold uniform. He was dirty-faced and bewhiskered and he had deep-set black eyes that snapped. He bowed low, and took up Mme. Viray's hand.

"Oh, do tell me, Monsieur," she said, "that I shall be vairee, vairee rich. Do, please, Monsieur; and say I shall not have some trouble ever any more." Then she laughed and added, "And say I shall have a nice husband, too—don't forget *that*, Monsieur!"

In a few moments the gypsy released her hand. He was scowling.

"Well?" asked the Señor. And we all chorused, "Well, what?"

Instead of replying the gypsy bowed and took up the hand of Miss Magister. He looked at it for some time, turned it over, dropped it, and shrugged.

"Am I fortunate?" she asked, and then she added smiling, "Lucky in love, I mean?"

He didn't answer. By this time his silence had become a bit oppressive. And when he had examined Berta Conley's hand with the same result, and Berta had laughed and said perhaps her hand was too dirty, Señor Corrijo spoke with authority.

"Tell us what you find in these ladies' hands."

The gypsy put his hand on his heart and bowed. "Pardon me," he said, and he spoke in such a low, hoarse voice that we bent forward to listen, "I prefer not to tell you, Señor."

There was a unanimous feminine protest. The Señor and Van Diegen and I were only amused, of course, but the ladies all declared excitedly that they wanted to know the truth, the whole truth and whatever it was. So the Señor took the gypsy outside into the corridor; and when he came back he shrugged his shoulders and said it was nothing at all, just nonsense.

But the ladies refused to be put off. And after their renewed expostulation it finally came out that the fellow had predicted, if you please, that every one of those three lovely ladies would die—and within a week.

That shocked us into silence until Maude Magister with an affected laugh asked, "How, Señor? Did he say how we'd die?"

"Well," said the Señor, "he called it murder."

I saw Berta Conley's teeth go over her under lip and she asked, "By whom?"

"Ah," said the Señor, "the man said he didn't know. I think he is a fool, or malicious. The best thing to do is to forget all about it." And he ordered more champagne.

The episode, after all, wasn't perhaps quite so serious as it sounds. It was unpleasant rather than really sinister.

"If I'm to be murdered," Berta said, "it will probably be done by myself. And, you know, I really did come near suicide some years ago, I even got some cyanide. I have it yet, in fact, right in my bathroom closet. But somehow I could never get up the courage to take it, or else my mood blew over, or something."

I asked her where she had ever got the cyanide. It was fairly hard to obtain nowadays, I thought.

Maude Magister remarked, "It can't be so very hard to get, I should think. People use it for lots of things,

cleaning silver, and everything, and you read about suicides by cyanide all the time."

Berta said that her brother, who was out West now,
used to be a pharmacist in Philadelphia. "And I used to
go into his laboratory sometimes," she said, "and he never
knew that I had pinched some of the stuff."

Then Maude Magister gave one of her rare smiles
and said in her bright English way, that if she had to be
murdered she hoped it would be done by someone who
wouldn't bungle the job and make her suffer. She sipped
her champagne and said,

"Now you, Señor Corrijo, would be able to do it beautifully, wouldn't you? It would be a real pleasure, I'm sure,
to die at your noble hands." And we all laughed.

"My dear lady," said the Señor, with a gracious gesture,
"if I were contemplating killing you, I assure you I should
kiss you to death." And we all laughed. We had all drunk
a good deal, and somehow it sounded droll.

Mme. Viray cried, "No! No, Señor, no! She is too cold!
Her lips would freeze you," and she drawled languorously,
"Kiss *me* to death, Señor! I taste so sweet, so vairee sweet!"
And we all laughed and laughed and kept on laughing and
drinking champagne, a little too much, I thought.

Even Karl Van Diegen had grown quite animated for
him, and he turned to Maude Magister and muttered heavily, "How would I do for a murderer? I think I might slay
you artistically. Do you prefer sudden death, Miss Magister, or would you like to die slowly—by inches?"

At that Berta threw up her hands. "Oh, for heaven's
sake, stop it!" she exclaimed. "It's getting on my nerves.
Mercy, fortune telling is all bunk, anyway. Why, I was told
last week by that psychic in Carnegie Hall, Pristine, her
name is, that I'd live to be eighty and marry twice and be
a famous artist."

"And a rather cruel artist, too, I'm afraid, my dear," Maude Magister laughed. "You know, Berta darling, your caricatures are positively marvelous, but—" and she glanced at the Señor, "rather heartless, aren't they? It's lucky for you that the originals seldom see them. You *might* get into trouble, you know!"

I saw Berta flush, but before she could retort the Señor asked us if we wouldn't like to see his collection of rings in the ball room.

First, however, the ladies withdrew and went upstairs to do their faces. We three men strolled out to a sheltered vine-covered loggia where we could look over a terrace across a spacious formal garden to the distant Hudson River shimmering in the moonlight. We sat awhile drinking coffee and sipping Napoleon brandy and it was worth coming, I thought, merely to enjoy one of Señor Corrijo's famous long cigars.

I was sitting at one end of the loggia, a little apart from the two men who were discussing the Señor's Argentine rancho and sheep lands. I could look across an open space, between two monkey pines, towards the garage. As I smoked I saw two men cross the drive. They were carrying a long box or crate. They soon passed out of my sight. I don't know whether or not the rather gruesome talk at the dinner table had colored my imagination but I swear that thing the men were carrying looked to me something like a coffin. Or was it more like the cases of rifles I had seen while I was with the Army in France? I wondered.

The Señor and Van Diegen were sitting where they couldn't have noticed what I saw, however, and I thought it best not to ask questions and appear inquisitive as to the Señor's affairs. It was just a passing fancy, anyway, I thought; and it went out of my mind when Señor Corrijo turned to me and began to talk. He asked me about my work, and seemed interested in my novels.

He was most cordial with me and told me that I, as an author, ought to see his library. It was a small but choice collection containing quite a number of incunabula, he said. I was writing something about the Pyramids at the time and I asked him if he knew of any book pretending to explain the precise method of their construction.

The Señor told me that he did have one curious old Latin volume on the subject and that he'd be glad to show it to me and the library itself at any time I cared to come.

He was telling me about the quaint wood cuts in the book, and his own ideas of Egyptian engineering, when the ladies, fresh and lovely and perfumed, came out to the loggia and joined us. Mme. Viray caught a little of the discussion as she entered, and she immediately exclaimed,

"Oh, are you so interested in Egypt, Mr. Gilbert? It is my grand passion, truly. I could tell you vairee interesting and mysterious things of Egypt. You know—listen, Mr. Gilbert, don't laugh at me—an astrologue told me one time that I was the incarnation of Cleopatra. It is true! What do you think of that? Isn't it thrilling?"

When I answered that it would be very easy to believe that she had lived a lurid and amorous life in the past, she laughed deliciously. Miss Magister and Berta Conley laughed, too, and watched her. Van Diegen watched her with a curious smile. The Señor folded his arms.

Berta said, quizzically, "How about Assyria and Babylon, Hélène? You must have slain your thousands there, too."

And Miss Magister remarked, with a toss of her head, "Oh, my dear, she simply ate them alive."

Then Mme. Viray's dark eyes flashed. She spoke in a low, tragic voice. "I murdered all my rivals and all my lovers; too. I was a bad, bad woman when I was a Princess." And she laughed and assumed a royal attitude that made us laugh again. Then she quickly turned to me and asked

me if I would come to luncheon some day soon at her
house, please, when she would tell me more.

"But not tomorrow," she added, "it is the day of *congé*
of my cook. She is a negress, my cook, and on Fridays I
think all day she is dancing the rhumba."

"She's a marvelous cook, nevertheless," said the Señor,
"I can swear to that."

I was struck again, as those three beautiful ladies stood
there on the portico conversing, with their striking dis-
similarity and their separate special attractiveness.

Mme. Viray, dark and lovely, with a few more pounds
would have been plump. The blonde Miss Magister with a
few pounds less would have been thin; but Berta Conley's
figure was perfect. Their movements too were as significant. Mme. Viray moved gracefully, all in curves. Miss
Magister moved scarcely at all. But when she did, it was
with great dignity and ease. Berta was as brisk and spirit-
ed, almost as jerky in her motions as she was in her speech.

Finally, laughing, chattering together, we passed down
through a vaulted marble corridor to the great ballroom.

The hall was in curiously grained maple with a barrel-
vaulted ceiling and was most interestingly proportioned
and detailed. On one side were eight fluted pilasters between panels with elaborate mouldings and connected by
arches. The wall opposite had seven arched windows re-
peating the same motive and divisions, and they looked
into a garden.

Van Diegen, always the connoisseur and critic, always
deliberate and detached, pointed out two fine old portraits, a Gainsborough and another which I think was a
Franz Hals. At each end of the hall were small ebony inlaid
cabinets, some let into the walls and there were others on
tables.

The dark Spanish looking girl I had seen when we first
got to the house came into the room, and Señor Corrijo

introduced his secretary to us as Señorita Tallia. She smiled continually, but scarcely spoke during the evening. The Señor called her Dolores.

It was she who got out the rings, going to a safe in the end wall, bringing a tray of them to a table in the center of the hall, and taking it away after we had inspected them. There were armchairs enough in the place, but when the rings were shown we all stood crowded around the table and the ladies began to "Oh!" and "Ah!" and were too excited by the display to think of sitting down.

I am not going to describe those rings. There were some two hundred, I imagine—we never saw them all—and each one was a wondrous work of art. Quite as interesting to me as the priceless precious stones were the more curious and historic poison rings and mechanical tricks in gold and enamel. But of course it was the gems, the diamonds, the rubies, sapphires, all of the very finest quality, all blazing with fires, that fascinated the ladies.

I saw their faces change curiously as they scanned them. A certain vague appearance of envy and desire, and a little hardness, too, I thought, crept into their expression—a faint, almost atavistic, savage look. It was the primitive lure of precious stones, I suppose, that has magnetized women since the world began.

Van Diegen was right, I thought, when he had said, on our drive out, that women's reactions are direct and simple. It seemed to me, though, that Berta Conley was less affected than the other two—or perhaps she concealed it better.

So we stood about, admiring, talking, exclaiming at this and that beautiful jewel, and the ladies swiftly tried on one ring after another, and held up their hands for us to admire them; and then took them off very slowly.

Señor Corrijo's eyes, I noted, never left them. Van Diegen watched the ladies, too, with his cold, cynical smile, as if they were children playing with toys. It was a good show. The women were much more fascinating than the gems.

I did get rather interested, though, in an Italian ring formed of three interlaced rings. I had separated them and was trying to get them together again but I couldn't seem to master the trick of it. Van Diegen took it, saying that it was supposed by experts to be a genuine Cellini, and we stepped a little away from the table while he deftly showed me the secret of its construction.

I was trying it again when we heard a crash.

A servant in livery had come into the hall just then with more bottles and glasses, and as he crossed the room he had slipped upon a small rug beyond the magnificent Kirman in the center of the floor and had fallen, scattering glass and liquids in every direction.

Señor Corrijo burst out in an abandoned torrent of fierce Spanish expletives and went angrily over to him. We all tried not to laugh.

In another moment the Señor had returned and he apologized profusely for his display of temper. He couldn't tolerate clumsiness, he said, and the servant would be discharged. He then collected the rings on the table and put them back onto the velvet covered tray.

Suddenly he stopped and looked searchingly at us, his eyes going swiftly from one to another. Then he pointed to a vacant space on the tray and said, quietly,

"Where is the Borgia ruby? The one with the chiseled gold lions?"

It was a horrible moment. We looked at one another aghast. Nobody spoke. Luckily, Van Diegen and I hadn't been near the table; Dolores was at the end of the hall, bringing up another tray; but the three ladies beside the table were visibly disconcerted and dismayed.

The Señor waited a moment. He waited more than a moment, as if trying to control himself, while we stood there transfixed. Then he spoke.

"Will the lady who borrowed that ruby ring kindly return it?" His voice was low but peremptory and I could see that he was trying to hold himself in. He handed the tray to Dolores.

Then, after another sickening silence he added, in a still more ominous tone, "Ladies, I am going to have the lights in this hall put out for two minutes. And when they are relighted, I trust that I shall see my ring there upon the table. In that way it can be returned without embarrassment, for nobody will know who put it back. I shall then have the pleasure of showing you my collection of dolls."

It was the classic solution of the problem; but this time it didn't work. When the lights went up again the table was still bare.

Berta was red; Maude Magister was deadly pale, and Mme. Viray's hands were moving nervously. None of them spoke. The situation was distressing and almost unendurable. I was sorry for them.

Dolores Tallia stood with the tray, halfway between us and the end wall, and didn't move. She stared, but there wasn't an expression on her face.

Van Diegen wiped his forehead and said, in his maddeningly slow precise way, "What are you going to do, Señor, have the ladies searched?" He chuckled. "If so, allow me to volunteer for the job, my dear sir. It will be a great pleasure."

Señor Corrijo said slowly, "I know who has the ring. I shall get it in my own way."

He smiled blandly now at the ladies. "You may take it away, my dear," he said, but without addressing any one of them in particular, "but I shall get it. If I don't, I'm afraid you will be sorry. You will be, may I say, extremely sorry."

And the slow way he brought out that word "extremely," made my blood run a little cold.

3

BERTA CONLEY

The rest of that evening, as you may imagine, was, to put it mildly, rather trying. After we had pretended to take an interest in the Señor's fine collection of dolls—it would have been an awful bore, I thought, at any time—I am sure that the ladies, every one of them, would have been glad to make some excuse for leaving. But it was probable that none of them dared suggest it because she feared that it might imply an attempt to get away with the stolen ring.

There was a prolonged and uncomfortable wait after that and then we all moved on, as cheerfully as we could, into one of the smaller salons to look projection of the motion pictures that had been taken at the dinner table.

The Señor had installed a dark room and laboratory, I believe, especially for the purpose. But not even the amusement of seeing ourselves pictured on the screen could ameliorate the constrained atmosphere in that room. Although the place, of course, was darkened, the ladies hardly dared even whisper to one another lest they be suspected of some guilty collusion. And perhaps each one, except the guilty one, feared that she would be speaking to a thief; and they appeared to be trying to cover their embarrassment with constant laughter.

I could hardly bear it. As the pictures flashed past, to see myself telling that silly fox story at the table in that ridiculous way was bad enough. But to find myself wondering which of those charming women laughing on the screen had pilfered that ring was pretty painful. I had an idea, though, that Van Diegen, in his cynical, ironic way, rather enjoyed the situation. Señor Corrijo hardly spoke during the show.

And so it was with considerable relief that the party finally broke up towards one o'clock in the morning. Not another word in all that time had been said about the missing ring. But I noticed the Señor, once or twice take his secretary, Dolores Tallia, aside and speak to her for a moment. No doubt they were exchanging suspicions.

Berta Conley drew me aside too and in a choked voice she asked me if I would drive her home. And at the same time Mme. Viray evidently had asked Van Diegen to accompany her in her car. I saw them whispering together. It was she who first suggested leaving, and she ran upstairs as if she were in a hurry to escape from the atmosphere of doubt.

That left Maude Magister alone to be taken into town in one of Señor Corrijo's cars and although he offered courteously enough she absolutely refused to put him to the trouble of coming with her. She as well as Berta Conley and Mme. Viray seemed anxious to part company from the other ladies. It was natural enough, I suppose. They were all suspected and probably suspicious of each other as well. There was no escape from the fact that one of the three had that Borgia ruby.

When I saw the Señor's chauffeur Pierre waiting outside under the *porte cochère* for Miss Magister I wondered if that handsome devil had anything to do with her evident desire to go home without an escort. Pierre was a foreigner of some sort, apparently, though I didn't hear him speak, and he had a dark skin, sleek brushed-back black hair and an olive skin. He looked something like the pictures of

Valentino—that dreamy, lover-like look. When he lighted a cigarette I noticed, though, that his hand trembled, and I wondered why.

After Berta Conley and I had got started in my car, and were out on the road, following Mme. Viray's dark green sedan, Berta looked at me and said,

"Wasn't it awful! I never went through such an evening in all my life. And now to be suspected, perhaps, of stealing that ring! Who d'you think took it, Mr. Gilbert?"

It was a queer question, I thought. Was it innocence or boldness, I wondered. I replied, of course, in the only possible way,

"I have no idea, Miss Conley. I was talking with Karl Van Diegen when it disappeared, you know, and we were a little away from the table. But I'm sure that whoever took it, it wasn't you."

She gave my arm a little impulsive touch, and said:

"Of course I didn't. I can't imagine either one of the others taking it either. The whole thing is perfectly shocking."

We drove along Riverdale Ave. for a while without speaking. I felt that she was telling the truth. And yet, why should I be so sure? I asked myself. Was it perhaps only because Berta Conley was the only real American amongst the three women, and I felt a closer affinity and sympathy with her? Other pretty Americans, though, I knew, had done worse things than that. Berta seemed so frank and sincere, though, how could I doubt her honesty? But I was almost as loath to believe that Maude Magister, so proud and aristocratic, could stoop to such a sordid crime, or that the exquisite, delicate Mme. Viray would be willing to descend to a theft that would not only be base, but would put her two friends under suspicion.

I asked Berta, after a while, just to get her reaction, if she thought it possible that Señor Corrijo for some subtle reason had been trying some psychological test, had ordered his servant perhaps to slip on the rug and drop the bottles and glasses.

"To give us a chance to get a ring?" she asked quickly. "Why should he think that any one of us was a thief?"

"Well," I said, "the ring disappeared, didn't it?" and immediately I was sorry I had said it. But no, on second thoughts I wanted to know how she'd take it.

All she said was, "Yes. That's the awful part of it— knowing that one of us is dishonest."

"It seems an extraordinarily reckless thing to do," I said, "stealing that ring. Whoever took it had to take the chance that the Señor wouldn't have the ladies searched."

"How could he do that?" Berta asked. "Señor Corrijo is a gentleman; and I'm sure he'd rather lose that ring than insult the two women who were innocent."

I said that the ring was historic and priceless. Of course it would be practically impossible to realize upon it, if kept intact. It would be instantly recognized. If the ruby were removed, I said, it should sell for a small fortune. But for safety's sake it would have to be cut up, I thought, and it would be difficult to find anyone in the United States to do that and become an accessory to the theft.

We drove along in silence for a while, through the night, watching the lights on the Jersey shore of the Hudson; and then I asked Berta about Mme. Viray—where she lived.

Berta didn't speak for a moment. Then she said, "Oh, Hélène has a nice little house on East 58th St. near the river. She must have an income of some kind, perhaps it's alimony, I never asked; anyway, she's not a poor working girl like me," and Berta laughed. "She's funny, though, in some ways. I'm awfully fond of her, she's a dear, and isn't she beautiful! But I never take much stock in what she says. Sometimes she says she's broke and can't pay her rent, and the next thing she'll show up in a new sable coat. Just now she says she owes money for dresses all over town. I don't know."

Was Berta trying to divert suspicion from herself, I wondered. Somehow I couldn't believe it. No, I'd follow my intuitions and believe in her. I asked her if she'd ever been to Mme. Viray's house.

"Oh yes," she said. "She has it beautifully fitted up. I've met some of her friends there, mostly men, Frenchmen. Hélène professes to be ardent for the Free French movement, and says she's working for De Gaulle. Half the time when I ring her up, though, she's out of town. She goes to Washington a good deal, I believe, I've no idea why."

"Is she intimate with Miss Magister?" I asked.

"Yes, and no," Berta said. "They get along, all right; but I have an idea they're not especially congenial, they're totally different types, you know. Hélène is warm and Maude's cold."

Then I asked her if it were true that Miss Magister had been on the stage.

Yes, Maude had acted, Berta told me, off and on, she thought, in New York productions in minor roles, mostly. And Maude had said she had tried to get into pictures without success. Berta thought Maude was too reserved and too proud. She didn't know how to make friends with the kind of men who could advance her. She valued herself too highly. Berta thought Maude attracted the more intellectual type, the better class of men; and that, she said, didn't get you very far in the theater. Maude lived alone, she told me, on East 46th St. in one of those smartish little apartments made over from an old family residence.

We were passing Grant's Tomb, and Berta's eyes were still on the river.

She said, "I think I know Maude as well as anyone, Mr. Gilbert; but we're not what you'd call intimate, the way a lot of women usually are. I mean that Maude manages, with that polite, formal English manner of hers, to hold me off, kind of—as if there were something invisible, like a sheet of glass, between us. You never get any nearer to her no matter how much you see of her. She's funny that way. When I first met her—at a party Señor Corrijo gave, a few months ago, I thought we'd be great buddies, and perhaps live together. But not Maude!"

Then she said suddenly, "Mr. Gilbert, you seemed to think Señor Corrijo capable of trying psychological experiments on us; do you think he could have planned that little scene with that gypsy, just to see how the three of us would take it?"

There was anxiety in her voice. The tzigane, you know, had predicted her murder; and I saw that the prophecy was troubling her; so I tried to relieve her by saying, yes, I thought the Señor was rather wily, but if that scene were planned it was in pretty poor taste.

After a while Berta asked me if I had noticed that remark Maude Magister had made at dinner, about her caricature of Señor Corrijo. Yes, Maude had said, I recalled, that Berta was heartless. That wasn't exactly like Maude, Berta said, and she thought that Maude may have drunk too much champagne.

"Do you think Miss Magister is in love with the Señor?" I asked.

Berta shrugged her shoulders. "I can't imagine Maude being in love with anyone," she said. "She's too cold and too well controlled." Then Berta sighed and said, "But I haven't a doubt that she's after his money, just as Hélène Viray is."

With some girls it would have been highly impertinent for me to ask whom she thought Corrijo was in love with. But Berta was modern and frank and American, and she didn't seem to mind it at all.

"I suppose Hélène and Maude each thinks she's got him," she said, "but naturally, I think he's in love with me. At least I think he likes me the best of the three of us. Because, I tell you, Mr. Gilbert, he has asked me to do him a great favor, and he wouldn't do that unless he liked me pretty well, would he?"

I glanced round at her and I said it depended somewhat upon what kind of favor.

"Why, he asked me if I'd get some information for him about some fellows I knew in the British Consulate. About wool, it was. Señor Corrijo has a big wool company in the Argentine, you know, and I think it's some business affair he's trying to put over. He may even want me to go to Buenos Aires, he said, with a good salary."

"Perhaps he's asked the others to do the same thing," I suggested.

She looked at me in surprise and, I thought, in some disappointment. "Perhaps," she said, a little doubtfully.

I would have liked to ask Berta, then, if she was in love with the Señor. But, to tell the truth, I was too afraid she would say yes. She had spoken well of him, anyway, and she seemed to admire and respect him, in spite of the disagreeable threat he had made about getting back his ring. I wondered why I should care so much about her love affairs. She was considerably younger than I, and after all, I had only known her three days. My considering her in an amorous light was absurd. But still, I did feel unreasonably happy when I was with her. I decided to go slow.

By this time we were speeding down lower Riverside Drive and Berta had grown suddenly very gay, I thought. She told me that she was an orphan and had always had to earn her own living, and she went on and on talking so fast and so excitedly that I could hardly follow her. I kept looking round at her.

All at once she said, "I'm telling you all this, Mr. Gilbert, because, honestly, I'm awfully upset, and I've got to
get my mind off that awful affair out there tonight. I've
just got to talk. I hope I'm not boring you too much."

"You were telling me," I said, "about your having been
a saleswoman in a department store, and how you had
worked your way into the fashion game. But you've done
a lot of other things, you said." I was sorry for her; I
thought she was trying not to cry.

And then in a moment she said, "I'm afraid I'm incur-
ably romantic, Mr. Gilbert. I'm really an adventuress, you
know," and she turned her lovely hazel eyes on me, and
there were tears in them, and I nearly ran into a taxi.

"I mean," she said, "I love adventures. I was an awful
tomboy when I was a little girl, and when I was fourteen
I got a job as office boy in a lawyer's office in Trenton."

I looked round at her again, amazed, and she said,

"Oh, yes, I dressed up as a boy, and my hair was bobbed
and everything, you know. And d'you know what that
darned old lawyer did when he found me out? He put me
right over his knee and spanked me with a big ledger—and
hard, too."

I can't remember all the odd things she said she'd done
to earn a living; but she had read to invalids and walked
dogs, and that young madcap had even got a job as recep-
tionist at an undertaker's just because she was dying to
know, she said, what a corpse was like. Her latest prank
was to write cute, flattering letters to well-known authors
about their books, and she had succeeded, she said, in
inveigling several of them into a prolonged correspon-
dence. I'd be surprised if I knew who they were.

It was that spirit of adventure, she told me, that had
led to her acquaintance with Karl Van Diegen. Then she
put her hand on my arm and asked me,

"Mr. Gilbert, what d'you really think of Mr. Van Diegen? Or wouldn't you care to tell me. I know he's your friend."

"Van is more an acquaintance than a friend," I said, "and I admire him, but"—and there I stopped.

"That's just it," said Berta. "I've got a 'but,' about him, too."

Then she told me that she was passing Van Diegen's door on 49th St., one afternoon and she stopped to look at a frame of photographs there. An impish impulse seized her, she said, and she went up to his studio and called on him.

"And I told him," she said, "that I was a whole lot prettier than any of those women whose pictures he had down at the door, and if he'd be good, I would consent to pose for him, and then he could put my portrait down there instead."

"Well, you should have seen the way Mr. Van Diegen looked at me, Mr. Gilbert. But he must have seen something in me, because he photographed me half to death that afternoon. I had on only a cheap street dress, but he said he didn't care, and he made me take off my jacket and then my waist and he even tousled up my hair, it was more artistic, he said. And then he took me to dinner, and I went to several places with him, after that, and then—" She stopped short.

I said, "That was where the 'but' came in, I suppose." I knew Van's tricks with women.

"Yes," she said, and was silent again. Then she said, "Of course nothing happened, Mr. Gilbert, really. You can manage Van if you know how, and I had no real trouble with him. After all, Van is a gentleman—of a sort."

I asked Berta if it was through Van Diegen that she had met Señor Corrijo.

"Oh yes," she said. "Yes." And she was smiling faintly again. "We met him at the Rainbow Room one night after the theater. I danced with him, and I don't know, I sort of fell for him. The Señor is really quite a person, you know. There's lots to him."

I said, "And with Señor Corrijo there were no 'buts'?"

"Oh, no," she said, "Señor Corrijo is a *real* gentleman—I *think*. Anyway, he has been awfully nice to me, and I do like him a lot. Do you like him, Mr. Gilbert?" she asked.

I said, "I don't quite know."

And Berta was rather quiet after that.

She waited for me in the Hotel Imperial lobby while I telephoned to have my car taken to the garage, and then we took the elevator upstairs. When we got up to the door of her suite she opened her blue silk bag and fumbled in it. Then she told me she couldn't imagine where her key was.

I asked her if she had had it when she left for the dinner that evening.

"I don't know," she said; she was still looking in her bag. "It seems to me I did, but I'm not sure."

I asked her when she had last used her key.

"Let me see," she said. "I had it, you remember, don't you, when you came up here with me on Tuesday afternoon. Now, yesterday— Oh yes, I remember, I was in all the morning and when I came back after dinner at about 9 o'clock in the evening the door was open and a chambermaid was putting towels in my bathroom so I didn't have to use my key. Today I didn't go out at all, I finished up some drawings and had my meals sent up from the hotel restaurant, so I don't know whether I had it or not."

"Did it have the hotel brass tag on it?" I asked.

"No, and no room number either. It was one I had made from the hotel office key. Of course the lock has a spring latch, like the one on your door, I presume, and so I don't need a key when I go out, and don't always think of it."

From a wall phone in the hall she called down to the front office for a key and I warned her to have her lock changed if she didn't find hers before she left the room again, in case someone should find her key.

She laughed and said she didn't have much of anything worth stealing; although she did admit that it was queer the way the perfume on her dressing table was used up so fast. *"Fleurs de Paradis"* was expensive, she said, and especially so now, as, on account of the war, there was no more imported. She said she suspected the chambermaid of helping herself to it occasionally.

After a key was brought up by the hall boy I asked to look at her caricature of Señor Corrijo again. Now that I had met him it had a new interest; and I remembered it as a marvelous exaggeration of his Spanish self-esteem and lordly manner.

But when she looked for it she couldn't find it anywhere. Then, of a sudden she stopped, and frowned.

"Oh!" she said, "so *that* was what Maude Magister meant when she took that crack at me, at dinner tonight." Berta stood a moment, thinking. "D'you know, I'll bet Maude sneaked that sketch out of here when she was here Tuesday night," she said. "She came up for me to go to Schrafft's you know—and do I know women! Yes sir, she intends to show it to the Señor and get me in bad with him." And Berta stood a moment thinking.

"Well, if that's so, I'll just have to get it away from her some way," she said.

Then the telephone bell rang in her room. I heard her protest, "No! Of course not! I couldn't see you now, anyway. Why it's after two o'clock!" and then, "No, I don't want to see you at all. I don't care *how* important it is," and then, "I won't tell you!" and things like that till she hung up.

She told me then that the man she had been engaged to, Hugo Vlack, had been making trouble for two days. Now he insisted on seeing her. He had written to her over and over, she said, but she had returned his letters unopened. He had been watching the hotel, and perhaps following her, she said; and now he had seen her with me perhaps, and he was probably half crazy with jealousy. He hadn't yet succeeded in meeting her face to face, she said, but she was afraid he would, and that he would do something reckless.

I didn't tell her, that night, about the man I had seen watching her window through opera glasses. I thought poor Berta had had enough to disturb her, without that.

The next morning at about ten, when I went out to buy some typewriter paper, I passed a man on 31st St. who seemed vaguely familiar. I turned and saw him go up the short steps of the entrance of the hotel Annex. But he didn't go in. He simply stood there.

I was pretty sure it was the man I had seen on Wednesday watching the windows of the hotel. It might be Berta's discarded lover, I thought, Hugo Vlack. He was tall and thin and dark and he had a light overcoat on and a very light gray hat. He looked worn and haggard. I felt that I ought to warn Berta, but I was in a great hurry and I didn't.

When I got back half an hour later there was no one near the doorway but Biddy Rumsey, the hotel pest, who was coming out. She shook a little fat finger at me and giggled and told me she was afraid I was smitten with Bertie, and she said Bertie was a lovely girl and she didn't blame me, and a lot of that sort of talk.

When I got upstairs and opened my door at about half past ten, the telephone bell was ringing. It was Berta.

"What d'you think!" she said. "Señor Corrijo just phoned me from his place. He told me that it was up to us three women to find out who took that ring, and to see that it was returned, or else he would hold us all responsible. Why, Mr. Gilbert, I don't know what to think," she said. "It seems so utterly unlike him. He has always been so pleasant—more than pleasant. His voice was different and he was angry. I was almost afraid of him. What d'you think I ought to do?" Her voice was trembling.

I told her I'd think it over and call her back in a little while. But before I could she had rung me up again to say that she had called Maude Magister on the phone and found out that Corrijo had made the same threat to her. And Berta asked me excitedly if I couldn't do something. She had terror in her voice.

I offered to go in and talk to her, but she said she was distracted. I suppose that perhaps she wasn't dressed, or had been crying and didn't want me to see her with her eyes red. But still, she said too, that she had to go out almost immediately because she was already late for a business appointment.

I didn't know what I could do, exactly, I told her. It was really none of my business, I said, and I was loath to interfere. But she said she was sure the Señor liked me and perhaps I could persuade him not to do anything unpleasant.

Well, I was so moved by her evident distress that, much against my better judgment, as soon as I had written a letter, about 10.50 it was, by that time, I went to the garage and got out my car.

I started out for the Corrijo place realizing that I was on a delicate mission, and I had no idea what I could do or say to the Señor. But as we had talked about his library, the night before, I finally decided to ask to see it, as an opening, and see how it developed from that. Well, I didn't hurry, I was expecting a rather trying half hour. But I wasn't at all prepared for the extraordinary experience I was about to have.

When I got to Riverdale I didn't drive into the Corrijo grounds, but parked my car at the curb at the entrance and walked up the drive through the gardens towards the front door of the house under the great portico. It was a cool, blustery day, and as I got near the porch there came a gust of wind that blew off my hat and sent it rolling along the grass towards the garden at the side of the house. I ran after it and finally caught it in a chrysanthemum bush.

I found myself then a little way from the window of the dining room. I looked up. And then I stood just staring. I couldn't believe my eyes.

I saw the Señor seated at a table which was set for luncheon; and with him were the three ladies who had been there to dinner the night before. Mme. Viray was in the same lacquer red dress with the gold sequins, seated in the same graceful, picture-like attitude. Miss Magister, in that same blue gown was sitting in an erect aristocratic pose, and impossible though it seemed, Berta Conley herself, in the yellow gown she had worn at the dinner, was there too, with her elbows on the table.

Well, that was inexplicable enough, since it wasn't more than half past twelve by that time. But what shocked and horrified me—I'll have to tell it, for it doesn't matter now—was that Mme. Viray was unclad to the waist; I could just see the skirt of her red dress, and Maude Magister's blue gown was hanging off one shoulder almost as scandalously.

And Berta—I simply can't tell you how she appeared— but she was calmly looking on with a faint smile. The Señor was laughing and talking to them.

For a second I watched his courtly gestures and then— well, it was just too much for me. It was like a bad dream; no, it was more like going insane. It couldn't be; and yet I had seen the women with my own eyes. There was time enough—I mean Berta might have taxied right out there after she had phoned me, for it took some time for me to get my car. But it seemed incomprehensible; she knew that I was going out there.

Of course I didn't go in to see the Señor. I drove back into town in a kind of sickened daze, hardly knowing what I was doing.

I had to have a conference with my publisher that afternoon, about a book I was at work on, and several times in his office he asked me to put down the pencil I was fingering, and listen. And once he said he didn't believe I'd heard a word of what he'd been saying.

I was asking myself over and over what the scene I had witnessed out at Riverdale could mean, and how it could have been possible. I tried to do several errands that afternoon and forgot where I was going half the time. I nearly ran over an old woman, I remember, before I put my car in the garage. I dreaded to see Berta Conley, yet I had to try to solve the mystery.

At my regular news stand, when I went to get my evening paper, I stopped, horrified. I snatched it up. I saw a picture of Mme. Viray, and in big headlines I read, *"Mysterious Death of Beautiful Divorcée."* And below it said,

"Mme. Hélène Viray, a well-known society beauty, once an opera star, was found dead in her house on East 58th St. at about four o'clock this afternoon by her maid. She evidently died of a dose of cyanide of potassium." The paper said that she left no known relatives; and that was all except the statement that she was of French birth and had come to the United States a few years ago.

I hurried home. I didn't wait to phone to Berta to ask if I could see her, but went directly to her room. It was then about 6.10. Berta opened the door; she was in a rose silk house coat and she looked ill and disheveled. She looked wild, bewildered. Her face was flushed and drawn as if she had been crying.

When I asked her if she had heard of Mme. Viray's death she screamed out, "Hélène? No, no, no!" and her face went white. She seized my hand fiercely.

"Are you sure it was Hélène?" she cried, "Hélène Viray? Was *she* killed?"

I showed her the paper. She looked at it. She looked at me, dazed. "Hélène!" she whispered, and she crumpled up the paper. "Oh, poor Hélène!" she wailed, and she stared at me so strangely. Then she began to tremble all over and I put my arm out to support her, but she pushed me away.

"Oh, I'm afraid!" she sobbed. "I'm afraid I'll be the next one," and her voice rose. "It was true, what that gypsy fortune teller told us!" she cried. "It was true! And I'll be the next one! Oh, I'm afraid! I'm afraid!" and she began plucking at the swan's down trimming of her house coat in a panic-stricken way, and I thought she'd tear it to pieces. She didn't know what she was doing, walking back and forth.

I pulled her down onto the couch and sat down beside her.

"Berta," I said, "I've got to ask you something. Were you out at Señor Corrijo's house this noon?"

I couldn't get her to answer. I doubt if she knew what I had said. She kept moaning that she'd be the next one, and she was afraid, and I took it that she was afraid of the Señor. I repeated my question but by that time she had grown hysterical, and I poured out a glass of water from the bottle on her table but I couldn't get her to drink it. She sat moaning and swinging her head.

I tried another direction. "Berta, why should Mme. Viray have committed suicide? Do pull yourself together, my dear! Have you any idea, Berta?"

"She's been killed," Berta cried. "I know she has. And I'll be the next one to go!"

"Do you really think she was murdered, Berta?" I asked. "What makes you think so?"

She jumped up and pushed me to the door.

"Go away!" she cried. "Oh, go away, please! I want to be alone! I've got to be alone!"

I went into my room and sat down, heart-sick, and tried to think things out. Then I snatched up the phone and rang up Miss Magister. I thought she might come over and give me some help. But there was no response. Then I turned on my radio hoping to get more news about the death of Mme. Viray. There were only reports of baseball games and bulletins about the war and Washington items until suddenly I heard,

"New York. Another sudden death of a young and beautiful woman occurred today in mysterious circumstances. Miss Maude Magister, 24, living on East 46th St., was stabbed to death this afternoon in her suite where she lived alone. Her body was discovered by a woman whom she employed to come daily to prepare her meals. The murderer is unknown."

I was stunned. A second murder! And in my dismay Berta's words came back to me. "I'm afraid! I'll be the next one, I know I will!" and I had a feeling of dread so strong that I ran back to Berta's door. I rang and rang again in a frenzy. I knocked, I pounded on that door.

There was no answer. I tried the handle, but it was locked.

I hurried downstairs to see the manager of the hotel. I begged him to investigate Miss Conley's room without delay. After considerable objection he consented to send the housekeeper up to Berta's room. I followed her up and the house detective came with me.

The housekeeper knocked and called through the door. Then she took a pass key and opened the door and went in. We heard a shriek and she came running out.

"Miss Conley is dead!" she cried. "She's lying on the floor. She must have committed suicide!"

4

IMPERIAL SUITE

The house detective rushed into the room. I looked in, and there she was. Berta Conley was lying face down on the floor with one hand under her head. She had on a blue knitted suit and a blue sport coat and she had her hat on.

I tried to go in, but the detective swore at me and told me to keep out. The housekeeper started to pick up an empty glass that was on the floor, but he caught her arm and swore again, and hell, didn't she know enough not to touch anything in the room?

Then he knelt down and felt of Berta's heart. "I guess she's gone," he said. "It couldn't have happened very long ago though, her body's still warm." Then he got up and looked at her and shook his head. "It's suicide, right enough," he said.

Then he wrapped the glass on the floor carefully in his handkerchief and picked it up gingerly and smelt of it, and set it upon the table in the corner by the bottle of spring water.

"Cyanide, probably," he said.

When the manager had been called up, he charged into the room, and gave one look at Berta Conley on the floor, and began to curse his damned luck at having a scandal in the hotel and now there'd be the hell to pay. Then he jerked up the telephone receiver and notified the police.

The house dick had rolled the body over. Her eyes were open and slightly bulging and her face was drawn as if she were in agony; and one cheek and her right hand that had pressed against it were bluish. I stood there looking at her. I couldn't keep the tears from my eyes. Poor Berta! I couldn't believe it—that lovely girl, so full of life such a short time ago! It made me almost sick.

The manager and the hotel dick poked about the room, looking at this and under that, and then went through all Berta's private things, all the time grumbling and swearing. Suicides often left notes, they said, and they seemed to be angry that they didn't find any.

Then the manager turned to me in a worried, impatient way and told me the police would undoubtedly want to question me and I'd better go to my room and wait there.

Out in the hall a chambermaid in a doorway was leaning on her broom and whispering to the elevator boy; and the elevator annunciator was clicking and clicking. I saw a door open and a half-dressed woman looked out and stared at Berta's door, and at us, looking frightened. I went back to my bedroom and rang up the District Attorney, Mr. Gross, at his home on Park Avenue.

I had got acquainted with Mr. Gross at my Club, you see, and I had seen him occasionally there and at his office. He was always very polite, and he had been good enough to give me considerable information for a book I had been writing. Someone at his residence, some woman, told me that he was investigating the murder of Maude Magister.

When I finally got Mr. Gross at Miss Magister's apartment, he told me patronizingly that he had already been informed of Berta Conley's death by the police. But when I told him that I had known all three of the day's victims and I wanted to tell him a lot of things he displayed more interest; and he said he'd come right over to the Imperial.

I went back to my door and looked out. A big police-man in uniform stood guarding the door of Berta's room and another policeman was in the hall at the head of the main stairway. He was pushing back a crowd of hotel guests who were gathering, and chambermaids and reporters. And every room door down the hall seemed to be open, with people looking out, and more were coming up the back stairs and being pushed back, and there was an excited murmur of voices in the corridors.

Two detectives from the Homicide Squad had arrived, and were bustling about; and inside Berta's room the house doctor and the Medical Examiner were consulting; I could see them through the open doorway. While I was waiting to speak to them two more detectives came hurrying in, and a photographer, too. He was carrying a queer, tall camera, and he was with a man whom I took to be the fin-gerprint expert.

Berta Conley's little room was now crowded, and every-body was talking, and the manager of the hotel was talking loudest of all. He caught sight of me lingering outside and he asked me irritably to go away. I told him I was waiting for the District Attorney, and he said I could wait for him in my room.

So I went back and sat down and went over and over the affair, trying to imagine what had happened. But no possible explanation came to me.

In a half an hour or so my doorbell rang. It was the District Attorney.

I had always liked Alfred Gross. He was tall and im-portant looking, a blond, a handsome chap, and he was always dressed as if he had just come from a society wed-ding. He seemed to know everybody and was invariably suave and affable. I took him into my front room where he drew a big gold case out of his pocket and offered me a cigar. We lighted up and he sat down in an easy chair. "Al" Gross affected a wax-pointed moustache and a camellia in his buttonhole, but he was a professional politician all over. He was rather too afraid of making enemies.

"I don't usually mix up with these preliminary investigations, Gilbert," he said. "I let the police get the evidence first. But these two sudden deaths and now this girl being tied up with them some way, as you intimated on the phone—well, it's rather sensational and it'll get a lot of notice from the press. The Viray woman was a cyanide case, too. We aren't sure yet whether it was a suicide or not. What d'you know, Gilbert?"

I was still somewhat dazed and shaking a little, I'm afraid, from what I had seen, but I sat down and told him as well as I could how I had met Berta Conley, and then I told him all about the dinner out at Señor Corrijo's, and the theft of the ring and everything, and my talks with Berta afterwards.

Mr. Gross smiled in a non-committal way, and twisted his moustache and when I had finished he smoked awhile. Then he said,

"Of course, Gilbert, I'm satisfied you're o.k., but it may be rather awkward for you, knowing this girl and living right next door to her, you know, and being the last person, apparently, to see her alive. It's certainly a strange story. Very strange."

I said, "It's stranger than you think, Mr. Gross." And then I told him about my driving out to Riverdale that noon and seeing the three ladies through the window with Señor Corrijo in his dining room at about 12.30.

Mr. Gross watched me with a frown gathering on his face.

"And they all died suddenly this afternoon," he said, doubtfully. "Rather peculiar that they should all three have been out there at Riverdale such a very short time before their death, isn't it?" Then he said, "See here, Gilbert, this Conley girl here, when you talked to her at half past ten, she knew you were going out to Riverdale, didn't she?"

"Why, yes," I said, "she asked me to go out and see the Señor—placate him, if I could."

"Then why should she have gone out herself?" said Gross. "Almost immediately, too. It's possible, of course, that something got into her female head and she took a taxi, and she could have got out there by 12.30, and into that evening dress you speak of. But it doesn't make sense to me. There must be some factor in the case you don't know, Gilbert, or else haven't told me."

I protested that I had told him everything I knew. He uncrossed his legs and leaned forward and pointed his cigar at me and smiled.

"You're not building up an insanity defense for yourself, are you, Gilbert?" he said, half jokingly. "I hope you haven't told anyone else this story, anyway. By jove, I can see what the tabloids would do with a fairy-tale like that!"

Just then the bell rang again, and I went and opened the door to find a solid, stocky man of sixty or so, with a clipped moustache and close-cropped white hair. He wore one of those colorless dull slate gray suits and a derby hat. When I saw his thin, lined, severe face and cold blue eyes I said to myself, he's tough, all right. He said he was head of the Homicide Squad, Capt. Joseph Little, and he looked at me suspiciously.

He limped into my front room, swearing at the rheumatism that had settled in his leg after he'd been shot in a fight with burglars, he told me. Mr. Gross greeted him as "Joe," and he sat down on the arm of a big chair, and accepted a portly cigar the District Attorney offered.

"Well," he said in a curt, decided way, "looks like suicide, Mr. Gross." He seemed to bite off his words.

"We found a bottle o' cyanide in her bathroom closet. The drinking glass smells of the stuff, too. Funny thing, though. This Conley girl, you know, had a bag all packed. Going away, apparently. Hat on, too."

At that word "suicide" something came back to me that I had forgotten, and I told the two men how at Señor Corrijo's dinner Berta had told us that she had at one time contemplated suicide, and that she still had some cyanide in her bathroom closet.

Mr. Gross asked me who had heard her say that.

"Why, all of us who were at the table that evening at the Corrijo place," I said, "the ladies, Señor Corrijo and Van Diegen. And the waiters too, for all I know."

"And don't forget yourself, too, Gilbert," the D.A. laughed.

Capt. Little looked at the District Attorney and said, "Yeah. That puts a different angle to it. See what I mean, Mr. Gross?"

Mr. Gross inspected his cigar and said, "You mean that someone may have poisoned the water in the bottle in her room, Joe?"

Capt. Little nodded. "Well, there's three men, anyway, Mr. Gilbert admits, who knew where to get the cyanide in the girl's room—if they wanted it." Then he looked at me and into me, I almost felt, and said in his precise, dogmatic way, "Mr. Gilbert lives right next door, too. He could easily be able to know when she went out of her room. Worth checking upon, anyway."

Mr. Gross put out his hand in a gracious gesture, and said, "Mr. Gilbert is a friend of mine, Joe, and he'll give you the whole story so far as he knows it, and answer any questions."

"O.k.," said Capt. Little, "I'll reserve judgment till I hear what he's got to say. I just don't want to overlook any bets, that's all. We'll know where we are better when we get the autopsy and a report on the finger-prints on the bottle and glass in the girl's room. Might be a homicide case, after all."

I had begun to feel pretty uncomfortable. I saw now that I might be accused of the murder. Capt. Little was already acting as if he suspected me. And suddenly I remembered pouring out that glass of water from the bottle in Berta's room only an hour or so ago, and trying to get her to drink it, when she was so hysterical.

Why, if the water in the bottle had been poisoned and Berta had drunk it, I thought, she might have dropped dead there at my feet. I felt a little faint. The only thing to do, though, I knew, was to tell the two men all about that last scene in Berta's room.

And so I did, while Capt. Little studied me as if I were a bug under a microscope.

"Very interesting," the Captain said slowly. "Very interesting."

Mr. Gross said, "I'm glad you told us, anyway. You're nice and frank, Gilbert. But I knew you'd be." Always smooth, like that, he was. I could see how he had got elected.

And then I said to the District Attorney, "Mr. Gross, I suppose I may be suspected in some way, and the police will undoubtedly want to corroborate my evidence. But since I knew all these women and something of their background, why can't I work with the detectives on this case and the other two? Go round with them, I mean, when they investigate. In that way the police can keep me under their eyes all the time, and I may be able to give them some help. I'm pretty sure," I said, "you won't get much out of either Karl Van Diegen or Señor Corrijo."

"Why not?" Capt. Little asked gruffly.

I smiled. "Oh, just one of my hunches, I suppose, Captain."

Capt. Little was trying to relight the stump of his cigar and I offered him a fresh one but he refused it a bit surlily.

The District Attorney smiled and said, "Mr. Gilbert is pretty well known as a novelist, you know, Joe. I imagine he can convince you that he's known these girls only a few days and he probably can have no motive."

Capt. Little still eyed me critically. He said, in his dogged way, "Wait till I hear his story, Mr. Gross. I'll soon find out." Then he added, "Of course, in any case you'd have to keep your mouth shut damned tight, Mr. Gilbert. We don't want the newspapers to get things before we're ready. At that, I'm always leery of writing men."

Mr. Gross said, "I'll vouch for him, Joe. But listen, Gilbert," he turned to me, "if you are taken round with 'em, don't go romantic on us. You know most homicide cases aren't broken in the picturesque and thrilling way people think. Usually it's this way," he said. "A murder is committed. See? Pretty soon some stool pigeon comes round or meets you on the quiet somewhere and he tips you off as to who did the killing, and he collects his ten or twenty bucks. Then you send out for the guy he put the finger on, and you bring him in and kick the guts out of him till he confesses. Isn't that right, Joe?"

Capt. Little ran his hand back through his cropped white hair. "Oh, I wouldn't say that, exactly, Mr. Gross; not for publication, anyway." But he had a sardonic grin. "Of course," he said, "we use all the latest scientific methods in criminology—chemical analysis, microscopic examination, spectroscopic identification, and all the rays of the spectrum—but still most of our work is pretty dull, Mr. Gilbert, a lot of footwork and asking thousands of questions of thousands of people. Good deal like placer mining. We pan out lots of sand and get damned little gold, usually. A thing like this triple murder by non-criminals, with all the victims linked up and a society angle may be plenty tough."

I said that I had heard it stated that the more unusual a crime the easier it was to solve.

"That's literature," snapped Little, and he glowered at me. "Like the idea that a murderer always revisits the scene of his crime. Bosh! And the smartest crook always forgets one little detail that trips him up. Bosh." He threw one leg over the other. "Hundreds of crimes are never solved," he said. "Same way with the popular superstition that detectives are something like clairvoyants and have some weird special sense that spots the criminal. Literature! Bosh! Police work is mostly routine, Mr. Gilbert. We don't work on hunches."

"All the same, Joe," Mr. Gross laughed, "Mr. Gilbert had a pretty good hunch that this Conley girl was killed."

"Too damned good!" Capt. Little grumbled.

"Well, Gilbert," said the District Attorney, "you see what you're up against, anyway. You'd better watch your step."

And then he got up and took his hat and brushed it off with his sleeve and put it on his head, carefully bending down the front of the brim. He yawned and said he'd been up till three the night before at a shindig. Then he asked Capt. Little how he was getting along with the other two murders.

"Why, at the Viray house looked like suicide, first-off," said the Captain, "just like this Conley girl's death." He pursed his lips and squinted. "The devil of it is," he said, "we haven't found any cyanide bottle, no glass near the body, either. That looks phony. Sergeant Pearson is at the Viray house on that job. At the Magister girl's flat you saw yourself, Mr. Gross, that there must have been a fight. Everything upset and pulled around, looked like a good long tussle. I've got my Sergeant, Dan Leary, going through the Magister girl's place, and checking up on everybody she knew that we can locate. Something's bound to break there any minute."

At the door the District Attorney shook hands and gave me the old political gag that if there was anything he could do for me just to let him know.

Capt. Little then took out his notebook and wetted the end of a stubby pencil. He fixed his cold blue eyes on me and he said, "Now, Mr. Gilbert, if you'll just spill all you know about this business, we'll see where you stand."

I began to go over the story of the last few days, for the Captain, as I had told it to Mr. Gross, and I was describing the dinner at Señor Corrijo's when he barked out,

"Which one of those three dames was Corrijo's mistress—or were all of 'em?"

I didn't much like his tone, and I said I didn't know that any of them were. The Señor appeared to like all of them, though, I said, and they certainly all liked him. Or they liked his money, anyway.

"Well," the Captain demanded, "who was the Romeo in this gang, Corrijo, or this fellow Van Diegen? Or were they rivals?"

I told him that the two men appeared to be good friends. Then I went on to the theft of Señor Corrijo's ring and the Captain listened intently.

"This Señor must have been plenty sore," he said, "but still and all, wholesale murder doesn't exactly seem to be the answer, not just for gypping a ring—not to me. Not yet, anyway. If there was any motive on Corrijo's part it's more likely to have been jealousy, I should say. Some of those Spaniards have got pretty hot tempers." The Captain puffed at his cigar. "But I don't see any reason for Van Diegen either—killing three women in a day, do you?"

I said I didn't see how it would be possible, even; and then I went on, telling about my driving Berta Conley home. Capt. Little didn't interrupt me until I told him about Berta's fear of Hugo Vlack.

"Good!" he barked. "Now we got something to work on."

He got up then and limped to the hall door and called in a tall, freckled detective with yellow hair who had been questioning the hotel guests. He called him Ferguson and Little told him to ask the elevator boys and chambermaids and everybody if they had seen the man I described. I told Detective Ferguson that this Hugo Vlack might have come up to Berta Conley's room—if he did come—several ways besides by the 31st St. elevator.

"Yeah, I know," said Ferguson. "This hotel sure does make it easy for anybody to get around and keep out o' sight. Look—you can come in three different ways—the 32nd St. main entrance, or from Broadway, through the bar, or by the Annex entrance on 3ist St. You can go up-stairs a lot o' ways—by the elevators in the main hotel, or by that little cable elevator side of the restaurant, or by the 31st St. elevator in the Annex, or by any one of three different stairways in the main hotel and two in the Annex. And on top o' that," he said, and Ferguson flourished his big, sprawling wide-open hand, "you can get through the main hotel into the Annex here on four different floors— ground floor, and the third, fourth and seventh floors. But," he said, "the best bet of all, in my opinion, is the little back stairway of the Annex. It comes up right past the Conley girl's door, you see, and it's out of sight all the way. Why, simply built for crooks, this place is! About the best get-in and get-out joint I ever saw!"

Capt. Little hadn't seemed to pay much attention. He said, "Well, Ferguson, go to it. See what you can get about this Hugo Vlack first, then check up on the Conley girl's mail and phone calls and find out who her friends were, and who she worked for, and see them all and dig up what you can about her. Locate her home folks too, if you can. Put all the men you can spare on it."

When Ferguson went out Capt. Little got up and stood at the window, looking out across the roofs, evidently considering the problem. I felt a sense of power in him, an intense concentration and determination. And I felt pretty sure that if I weren't innocent, I'd be likely to have a hard time with him.

I asked him if he thought the three murders were committed by the same person, but he didn't answer.

Finally he came slowly back and sat down and silently relighted his cigar. Again I offered him a fresh one, but he just shook his head without answering.

I decided then, in spite of the District Attorney's caution, to tell the Captain about the scene of the three ladies I had witnessed that noon in the Señor's window out at Riverdale. I wanted to see if he had any explanation; but I fully expected him to laugh or sneer at me, or accuse me of trying to mystify him. Instead, he listened with apparent interest.

"Well," he said, "I've been too long on the force, Mr. Gilbert, to be amazed at anything, no matter how improbable. On the face of it, of course, your story sounds kind of phony. Now, you say you were with Miss Conley at 10.30 this forenoon—"

"No," I said, "I didn't see her then, you know. We only talked over the house phone."

The Captain kept his eyes on me. "And yet her rooms are just a step down the hall from your door—how's that?"

I suspected that he was trying to catch me in a contradiction, as he had, in fact, tried before several times during the conversation, and I told him that Miss Conley had asked me not to come to her room. She was probably dressing, I said, as she had told me she was going out immediately to keep a business appointment.

The Captain was silent for some time, but his eyes were on me. Finally he said, "Well, let's see just when the Conley girl's key could have been lost or stolen. From what you tell me, Mr. Gilbert, she had it when you came up to her room with her on Tuesday evening at about six o'clock. All right. On Wednesday, she went out at about four in the afternoon, the chambermaid told me. When she came back at about 9.30 in the evening the maid was in her room changing the towels, and as she had left the door open Miss Conley didn't use her key. She may have had it, and she may not. On Thursday the maid said, and you say she said, too, Miss Conley didn't go out at all until this Señor Corrijo's car came for her at about six o'clock to take her out to Riverdale. But when she got back, you say, Mr. Gilbert, she didn't have her key. It seems probable that it was lost in the Corrijo house out in Riverdale." He looked at me questioningly.

"It's possible," I said, "though I don't know who could or would have taken it." And then a thing flashed into my mind that rather terrified me. I didn't know whether to tell it or not; but finally I said,

"Capt. Little, about a year or so ago, while my apartment here was being painted and papered, I occupied that little suite where Miss Conley was for a couple of weeks, and I believe I still have an extra key I had to it."

"You have!" He glared at me. "What's this? Trying to put the noose around your own neck, now, are you? Well, did you ever use that key since you left the suite?" he asked.

"No, certainly not," I said, "but it has occurred to me that maybe other people have occupied that suite and may have kept a duplicate key to it."

Capt. Little's cold blue eyes were still fixed on me. "You certainly have got yourself badly mixed up in this thing," he said, and his voice grew hard. "I suppose you figure that we may go through your place here and you'd better get the credit for acknowledging it before we find that key to her room."

I didn't answer. Capt. Little hitched his chair nearer to me.

"The Conley girl," he said harshly, "was out of her room from about 4 P.M. Wednesday, till 9 or 10 P.M. Where were you at that time, Mr. Gilbert?"

I told him that I was out all the afternoon. I had dinner at my club, I said, and got home at about 8.30 in the evening.

"Well then, you had a good hour on Wednesday to get into the Conley suite and administer the cyanide," said the Captain with a grim grin. "You're certainly making it pretty tough for yourself, Mr. Gilbert."

I tried to smile and I said, "If cyanide had been put into the water bottle on Wednesday, Capt. Little, don't you see, she would have died that day or yesterday, in all probability. Miss Conley told us, you know, that she drank six or seven glasses of water a day. So it's a hundred to one the cyanide was put in while she was out of her room today. At about 10.50 though, and before she had left for her business engagement, I had gone to get my car; and I was out with it all the afternoon till near six o'clock, when I saw Miss Conley alive."

"How do I know you saw her alive?" snarled Capt. Little. "Perhaps you saw her dead. Perhaps that's why you notified the hotel manager that she was dead, an hour later, before anybody else could know anything about it. How do I know you didn't?"

Then he leaned back in his chair and crossed his legs and nodded.

"See here, Mr. Gilbert," he said sarcastically, "of course you couldn't possibly have slipped the cyanide into Miss Conley's glass while you were there in her room at six o'clock. You couldn't possibly have seen her drink it and die, and then quietly sneaked back into your room, just a few yards away, now could you?"

"I suppose I could have," I said, "if I had been able to get that cyanide out of her bathroom closet without her knowing it. But I certainly didn't. Why should I have killed her, Capt. Little? I'd known her only three days. And when I went into her room she was so hysterical that I couldn't do anything with her. She wouldn't even answer my questions."

A fire engine, just then, went charging and screeching up Broadway and Capt. Little had almost to shout at me.

"How do I know she was hysterical? All I've got is your word for it, isn't it?" And then he jumped up and came over to me and pointed at me. He shot a question at me like a bullet.

"How did you happen to know so soon, Mr. Gilbert, that Miss Conley had been poisoned? Less than an hour, apparently, after she took the poison."

"I didn't know," I said. "It was more like an unreasoning dread that she might be killed, I suppose, after I heard of the death of the other two ladies in that party. Perhaps too," I said, "there was some suggestion put into my mind by that gypsy fortune teller at the Corrijo dinner. You know the old saying, 'Where there are two, there'll be three.'"

"Literature," he barked. "Bosh!"

The Captain asked me a lot more questions after that, evidently trying to make me contradict myself, but by the time we had finished the interview he had evidently pretty well made up his mind that I was telling the truth, for his manner towards me changed somewhat. Before we left the room he even accepted one of my cigars and lighted it.

Then he limped to the door, glanced up at an antique
clock on my wall, and turned to me and said he was going
to have another look at the Conley girl's room. Then he
was going back to the house of Mme. Viray and see what
Detective Pearson, in charge there, had turned up. They'd
try to put things together, he said, so that they'd make sense.

I asked him if that meant that I could go along with
him. I'd like to see the Viray house, I said, before anything
there was changed.

He nodded reluctantly without looking at me, and I
got my hat and followed him out.

In Berta Conley's room the body was gone. The photographers had gone, and everybody else except two detectives who were rummaging in the two rooms before packing up Berta's clothes and personal effects to send to the
Morgue. The finger-print man had dusted the drinking
glass and the water bottle and I don't know what else, and
he had carried them off to Police Headquarters.

Capt. Little scowled at me and said, "It's damn lucky
for you, Mr. Gilbert, that you're a friend of the D.A.'s, or
by this time we'd have had you locked up. You've admitted
that your finger-prints may be on that glass and the bottle. So I'll have to ask you to come round to the Station on
West 30th Street and we'll take 'em for you, to make sure."

I shrugged my shoulders and said, "Then I'll be all
ready for the Rogues' Gallery, I suppose."

The Captain grinned with a sort of surly good-nature.

"Only trouble with you, Mr. Gilbert," he said, "you
got no apparent motive. But give us time, give us time.
We may find one. Were you in love with this Conley girl?
That would help some. She was sure pretty enough. They
was all good-lookers, all three. The Señor sure knew how
to pick 'em. Swell story for the papers. It'll beat the war
in the headlines tomorrow. The reporters will be after us
hammer and tongs till we break the case."

While the detectives went about their search in their callous business-like way, I looked about Berta's little living room and I couldn't help being moved by its pathos. Everything there showed the effect of her personality.

There were her sketches on the walls, and her books in a small case. There was even one of my books, I found; it was new, and she had probably bought it after she had met me. An unfinished fashion design in crayon was on her easel. I looked at the dictaphone on its stand with a pile of cylinders, and I wondered what those records had to say. It would be uncanny, I thought, to hear her voice again after she was gone.

I went into her bedroom. A detective was taking the bottles and brushes and cosmetics from the top of her dresser and packing them up in a carton. He picked up a curious shaped flask and took out the glass stopper and smelt of it. *"Fleurs de Paradis,"* he read on the label, and he said it was nice stuff.

I don't know why, but that perfume, I think, affected me more than anything else—more than the tumbled undergarments thrown onto the bed, more even that the lemon yellow satin gown that she had worn at the Corrijo dinner.

I stood there wondering why her airplane bag had been packed for traveling. Where had that girl been intending to go, just before she drank that glass of poisoned water, hardly an hour after I had last seen her? And why was she going? Was she running away for fear of being killed like her friends Maude Magister and Hélène Viray?

The yellow-haired detective, Ferguson, came into the room and said to the Captain,

"I ain't found anyone yet, Chief, who remembers seeing this Vlack guy, but say, Chief, seems they was another guy here in the Annex this afternoon, snooping around. Why, the elevator boy here just told me he seen a foreign lookin' guy goin' up the stairs, about two o'clock, it was. He walked up one flight; and when the boy went up in his elevator he said he seen him walking along the corridor on the second floor towards the Beauty Parlor. Them back stairs come down into that corridor, you know. This gent might have gone up them back stairs to this room here. Nobody could see him from the main stairway, you know, or the elevators."

Capt. Little asked him if the elevator boy had seen the man come down.

"No," said the detective, "not comin' downstairs, but he seen him again goin' out the street door about half an hour later. He looked like a man who'd have money, well-dressed, he said, dark suit and hat an' a black moustache an' a goatee. The boy went to the doorway and looked out, an' he seen this guy, a swell he was, too, looks like, go across Broadway and get into a car that was parked there by the Chinese laundry, this side o' Sixth Avenue."

"Private car or taxi?" Little asked.

"I asked the boy, but you know 31st is a Westbound street so the car was headin' towards Sixth Avenue and he couldn't only see the back of it, an' he wasn't sure."

I said right away that the man's description might fit Señor Corrijo. Perhaps, I said, he went up to see Berta Conley, and frightened her, and maybe that was why she was so hysterical when I saw her at six o'clock. And perhaps that was why she had packed her grip—to run away from him. The Señor had rung her up in the forenoon, I said, and had threatened her. He had threatened Maude Magister as well. He was furious about the theft of his ring, and he might have even insisted on searching Berta Conley's rooms. He may have gone to see Maude Magister also, I said, on the same errand.

"That's a line, anyway," said Capt. Little. "I'll have to see this Señor Corrijo, that's sure."

And then he remarked that, after all, this didn't eliminate the Hugo Vlack fellow. He'd have to send out an
alarm for him.

I suddenly happened to remember then about Biddy,
Mrs. Rumsey. I had forgotten to mention her. She had
seemed to know Berta fairly well, and she might be able
to give some information, I thought. Capt. Little said he
would question her immediately, and he sent for her. We
went into a small unoccupied room near the elevator.

Biddy came in with her eyes red and swollen and she
seemed frightened out of her wits at meeting the police.
She wrung my hand as if we were at a funeral and she whispered wasn't it awful!

And then the Captain asked her if she knew Miss Conley well.

"Bertie Conley?" She turned her great staring eyes on
him and said, "Oh yes! I knew her *very* well indeed. Oh yes,
Bertie and I were *great* friends. In fact, I think I was Bertie's very *best* friend. Best *girl* friend, of course, I mean."

"How long have you known her?" the Captain asked.

Biddy worked her lips and tilted her head and said,
"Well—why, quite some time, and we got so intimate, why
I felt just like a sister."

Capt. Little repeated it. "Exactly how long have you
known her?"

"Oh, I've known Bertie ever since she came here to the
Imperial," Biddy declared.

"When was that? Answer the question, please."

Biddy seemed confused and frightened. She looked at
me as if for help. "Why, I don't know, I don't just remember just when exactly, but why, I feel as if I'd known her
all my life, really I do. We were just like sisters. Why, I
even used to read some of my novel to her I'm writing,
and she said it was extraordinary. I'm a writer, you know.

I write all night sometimes till the dawn comes in at the window!"

"Never mind the dawn," Capt. Little snapped. "This is a murder case, madam." And the Captain asked me if I knew when Miss Conley had come to the hotel and I told him ten days ago.

Biddy bridled and smirked and said, "Well, it seems much longer than that to me. Oh, much longer! Why, we were just like sisters."

"Yes, you said that before," snarled the Captain. "And speaking of sisters, d'you know anything about this Conley girl's relatives?"

After much more circumlocution, he finally got it out of her that Berta had a sister in Philadelphia and a brother out West somewhere, but of course Biddy didn't know either address.

"D'you know this Hugo Vlack, a friend of Miss Conley's?" the Captain asked.

"Hugo? Oh yes. Very well."

"Are you sure you do?"

"Oh yes. Why, I've heard Bertie talk about him loads of times."

"Have you ever met him?"

"Why," said Biddy, "I don't know as I've ever actually *met* him, but I feel as if I knew him, you know, because Bertie told me about him so much, and I've seen him— that is, I think I have. I'm almost sure I have."

"When?"

"Now, when *was* that?" said Biddy, and she looked at me as if I ought to know. "Oh yes, I remember now"— She had to screw up her face to remember. "Why, of course! It was Wednesday morning. No, wait a minute. Was it Tuesday?" And again she appealed to me.

"Hell!" said Capt. Little. "Don't you know anything?"

"Oh yes!" she said, seriously. "It was Wednesday morning, I'm almost sure, because I went downstairs at about nine to phone to my Beauty Parlor about my bang—"

"Never mind the bang. Get to the point, please. Did you see Vlack?"

"Why yes, I just told you I did, didn't I?"

"Where did you see him?"

"Why, right on that wide step there outside the door." She turned to me. "You know, Mr. Gilbert—where the two lamp posts are on the buttresses, don't you?"

Capt. Little was getting more exasperated every moment. "Well, well, what about him? What did he do?"

"Why, he didn't do anything at all," Biddy said. "He just stood there, and I went over to the Automat—"

"Good god!" the Captain exclaimed; and then he asked her if that was the only time she had ever seen him, and to answer Yes or No.

"Why—" she stared at him. Then she said in a subdued voice, "Yes, I guess so."

"Did Miss Conley have any enemies that you know of?"

Biddy looked at him with her big dog eyes as if he had insulted the dead. "Why no, of *course* not!" she said. "Bertie was a nice girl. She was an awfully nice girl. Everybody just loved her."

The Captain threw up his hands in despair and when Biddy was dismissed I saw her pounced upon by reporters out in the hall, and I certainly felt sorry for them.

And then, after Capt. Little and I had gone back to Berta Conley's rooms and were preparing to leave, something happened that so shocked and sickened me that I was almost unable to believe my eyes.

One of the detectives who had been searching the bedroom came up to the Captain with a grin on his face. He had something in his closed fist.

"Say, Chief, what d'you think we found?" he said. "It was jammed into the toe of one of her white shoes in her suit case there, and we missed it at first."

He opened his hand, and held it out.

And there was the gold ring of Señor Corrijo, with the chiseled lions and the blazing Borgia ruby.

5

HÉLÈNE VIRAY

That evening with Capt. Little I had my first ride in a police car to the accompaniment of a continually screaming siren. At another time the excitement of dashing through the streets, without regard to traffic lights might have elated me. But, after the shock of Berta's death, the finding of the Señor's ring in her room had so dejected me that I was quite indifferent when we got to the 14th Precinct and they took my finger-prints. I was well aware though, that I wasn't yet by any means free from suspicion.

As we hurtled up Fifth Avenue the car's police radio was calling:

"Look out for a man, about thirty years old, rather tall and thin, face somewhat emaciated, thin moustache, dressed in light overcoat, light felt hat. The name is Hugo Vlack. Wanted for the murder of Berta Conley at the Hotel Imperial. Bring him in. That is all."

Capt. Little broke a long silence by saying,

"We checked up on this Conley girl's telephone, and she called up Miss Magister this afternoon at 3.25, but Miss Magister didn't answer. She called up Corrijo's number at 5.10 P.M., and he was out, too, the operator said."

I said, "Then if the Señor did go up to her room at two o'clock, and if he did threaten her or frighten her, why

91

should she call him up later? Something must have happened that she wanted to tell him."

"Lots of things were happening today," said the Captain. He made a quick, deft turn to avoid a truck. "One of the chambermaids told Ferguson that at one o'clock she was in that end hallway and she saw the Conley girl's door closing just before she could see who it was inside. The maid said that she assumed it was Miss Conley. And so she was surprised when she saw Miss Conley come in about half an hour afterwards. The elevator boy corroborated her, as to that."

"Then someone must have entered the room while Miss Conley was away," I said, "an hour before Señor Corrijo called—if he did really call. Who could it have been?"

"Hugo Vlack, maybe," said the Captain, and he didn't speak again until the car stopped in front of a quiet-looking four-story brick house on East 58th St., not far from Sutton Place. Mme. Viray's green sedan was at the curb and there was the usual curious crowd staring at the house and discussing the tragedy.

We went up a low flight of wide stone steps, with a concrete urn at the top of each buttress. Inside we found Sergeant Pearson, a long, loose, round-headed chap with sleepy eyes. He was with a burly bristly redheaded detective with a hard, dog-like face and hardly any eyebrows. The two were in a small reception room off the front hall, examining a window. The room was littered with pasting tables and step ladders and rolls of wall paper, and scraps of paper were all over the floor, and tracked out into the hall.

"If the tragedy occurred while the paper hangers were here," I said to Capt. Little, "why wouldn't they know something about it?"

It was Sergeant Pearson who answered me. "Hell, think we wouldn't go after that the first thing?" he said. "Why, the workmen weren't here only half a day, today. They run out o' stock, they said, and knocked off work and went some place else, some other little job. We checked up on 'em all right." Then he fished into his pocket for a green gumdrop—he seemed to have a paper bag of them—and popped it into his mouth.

Capt. Little asked him if the front door was locked when he came.

"Just the spring lock," Pearson said, chewing, "Question is, did somebody have a key to come in, or did this Viray woman let him in."

"I thought she had a negro maid," I said, "or a cook, whatever she was. Mme. Viray told me so last night, anyway, at the Corrijo dinner."

Seeing that I had known her, Pearson took more interest in me.

"Yeah," he said, "but the girl was away today," and he kept on chewing. "Her day off, she says. We checked on that, too, Chief," he said. "She was shakin' her legs in a rhumba joint up in Harlem—and her behind, too, I guess."

I recalled, then, that Mme. Viray had asked me not to come today, as it was her cook's day of *congé*. And then Pearson said he had the woman here in the house, and had been questioning her. Her name was Dahlia Jones, he told us.

Capt. Little said, "She has a key to the house, I suppose?"

"To the lower door, below the front steps," Pearson said. He took another gumdrop. "Question is, which way did the murderer come? Believe me, Chief, that gal Dahlia is one flip negro. Why, Chief, she claims—"

"I prefer to hear it first hand," said Little curtly. "I want to see the place first."

Mme. Viray's living room in the back of the house was a beautiful place. It was full of color, quite the sort of home you might expect of a Frenchwoman of such grace and charm. I greatly admired the richly-flowered silk curtains and hangings—crimson and yellow, white, green, and the sleek walnut woodwork. The brick fireplace was in pastel shades of dull, tapestry brick, and it seemed intimate and friendly and the sepia brown walls were so warm, too. It was no place for death, that lovely room, I thought; and in spite of what had happened, in some curious way I felt elated, almost excited as if by her invisible presence. I seemed to hear again the rich contralto of her French voice.

"You nevaire know what I am going to do, either, Mr. Gilbert,—I hope." And then her seductive laughter, her half-closed eyes. "I should be *desoleé* if I thought that no longer I could give you a surprise. . . ." I hadn't realized before that her personality had affected me so deeply.

"Here's where the body was found," Pearson said, in his whining drawl. "Right over here." He began another gumdrop and pointed to the floor near a green tapestry couch in the middle of the room. "She certainly was one peach of a dame!" he said. "I been mixed up in a powerful lot o' murders in my day, Chief, but I swear I never see nothing like her, the way she laid there kind o' graceful, just like she'd gone to sleep. It kind o' got me, at first."

Capt. Little said then that he would talk to Mme. Viray's negro maid; and she was brought up from the kitchen on the basement floor where she had been held during the preliminary investigation.

Dahlia Jones came into the room with her hips switching. She had a half-frightened, half-defiant look on her face. She was a rather attractive yellowish negress of about twenty-three or so, with a good figure; and she had a sort of feline charm, like a graceful, half-tamed animal. She was well dressed in what were probably Mme. Viray's cast-off clothes.

The Captain asked her first how she had happened to come to the house that afternoon. He had heard, he said, that Friday was her day off.

"Yassir, that's right," she said, in a sort of singsong tone. "Fridays I mos' generally dance. I works hard all the other days, an' come Friday I gits so mopin' tired I jess got to dance it off. Yassir, I suttinly does love to dance. I reckon I got it in ma bones."

"The hell with your bones," the Captain exclaimed. "Answer the question. What were you doing here in the house on your day off?"

"Ain't I jess tellin' you, mister?" Dahlia answered. "Don' ma Madam tell me yisterday I kin have a pair o' her nude pylon stockin's what they done jess begun to run a little in the back? So I jess nacherly gravilates aroun' this afternoon to ask her could I have 'em to dance in tonight." Dahlia thrust out her foot. "I look jess grandelegant an' kinder who-cares in them stockin's. I suttinly does. I got laigs."

"Never mind your legs," the Captain barked. "Pull down your skirt and tell me how you discovered the body."

"Wall," said Dahlia, "jess like I told this gen'leman, I tol' him a dozen times, I come in by the door under the steps, an—"

"What time was this?" Capt. Little asked her sternly.

Dahlia was unimpressed. "Why, 'bout ha' past three o'clock, I reckon," she said, calmly. "I ain't got no watch. An' I come in through the kitchen, they ain't no other way to come, so that's jess the way I come, an' I come up them little back stairs up into that there pantry."

She pointed to a door near the corner of the room. Near it was a service window into the room we were in, and it had a panel that slid up and down.

"Then I come into this here room," she said, "lookin' for ma Madam. I didn't know was she here or upstairs, an' the fust thing I see, I see ma pore Madam layin' there on the floor. An', holy boy, was I scairt!"

The Captain asked her how the body was lying. He hadn't yet seen the photographs.

"Why, she was all sort o' flapped over," Dahlia said. "An' I see right off somethin' was the matter, sure nuff. Her eyes was open, starin' at me somethin' awful, an' her face was all black on one side an' her mouth was frothin' like a racehoss. I felt o' her hand an' it was ice col', an' I reckon I let out a screech, I was so scairt, yassir, shakin' like a palsy, I was; an' that's all I know, 'cause I made one jump for the phone an' tol' the police jess as quick as I could, but I couldn't hardly speak oddible I was so scairt."

Capt. Little then told her to lie down on the floor in exactly the same position in which she had discovered Mme. Viray's body.

"Oh, my god, Mister, don' make me do that!" Dahlia implored. "I's scairt that's goin' to make me bad luck, if I do that!"

But she slowly dropped down, rolling her eyes, and, negress though she was, realizing that the beautiful Hélène Viray had lain there dead, like that, only a few hours ago, it was a ghastly sight—to me, at least. To the Captain, I suppose it was a mere experiment. He studied her awhile, then told her to get up, and he asked her if Mme. Viray had many callers.

"Yassir, she done have loads an' stacks o' folkses comin' round. More gen'lemen than ladies come, though."

"Any of them stay all night?" barked the Captain.

Dahlia tossed her head defiantly. "I dunno whether they does, or whether they doesn't," she said in her pert way. "I go home when ma work's done, an' ma Madam, she do what she wants to do, I reckon, jess like I do."

"What sort of people called here, Dahlia?"

"Wall," Dahlia said, "furrin peoples mostly. They speak some o' this jabber-talk, I don' know what they say."

"What nationality—French? Spanish? Italian?" Pearson asked.

"Oh, lawd, I dunno no difference that way." Dahlia tossed her head again. "They jess all talk jabber."

"Well," said the Captain, "did they seem like,—well, nice folks?"

"They suttinly did, sir," Dahlia said. "Only they kinda rich an' ain't rich, too, most of 'em."

I put in, "You mean they acted as if they had had money, but hadn't so much now?"

"Tha's it, tha's what I means," she cried, eagerly. "They got furs all kinda wore an' mangy, an' yet they's swell furs. They got kinda three-year-old hats. Kinda people who knows they knife an' forks—I know 'em. Quality folks, ma ol' mammy used to call 'em."

"Did Señor Corrijo ever call here?" Capt. Little asked.

"Yassir, off an' on," Dahlia said, "mainly on."

"Did Mme. Viray seem to like him?"

Dahlia grinned and said, "Yas sir! Ma Madam was crazy about that Senior man, she suttinly was. She always smile when he come, she suttinly smile mighty pretty on that Senior man. Sometime she gimme a dollar so I go home early."

"Did he ever stay all night here?" Capt. Little shot at her.

Dahlia rolled her eyes. "How I know that? Ain't I done tol' you she allus scoot me home when he come? That Senior man he allus gimme a dollar, too, he suttinly is a magnificent gen'lman. Once he gimme a five," and she grinned.

"Did Mme. Viray ever quarrel with the Señor?"

"I don' know nothin' about no quarrels, nossir, but they did git to kind o' argifyin' like sometimes, specially lately. Seem like the Senior man, he tryin' to git her to do somethin' what she don' want to do. I don' know nothin' about it, though. How I know? I got ma work to do, an' I does it. I guess it was about money, might be. Ma Madam she was mopin' about money all the time, mostly."

The Captain then asked her if she knew of any enemies Mme. Viray could have had.

"Huh! Mos' everybody done got some enemies, ain't they?" Dahlia said impudently. "They don' amount to much if they ain't. I got a heaps o' enemies. What I care?"

Capt. Little asked Dahlia if she were married. "Deed I is, sir, yassir, I got a man, but he ain't no good."

"You mean you have to support him?"

"Nossir, I don' s'port him, *no*sir, not that bum, I don't. No *sir!* He s'ports hisself. You don' ketch me workin' ma hands off, not for no no-count negro like he is. Let him git along hisself if he won't work, tha's what I say."

Pearson asked in his drawling way, "But he lives with you, doesn't he, Dahlia?" And he offered me a gumdrop, and winked at me.

"He got a kinder broke-down truckle cot in the kitchen, yassir, if you calls that livin'. He can't clutter up ma room, nossir. I pays the rent but I don' git him no meals nor nothin'. I tells him, 'You go git a job if you want to eat, an' earn money like I does. Don' you spek me to stuff yo' hide. You can't have none o' my money. I works too hard for it, while you's jess shootin' craps.' He got his health, ain't he? Let him work if he want to eat, or go empty, tha's jess what I tell him."

"But you have some of your meals at home, don't you, Dahlia?" Pearson insisted. And he bit into another gumdrop. "There must be food in your house, isn't there?"

"Huh! They sure is food an' plenty of it, too. But they's padlocks too, an' plenty of 'em. I done got one on ma kitchen closet door an' one on the ice box. Everything's locked up shut like dimonds an' that bum he don't git none o' ma food, nossir! He jess rarin' hongry all the time, I don' care."

"Has your husband ever been in this house?" Capt. Little asked.

"Him? Huh! Why, he was here on'y last night," Dahlia said.

"Here last night!" Capt. Little exclaimed. "What for?"

"Ain't he ma husban'?" Dahlia answered. "How come he can't come here if I want him? I tol' him to come, tha's why he come. Ma Madam, she done gimme a old armchair what was broke an' ma man Sam, he done come an' fetched it home for me last night. Tha's why he come, yassir."

Pearson had been questioning her in a quiet, friendly enough way, so far; but now he took a hand and he startled me almost as much as he did Dahlia when he shouted,

"What did you leave that basement window unfastened for last night, Dahlia Jones?"

Her eyes rolled and she whimpered, "I ain't left no winder onlocked at all, nossir. What for I leave it onlocked? I locks 'em up every night when I goes home, don't I?"

"You mean to say," Pearson snarled, "you didn't know the window in the kitchen, next to the basement entrance there was unlatched last night? Who did you leave it that way for, Dahlia? Come on, now, who was it? Your husband?"

"That no-count bum? No *sir!*" she shouted, swaying in her chair. "Not him an' not nobody, neither."

Capt. Little went at her. "You got some other feller, Dahlia, you go with? Come now, have you? Haven't you? Answer me!"

Dahlia almost screamed. "No *sir.* I ain't got no boy fren', deed I ain't. I's a speckable married woman, I is, even if ma husban' is a bum. I don' never s'picion tha' winder git onlatch, nohow, no I don', nossir." She pawed with her hands. "What I want to leave that winder onlatch that way for, anyway? Ain't I got a key? What I got a key for? I don' have to crawl through no winder like no monkey, is I? Ain't I done tor ma Madam a hundred times she oughter git bars put on them winders? I don' know who done lef' that winder onlatch, but I knows one thing, mister, it suttinly ain't me. No *sir!*"

And when they had finished their questions, Dahlia swung herself out of the room like a lithe animal, growling, and I thought that if she'd had a tail she would have been switching it.

Capt. Little and Pearson sat there some time discussing her story. I was only half listening. I was looking down at that place where Helêne Viray had been found on the green carpet. Then I thought I saw something glistening, something like sparkling dust. I asked Pearson what it was.

He got up and went over, kneeled down and inspected the carpet. Capt. Little came over and looked, too.

"Broken glass," he said. "Must have been stepped on and ground into such little fine pieces I can't make out what it was. Too thin to have come from a drinking glass, though."

The Captain asked Pearson to cut out that part of the carpet carefully and have it sent to the laboratory for microscopic examination. Then he asked Pearson if the fire had been burning in the fireplace when he first got to the house.

"No, but the ashes were still warm," Pearson said. "I guess I'll have a look at 'em now."

Just then one of Pearson's men came into the room, a little short, snappy, keen-eyed man. Coy, his name was. He had been going from house to house interviewing the people living on the block. He read from his notes.

"Mrs. Splicer, widow. No. 954. Opposite side of street. Saw a man at Viray's front door today. Black moustache, black soft felt hat, dark clothes. Time, about three o'clock. Doesn't know whether man went in or not. Reason: Next time she looked over here, he wasn't there."

Capt. Little asked me if the description sounded anything like that of Señor Corrijo; but I thought it too vague for identification, and besides, there was nothing about a goatee.

Detective Coy read on. "Ernest Dibling. Janitor at 958. Saw man at Viray's door about three o'clock. Lightish overcoat. Light soft felt hat. Overcoat collar turned up. Couldn't see much of his hair. Thought it tousled. Couldn't identify clothes. Reason: Buttress of Viray's front steps partly hid man. Time. Not sure. Thinks it was little after three."

And then Sergeant Pearson called out from the fireplace he had been searching and held up a charred lump attached to a short broken piece of glass tubing. Capt. Little examined it carefully.

"That charcoal stuff looks to me like burned rubber," he said.

Finally he snapped his fingers and said, "I got it! You know what this thing was?—a medicine dropper. D'you see, Harry? That's how they gave her the cyanide. That's why we didn't find any drinking glass or bottle. The stuff was brought here in a dropper and forced into her mouth. No doubt about it."

The red-haired, dog-faced detective I had seen with Pearson now came into the room. He had been searching Mme. Viray's bedroom upstairs. He handed Capt. Little a cigar box containing about a dozen cigars. The Captain smiled and asked me if I knew what kind of cigars Señor Corrijo smoked.

"A good deal like these," I said, "specially made extra long Panatelas, very dark—Maduros, I think."

"I guess he was pretty good friends with this Viray woman," the Captain said, dryly.

And then the detective handed him a photograph, saying that he had found it in one of the bureau drawers. It had been, he said, with photographs of the city and harbor and the Plaza of Buenos Aires, and other scenes in Argentina.

Little looked at the photograph and I saw his face change. He studied it for a moment with a pursed mouth. Then he turned to me.

"Well, Mr. Gilbert," he said, without a smile, "I'm afraid your girl friends weren't quite so nice as you seem to think. Pretty gay, I should say, by this photograph, all three of 'em. Pretty damned gay. That story of yours about seeing them when you looked through the window of Corrijo's dining room out at Riverdale seems a little more plausible, now."

I went over to look at the photograph, but he shoved it into his pocket. "Well," he said, "you never can tell about women."

And I followed him out of the house still puzzled and wondering about those lovely women. Was it possible that I had been mistaken in them?

There was still quite a crowd out on the sidewalk; and I saw a young fellow in white trousers and white sport shirt crossing the street. He didn't have any hat on. He stopped one of the cops and spoke to him. Then the cop came up to the Captain's car where we were talking and said,

"A guy here thinks he's got something for you, Captain Little. Want to talk to him?"

The young chap was quite a swell, in a way, good-looking and intelligent. He was smiling with the debonair insolence of youth and smoking a cigarette. He was evidently quite amused by the affair. He said he lived in a house across the street.

He was sitting at his window on the second floor, he said, in a rather patronizing way, at about 2.45 it was, he thought, and he was studying. He explained, as if it were important, that he was a senior at Columbia.

"I happened to look out the window," he said languidly, "and I saw a dusky individual descend those steps of this house under the front entrance there. He must have entered by the basement door, I surmise, because I didn't see him again for about ten minutes. Then I saw him emerge up onto the sidewalk and start to run. He ran to the corner and round into First Avenue, I think. He was a tall chap in shirtsleeves. Lanky, I might say, and cadaverous. I've been in my room writing ever since, you know, and I've been so busy I never heard anything about the murder till just now. Was it a bloody one, may I venture to ask?" he added, cynically.

Capt. Little shut him up with a sharp remark, and took his name and address and then said to the police officer,

"Go in and tell Sergeant Pearson to send somebody out and get that colored cook's husband, Sam Jones. Bring him into my office tonight sure."

While the young fellow was talking I had happened to notice, in the crowd on the sidewalk, a tall, thin, ungainly negro in an old battered straw hat. Then I noticed that he was in shirtsleeves. He was staring, with his mouth open showing glittering white teeth; but before the young fellow had finished talking to the Captain I saw that negro slink off and walk rapidly down the street.

I caught Capt. Little's arm and pointed at the retreating figure. "Say, I believe that negro there may be Jones!" I said. "Don't let him get away."

Little shouted, "Jones! Sam! Come back here!" and a policeman started after him on the run, and he shouted, too.

The negro ran a little way and then stopped short, and looked back, terrified. The officer brought him back, and the crowd stared at him and muttered.

"Is your name Sam Jones?" Capt. Little demanded none too gently.

The negro took off his old straw hat. He hesitated a moment, rolled his eyes about and then he said, "Yas. sir. Yas, I's Sam Jones. I suttinly am. Tha's my name. What you want? I don' know nothin'."

The Captain ordered him taken into the Viray house, and we all went back into the living room again. Detective Pearson was seated there at a table making some notes, with his hat on the back of his head and his bag of gum-drops beside him almost empty.

"Now, Sam," said Capt. Little, "did you kill Mme. Viray?"

"Who, me? Nossir, nossir. No *sir!* I swear to holy god I don' never kill nobody, nossir. I don' know nothin' about it. I don' know nothin' about nothin'."

"Well, you'd better know something pretty damn quick, Sam."

Sam rolled his eyes, scared almost stiff. "How I gwine to know somethin' what I don' know, when I don' know nothin'?" he whined.

Pearson laughed. I didn't.

Capt. Little made a gesture to the policeman who held Sam's wrist. I saw him give it a screw and the negro screamed.

"Oh, my god," he cried. "Oh, don' twist me, mister! Please don' twist me, mister, for god's sake, mister, don' give me no third agree, please don'! I's gwine talk all I knows. Yassir, yas sir, I gwine talk, I is, yassir.

Sam Jones told his story then with many rambling words and much questioning. He confirmed all his wife Dahlia had told about his home life, with every bit of food locked up. And as he had no job and hadn't a cent to his name he was half starving, he said, on only a sandwich or two a day. The poor devil was wrinkled like a raisin and as thin as an alley cat.

When he had come here to Mme. Viray's, the day before, he said, to get the chair she had given his wife Dahlia, he had noticed the well-filled refrigerator, not to speak of lots of food and fruit in the kitchen, and, as Mme. Viray was then away, he had found a chance to grab something to eat. But he said Dahlia had caught him red-handed and she had taken the cheese and cake he was stuffing into his pocket away from him.

He carried the chair downstairs after that, he said, and took it out through the lower door, under the front steps. But Sam said that while his wife wasn't looking, he had slipped open the catch of the window nearest the basement door.

And so the next day (which was today), as Sam knew that his wife would be off in some dancing dive, he told us, he came here to the house at about three in the afternoon. He thought that Mme. Viray would probably be upstairs or away, but as she was seldom in the little kitchen anyway, he said he expected to be able to sneak to the refrigerator without her knowing he was in the house. All Sam wanted, he said, was to get something to eat.

And so, when he got to the house here, he went down the steps to the basement door under the front entrance and waited till no one was visible on the block. Then he raised the lower window and slid in. He tiptoed up the back stairs. He opened the refrigerator door. He was just about to snatch a dish of ham and some sweet potatoes, he said, when he heard a noise.

It was evidently Mme. Viray running down the front stairs, for he then heard the front door close, and Mme. Viray's voice talking as she and her caller came down the hall.

Sometimes Mme. Viray received her guests in the small reception room near the front door (so Dahlia had told Sergeant Pearson); but as it was being redecorated, Mme.

Viray took whoever called into her big living room where we now were. This living room, as Dahlia had shown us, was connected with the pantry by means of a service window with a sliding panel. Sam told us that by raising this panel half an inch or so, he, out of sight in the pantry, could look through the crack into the living room. And Sam said that what he saw terrified him.

"Madam, she talk an' laff with this feller all the time they come along the hall," Sam said. "But jess the minute they git into this room, all of a sudden this feller he throw a arm roun' Madam's neck an' look like he pinch her nose. He never say one word, he don', nossir, not one word. I's behind in there lookin' all the time. An' then this feller he done shove somethin' into Madam's mouth, an' Madam she give a gulp like she choke, an' she walk jess a step or two staggery, then she drap down on the floor plunk jess like she done got shot."

"Who was the fellow, her caller?" Capt. Little demanded. "Would you know him again if you saw him? What did he look like?"

Sam looked at the Captain blankly. His eyes were bulging. "I don' know," he said. "I don' never see him."

"Why, you just told us you saw them come in, the two of them."

"Yassir, I sees 'em come in, I suttinly did, yassir, jess like I say; but I don' ketch no sight o' the feller."

"Why not?" shouted the two detectives almost together.

Sam was trembling with fear by this time, and he whimpered,

"'Cause when they come in the door, Madam, she in front of him, kinda, so I don' git to see much of him, on'y he got kinda light hair, an' when he grab her round the neck his back kinda git turned on me so I don' see nothin', on'y his back. Boy, I's so scairt I don' sca'cely dast to look, nossir, I don'."

"But when Mme. Viray dropped, as you said, you could see the fellow then, couldn't you?" Capt. Little wanted to know.

"Nossir, I can't see him on'y back to," Sam said, "an' that there sofy kind o' hide him part way down, too. An' anyways, I don' git on'y jess a leetle crack to see through, an' holy boy! was I scairt!"

"What did he do after Mme. Viray fell, Sam?"

"Golly, I don' know. Don' ask me, I don' know what he done done. How I know that?" Sam said. "Lawdy god, I don' never wait for nothin'. Boy, I was scairt out o' my gizzards, I was."

Capt. Little asked him why he didn't try to help Mme. Viray.

"Oh, lawdy god!" Sam cried. "I's scairt, I don' want to git mixed up in no killin' mess. I jess want to git away quick."

Pearson asked impatiently, "Don't you even know what kind of clothes this feller had on, Sam?"

Sam fumbled his old straw hat. "Seem like he got a light overcoat an' a light hat, a felt hat; yassir, tha's jess what he got on, but I so scairt I don' pay no 'tention about his do's."

"And you don't recall anything you would know him by, Sam—nothing special?"

Sam said uncertainly, "He got his coat collar pulled up roun' the back of his head, an' look like he got some kind o' little spot in his shoulder o' his coat, yassir. Little roun' spot."

"Are you sure, Sam?" Capt. Little said sternly. "How d'you know? Don't try to make up anything, now. We'll know if you're lying."

"Yassir, I ain't gwine tell no lie. No *sir!*" Sam declared loudly.

I made bold to ask him why, if he was so scared, did he happen to notice a little thing like a spot on the man's coat. And Pearson nodded and said that was just what he was wondering.

Sam said in a low, trembly voice, "I done see that spot most suttinly sure, yassir. Ain't the sun shine in the winder? Ain't that sun light him up good, plum on the shoulder. Yas *sir!* Little roun' spot like it mos' washed out, kinda like it ain't hardly there. I don' hardly see it when I see it, I's so scairt, but I see it now, plain. Yassir. Little roun' spot."

"Well, go on," said the Captain, wearily. "What did you do after you saw Mme. Viray fall?"

Sam rolled his head and grinned sillily. "Who, me? I scramboodle. I done git out o' this house like I's bein' shot at, yassir."

"And when you were out on the street," Pearson whined, "did you see anyone coming out of the house?"

"Nossir, I isn't lookin' for nobody, no *sir!*" and Sam shook his head a dozen times. "I's in a pow'fle hurry to git away, yassir. I jess scramboodle."

The telephone bell in the room rang just then. Capt. Little yelled "Hello!" and then he said, "What's that? The German-American Bund?" Then he listened for some moments. Then he said, "O.K., Dan, I'll be over as soon as I've finished here." Then he hung up and said, "Dan Leary, over at the Magister place. Go ahead, Harry."

Detective Pearson pointed his finger at Sam and whined, "Sam Jones, why didn't you notify the police at once of what you'd seen?"

Sam cowered and fingered his loose-lipped mouth. "Me? I don' want to git mixed up in no killin' mess, nossir! Not me! No *sir!*"

Pearson drawled, "D'you realize, Sam Jones, that you can be sent to jail for not reporting this crime?"

Then the Captain went over to him and shook his fist. "See here, Sam Jones," he shouted, "didn't you kill Mme.

Viray? You might as well say so before we go to work on
you, you know!"

"No, no, no!" Sam let out a yell. "Don' beat me up,
Mister, I ain't done it, I swear to god I ain't! No *sir!* I jess
git into that winder to git a bite o' somethin' to eat. I ain't
no killin' negro, mister, I's peaceful, I is. I ain't no razor
man, I's peaceful."

Pearson whined again, "What did you come back to the
house for, tonight then, if you was so scared?"

"Why I come back?" Sam said. "Don' the police they
come git ma Dahlia? Tha's why. Tha's why I back. Don' I
want to know what gwine happen nex'? Yassir, I want to
know what they gwine to do to ma Dahlia. Tha's why I
come back."

Capt. Little remarked to me dryly. "There's your literature, Mr. Gilbert. 'Murderer revisits the scene of his
crime, drawn back by the irresistible urging of his con-
science.'"

Just as the phone rang again a big policeman took the
blubbering negro away to be locked up. Capt. Little took
up the receiver. "What's that?" he said. Then, "All right,
Dan . . . Yes, about fifteen minutes," and hung up.

"D'you really think, Captain," I said, "that that negro
killed Mme. Viray?"

The Captain was standing and he said that they'd have
to hold Sam as a material witness, anyway. And as we all
walked to the front door he said, "In a homicide case
you've got to suspect everybody who has had an opportunity to commit the crime, whether you can find a motive
or not and regardless of how they act."

"O' course it ain't likely this poor negro done it," said
Pearson. He swallowed his last gumdrop and threw the
paper bag onto the floor. "Too hard to get the cyanide,
for one thing; and I can't seem to see Sam jumpin' all over
town killin' women."

"Well," said Capt. Little, "there's a lot about that negro we don't know yet." He leaned back and looked up thoughtfully at the ceiling. "He may be a psychopathic case with a killer complex—a sadist. He might even have been paid to do in this woman, for all we know." He laughed.

"Well, anyway," Pearson drawled, "we got a kind of a description o' the murderer, if that coon ain't lyin'—light hair and light coat, light hat. An' it tallies with what that janitor, Dibling, across the street said the feller was like that called here at the front door this afternoon."

The Captain got up then and yawned and said he was going upstairs to have a look around. I got up too, but he told me to wait there in the living room. I was disappointed. I should have been glad to see what sort of a place an exquisite creature like Hélène Viray, so fond of beauty and comfort, would have for her intimate life.

But after all, I thought, this room was where she lived, too. It was where she entertained her friends. How did she entertain them? It made me queerly sad to think that I should never call on her here. Where would she have sat, I wondered—in that gay armchair by the window, perhaps, while I talked to her in this other gay armchair. Unless we both sat on that big couch with the red cushions. We might have sat pretty close together. How could I ever keep away from such a delicious and seductive creature? I wondered if I would have kissed her—of course I would—and what then? And then I looked down at that spot on the carpet and realized again that lovely Helêne was dead, dead, dead!

I couldn't bear to think about it, so I got up and went to a long book case along one end wall. Mostly yellow paper covered French novels, and daring ones, too. A Stendhal, bound in morocco. Paul Morand, Gide, Birabeau, Delteil, Sartre—a mixture.

Then I saw a row of books on Egypt in German, French and English. I took out *"Le Secret des Pyramides"* and I smiled as I turned the foolish pages. A sheet of paper fell out. I picked it up and looked at it.

On it was written, in a fine, elegant, European hand, her writing, I thought, *"Com. des Relations Etrang."* And after it were a list of names. Some of them I recognized as the names of Senators. And some, I knew were on the Committee of Foreign Relations. Washington! Hadn't Berta told me that Mme. Viray made frequent trips to Washington? I put the paper into my pocket and sat down again.

I was still wondering about it when Capt. Little rejoined me. I asked him if he had found any clues.

"I don't know," he said. "There was an old cardboard shoe box in her closet, filled with silk stockings. They all had holes or runs in them and probably she was keeping them to be rewoven. These were in the bottom of the box."

He handed me two letters in envelopes.

"They're from the French Consul General in New York, evidently," he said. "I doubt if they'll help much, but you never can tell. Unfortunately I don't read French, so I'll have to get them translated."

"Let me see them," I said. "I think I can tell you what they're about, I've lived some ten years in Paris."

He was delighted, and I unfolded the sheets, and looked them over.

"This one is about some cousin she has, living in occupied France, evidently," I said. "The Consul says he hasn't been able to get any information about her. He says he may be able to get a letter to her through a friend in Vichy, though. This other one is an invitation to dinner from the Consul. He says he has good news about that *canaille*, that means a rotter, you know, and he says 'We'll soon manage about Dak.' Oh, wait a minute! Listen to this. 'Delighted that you are making progress in W.'"

"It's all Chinese to me," said the Captain.

"Of course," I said, "but just wait till I show you what I found." And I showed him the sheet of paper that had dropped out of the book.

Then I explained to him that, although Mme. Viray had told Berta that she was for De Gaulle, and was working to free the country from Hitler, these papers pretty well proved that she was, instead, working with the Vichy government.

"If she weren't," I said, "she wouldn't be getting friendly letters from the French Consul here. He's a Vichy agent, of course. If she is friendly with him, then what she's going to Washington for, is probably to try to influence the Foreign Relations Committee of the Senate *not* to recognize De Gaulle and the crowd working for Free France. In his letter 'W' stands for Washington, of course; *canaille* must refer to De Gaulle, and 'Dak' is obviously Dakar, the port on the west coast of Africa that we're all worrying about just now. In other words," I said, "Mme. Hélène Viray was a traitor and worse. She was a spy."

The Captain nodded, evidently pleased with me, and he said, "Very interesting theory, anyway, Mr. Gilbert, but I'm not too sure of it. The D.A. warned you not to go romantic on us, you know. Perhaps your fiction training is carrying you away."

"There's an easy way to prove it," I said. "Ring up the French Consul General and ask for information about her."

He said that's just what he'd do and went to the phone.

It was well on in the evening by this time, and the Consulate, of course, had long since been closed. But the New York Chief of Police found a means of ascertaining the Consul's whereabouts, and after considerable waiting and fruitless trials, he was located at the Rainbow Room.

I heard the Captain ask him if he could give any information about Mme. Hélène Viray, who had been murdered this afternoon. There was a pause. Then I saw the Captain's face change almost imperceptibly, and he said, "All right. Thank you, sir," and he hung

"Well, Gilbert," he said, "I've got to hand it to you. That damned Consul said he had never heard of such a person."

"In that case," I said, "I'm very much afraid you'll find the lady was pretty badly mixed up with the Nazis."

6

MAUDE MAGISTER

As we drove away from the Viray house in Capt. Little's car, he said,

"This spy complication, true or not, is an interesting angle, and you've helped some, Mr. Gilbert, I acknowledge. And it may lead us somewhere, in the end, at that. But my immediate business," he said, "is to solve these murders in a hurry. You see, whoever killed this Viray woman must have known her pretty well, because she let him in and talked with him—always assuming, of course, that Sam Jones was telling the truth."

Then he said they'd have a lot of routine to do—checking up on all Mme. Viray's friends and acquaintances. Then they'd eliminate the alibis, and boil it all down to possibilities and then to probabilities.

"That's the regular way," he said, "the hard way. We have to go at it like a machine, you know, unless we happen to get a break with some new evidence. Or one of your hunches," and he smiled grimly.

"And by the way," he said, "as you know French, you might see what you can make of this." He handed me over a small packet of papers tied up with a red ribbon. There were several newspaper clippings, creased and worn, and a letter or two. He said he had discovered it in a small tin cash box with a few rings and pins and things.

I glanced them over and said, "By the paper and type I should think these clippings might be from some of the Parisian weekly papers, *Candide* or *Gringoire,* they both specialize in rather spicy and scandalous personal anecdotes, you know. This clipping is about the divorce of Colonel Claude-Jean Viray, probably Hélène Viray's ex-husband. The letters look like love letters. They're addressed *ma chèrie* and signed 'CJ.' That would be Claude-Jean, undoubtedly. The ink is pretty badly faded, though, and the writing is hard to read. I'll let you know what they are tomorrow."

That little package didn't, as it turned out, help much towards solving the mystery of Hélène Viray's death, but it did bring her to life for me, and gave me a vivid glimpse of her romantic past.

And this was the romantic story that I pieced together when I translated those letters and clippings in my room, later that night:

Hélène and her sister Marie were identical twins. They lived, when they were girls, at Tours, in central France, where their father, Dr. Le Cou was a modest family physician.

There was a middle-aged artillery officer, Col. Viray, stationed at Tours, and he made the acquaintance of the beautiful Le Cou twins. They were then seventeen years old, and they resembled one another so closely that few— and hardly the Colonel himself—could tell them apart. He saw most of Marie, as it happened, and although she was penniless, he fell desperately in love with her. As he was rich and of an old and distinguished Norman family, Marie's parents urged her to accept him, and she was duly affianced.

Then came the drama. The Colonel was transferred to Morocco; and Marie, who had never cared too much for him, anyway, promptly fell in love with another man, a brilliant, handsome young surgeon.

Marie was in despair. She wanted to throw the Colonel over, but her parents refused to permit her. They not only feared a scandal, but the wealthy Col. Viray was a most desirable *parti,* especially for a young girl without a *dot.*

The two sisters talked it over. Hélène, who was ambitious and loved luxury, proposed that she marry the Colonel, instead of Marie, but without his being aware of the substitution of the bride. Not even the parents were aware of the plot.

And so, when the happy bridegroom returned from his African post for the wedding, Marie saw him as before, though as little as she decently could. She made all her preparations for the ceremony just as if she were really going through it. Hélène, meanwhile, kept out of the Colonel's sight as much as possible.

The girls' problem now was to prevent the Colonel from suspecting that he was marrying the wrong twin. But Hélène was what the French call *fine;* she was clever and resourceful. And so, the day before the wedding, she scratched Marie on the cheek with a needle, and cut her ring fingernail square across short, as if it were broken.

That evening Marie lamented to the bridegroom that both her pretty face and her finger were so disfigured, just when she wanted to be most beautiful.

If it should enter anyone's mind that there had been a change of brides, you see, these two little tricks would be likely to quiet their doubts, and positively identify Marie, the bride.

The day of the wedding Hélène was to help Marie dress. But instead, it was Marie who helped Hélène put on the bridal veil, after the mother had been laughingly excluded from the room. Hélène then cut off the nail of her own ring finger, and gave herself a scratch on the cheek exactly like Marie's. And Hélène then artfully painted over and hid Marie's scar with some concoction she had obtained of a pharmacist. White gloves would of course hide Marie's fingernail until after the ceremony. Who would notice the bridesmaid, anyway? It would be the bride who attracted all eyes that day.

And so it was that Hélène became Mme. Viray.

It was almost a year, I read, before the tricked bridegroom discovered that he had married the wrong twin. He was shocked and enraged and his pride was deeply wounded. One of the clippings showed how the sensational story was brought out at his divorce proceedings.

But there was, it appeared, a happy sequel. Happy, that is, for Hélène. In one of the letters from Col. Viray, I read: "I will never forgive you, but I shall never forget you, Hélène. I never wish to see you again. But, *ma chèrie*, you are too beautiful, I cannot let you suffer. I want you to shine always," and he ended by saying magnanimously that although he would not leave her anything in his will, he had settled an annuity on her that would always keep her from want. It was true *noblesse oblige*.

A worn old clipping told of Gen. Viray's having been killed in the disastrous Battle of France. And another one had a mildly flattering notice of Hélène's singing in a second-rate opera company in New Orleans. How she ever gravitated into French politics and espionage, I don't know. But the lovely Hélène was too fond of money, I'm afraid, and the good things of life.

And as we dashed through the streets of New York in Capt. Little's screaming car, I wondered if it would turn out that Maude Magister, too, had taken that easy way.

I said to the Captain, "I don't want to be too inquisitive, but can you tell me what it was you heard on the phone, a little while ago, about Miss Magister, in connection with the German-American Bund?"

Capt. Little had thawed out still more towards me since I had translated the letters from the French Consul at Mme. Viray's house, but it wasn't so much for my help as to keep an eye on me, I suspected, that he was taking me along. Especially as his answer was a curt, "We'll see when we get to the Magister place."

Anyway, I was glad enough of the opportunity of seeing how that proud, aristocratic beauty had lived. It was a made-over four-story residence on East 46th St.; one of those places where you press a button under a row of letter boxes in the vestibule, and the front door is buzzed open. We hurried up a flight of blue carpeted stairs to the second floor.

Detective Dan Leary, who met us at the door, was a bulky big man with a round red face and round eyes, one of the old-timers on the Force, I guessed, and a bit slow-minded, who had a pretty good opinion of himself. He said that there were some Press photographers taking pictures in the living room. And so, head in the air, he led us into the dining room of the flat.

And there, with a gesture that seemed to say, "I guess that'll hold you," he took from his pocket a folded paper and handed it to Capt. Little. It contained a list of names and addresses written in violet ink. "We found it in one of the drawers of her secretary out in the front room, there," he said.

Capt. Little rolled his cigar around in his mouth and studied the paper. "Mostly German names," he said. "But the Magister girl was as English as the Tower of London."

"So's Lord Haw-Haw," said Leary. "But don't he broadcast Nazi propaganda in a pure Oxford accent? Looks to me, Cap., as if the gal was linked up with the Nazi crowd

here, and those names are maybe members of their under-
cover organization, all over the Eastern states."

"Yes," said Capt. Little, "and she may have peddled life
insurance too, and these are the names of her prospects."
Then he stopped rolling his cigar and looked at Leary and
asked, "You got something else up your sleeve, Dan?"

Dan Leary threw up his head pompously. "Only a map
of New York with all the police stations marked in red circles," he said; and he produced that, too, from his breast
pocket and handed it over.

Capt. Little nodded, his eyes on the map. "Looks like
something for the F.B.I.," he said. "It does begin to look
as if there was a spy tie-up between the two girls. This
Mme. Viray, you know, was probably working with the
Nazi bunch, from the French end of it. What else you got,
Dan?"

Detective Leary took a cardboard box from the mantel and opened it and displayed some small transparent
stones.

"We found 'em scattered round on the floor an' rug in
the front room," he said. "They're cut glass, or rhinestones
or whatever they use in this cheap costume jewelry the
women are all wearing nowadays."

"Well, what about 'em?" the Captain asked. He got up
and inspected them.

"Here's the point, Chief," Leary said. "The Magister
woman had on a flowered rayon gown when we found her,
a hostess robe, I believe they call 'em, and she had a fancy
clip on it, with some stones missing. I figure that in the
tussle they had, whoever it was pressed hard up against her
and scraped against that clip and loosened the stones so
they fell out. You get it, don't you, Chief?"

I asked Leary if there were any finger-prints on the
knife Miss Magister was stabbed with.

"No," he said, in a disappointed tone, "it was one of those curved Norwegian hunting knives, you know, with a stag horn handle, and it was all broken up into little grooves, you know, with no flat surfaces on it big enough to hold a print. They tell me she kept the knife in a sheath on her writing table, probably for a paper cutter or something."

Capt. Little sat down and relighted his stump of cigar. "If the killing were premeditated," he said, "of course the fellow would be likely to bring his own weapon. The key to the whole business is the fight the girl had before she was stabbed." The Captain ran his hand back through his white hair. "Might have been some sneak thief get in and she caught him at it, and he killed her for fear of her testifying against him. Is that all you got, Dan?"

Leary became more important than ever. He took a plate from the sideboard and brought it over. On the plate were three cigarette butts.

"Know what these are?" he asked, like a professor. "We found 'em on the floor there where the girl was killed. Must have been in the ashtray when the table tipped over. They're hand-made cigarettes, Chief, and you know what? I'm pretty sure they're some o' them reefers."

Capt. Little whistled. "Marijuanas, eh? Well, that's a new angle."

I knew of course from the newspapers and magazine articles that smoking marijuana cigarettes, or "reefers" as they are popularly called, lowers the psychic centers and inhibits all sense of responsibility. The victims of the habit do all sorts of uncontrolled things and go to excesses of which, normally, they would be incapable. I had heard too that the police were trying to suppress not only the sale of reefers, but were also all the time hunting for and extirpating the weeds from which they were made.

Capt. Little said that he had had considerable experience with reefer addicts.

"When a chap gets hopped up on those things," he said, "what they call 'high,' he's liable to do anything. He's just the same as crazy. Looks to me here something like a case of attempted rape."

Capt. Little sat back in his chair and tipped his head and thought it over.

"Suppose," he said, finally, "some guy gets struck on this Magister girl. She's a good looker, but cold, and she high-hats him. What does he care after he's inhaled a few reefers? He'd tackle the Queen of England. All he's got to do is punch her call button in the vestibule downstairs and phone up that he's the gas man to read her meter, or got a package to deliver or something, and come right up. All right. He makes a pass at her and he tries to get gay. She grabs up a knife to defend herself."

"I get it," said Leary. "Maybe he gets the knife away from her, then he goes wild and lets her have it to keep her quiet. It's easy. Remember that murder in that apartment in Sutton Place? The Italian chap got into that woman's place easy enough, didn't he? And that's just what happened here, except that this Magister girl was knifed instead of strangled."

"Take it easy, Dan." The Captain was smiling. "It's just a snap theory. I'm not ready to go to town with it yet so you needn't get excited. Why, I'll bet even Mr. Gilbert here can see the holes in it."

I said, "I see one thing against it, anyway. If those cigarette butts—"

"Sure," said Capt. Little. "If this chap was so busy making love to her, how about his smoking those three cigarettes while he was here? Looks as if either she knew the chap pretty well or he was attractive enough for her to be willing to entertain him a while, before he got too fresh with her."

He started to discuss the affair with Detective Leary, and I went up the hall to look at the scene of the murder. There was a patrolman in the front room who had been watching the photographers.

I wasn't allowed to enter; but through the open doorway I got a glimpse that sickened me.

Now the other two places, despite their tragedy, had suggested life and happiness. At the Hotel Imperial, I mean, it was as if Berta Conley might come laughing into her modest, artistic, happy-go-lucky room at any moment to finish a sketch. And in Hélène Viray's lovely home she seemed to have just left and you could almost hear her rich contralto voice. But this square, blue-and-gray Empire living room of Maude Magister's, with its high ceiling and two windows on the street, suggested only violence and death.

A round mahogany table with brass decorations was lying on its side in the center of the room, and two chairs also had been upset, and the blue rug was scuffed and trampled into wrinkled folds and shoved to one side, showing the hardwood floor. I didn't see any trace of blood, but there was a splotch of black ink on the rug, and books and magazines were strewn about and I saw an ashtray on the floor, too, and some pens and sheets of note paper.

The policeman pointed out a large Empire armchair near the mantelpiece under a fine large pastel portrait of Miss Magister.

"That's where she was found," he said, as if he thoroughly enjoyed it. "She was hanging over backwards across the arm of that chair. She had been stabbed through the heart and the knife was still sticking into her. Mrs. Ball—that's her part-time maid—she was too scared, she said, to pull out the knife. But she said she knew the girl was dead anyway. She ran right out and got a cop on the corner."

I asked the officer where this Mrs. Ball was now. I should have liked to talk to her, I said.

He laughed and shook his head and said, "If you get to talk to her, you'll have plenty hard time. And can she throw words at you! Why, she's half-witted," the cop said, "if she's even as much as that. In fact I think she's plum crazy. Dan Leary couldn't do nothing with her; it was like talkin' to a Portuguee." Then he told me that Mrs. Ball was at her home, a few blocks away, but she was being taken care of by a plain clothes man and wouldn't get away. Dan Leary, he told me, was going to try her again in the morning and see if he couldn't get a straight word or two out of her.

On my way back to rejoin Capt. Little, I opened a door in the hallway. It was Miss Magister's bedroom. I thought it best not to go in, but I stood a while there looking at it curiously.

Berta's bedroom had been informal, almost to disorder. Sketches were pinned up here and there haphazard, and table tops were crowded with books and papers and the whole air was rather Bohemian. But this chamber of Miss Magister's was like one of those sample bedrooms you see up on the 9th floor of a big department store. It was severe but artistic in its blue and white decoration and every article of furniture placed just so. Everything, of course, was perfect and of fine quality and taste, but the room seemed cold and impersonal. There was nothing intimate or familiar or cozy about it. It might be the sanctuary of a modern Vestal virgin.

As I got back to the dining room the front door bell rang, and in a few moments the cop I had been talking to brought in a smallish, wrinkled old letter-carrier with bright blue eyes. He took off his cap, showing an almost

bald well-shaped head, and he remained standing respect-
fully.

The cop said, "This feller says he see somebody goin'
into the vestibule downstairs here this afternoon." He
turned to the carrier. "What time was it you said, Buddy?"

"Three forty-five," said the postman, in an honest, precise voice. "I heard the murder is supposed to have taken
place at about four o'clock, and so I thought it might be
important, because I know the people on the first and
third floors are away in the country, and the fourth floor
is vacant at present."

"What did the fellow look like?" the Captain asked.

"He was a tallish chap," said the postman, who seemed
very intelligent, "about forty or so years old perhaps.
Seems to me he had a beard, but I'm not sure. I only got a
quick glimpse at him."

"Was he round-shouldered?" I asked him.

"That I couldn't say," he answered, "he might have
been, yes, sir."

"What was he wearing?" Dan Leary asked.

The postman thought it over a moment very calmly.
Then he said,

"Black felt hat and—no overcoat, I think. Not sure,
though. Dark clothes, seems to me. Of course I paid no
particular attention to him."

Capt. Little asked him if he had seen the man come out
of the vestibule afterwards.

"No," he said, "I had no mail for Miss Magister today
and didn't go into the vestibule. And of course I don't
come back this way."

When the postman left I said that the caller might
possibly have been Van Diegen. The description sounded
something like him.

The Captain said, "Yeah. Didn't you tell me, Mr. Gilbert, that you thought he and the Magister girl had had

some disagreement? Well, anyway, we'll give Mr. Karl Van Diegen a chance tomorrow to tell us where he was this afternoon at 3.45."

Then Leary led the Captain, and I followed, back through the kitchen into a large closet. It was filled with dishes and cooking utensils, and there were a lot of cans and other provisions there, too. Detective Leary pointed up to a top shelf. Back in a corner, hardly visible, was a small black walnut cabinet with several drawers, and beside it was a glass jar with a glass cover.

"Butterflies," he said. "Four drawers of 'em, all carefully arranged and labeled."

"H'm!" said the Captain. "So this Miss Magister was interested in Lepidoptera, was she?"

"Not so terribly interested," said Dan Leary, and he laughed. "The cabinet and jar are both covered with dust. I'll bet they ain't been touched for a year."

When we got back to the dining room there was a plain clothes man, I suppose he was a kind of detective, waiting for us, and he was grinning.

"Well," said Dan Leary, "did you get anything?"

The man said, "Sure. A woman across the street claims she'd seen men in the winders here sometimes late at night."

"How late?" Capt. Little asked.

The man laughed. "Oh, two and three o'clock, she says."

"How many men?" asked Capt. Little.

"Oh, only one at a time, she says," the man answered. "She couldn't describe 'em though. Just passin' the winders, like, she says. And then I found a bird on 47th St., too. He's got a back room an' he can look across at the bedroom winders here. He's one o' those opera glass snoops, I guess. Anyway, he's seen a man in the bedroom here late at night once or twice. Seen him pullin' down the shades."

Dan Leary laughed and said, "Well, I guess this Magister dame was a pretty lively piece, all right."

Well, I was feeling pretty sick about it. I simply couldn't imagine the aristocratic Miss Magister in any such vulgar role. But Capt. Little finished me when he winked at Leary and told him to bring the box Leary had shown him while I was in the living room. Leary had found it, he told me, in a bureau drawer in Miss Magister's bedroom.

It contained a suit of men's pajamas. They were not new pajamas. They must have been worn several times at least.

7

KARL VAN DIEGEN

At ten o'clock that evening I was weary and faint. I walked
along East 46th St. looking for a restaurant. I hadn't had
a chance to eat a thing since luncheon, but I hated to take
the time for a regular supper even now, because I was bent
on a plan.

I had decided to try to see Karl Van Diegen that night,
as he knew all the three women who had died that day. I
wanted to get his reaction to the tragedies. I hadn't said
anything about my intention to Capt. Little, though, when
I had left him at Miss Magister's apartment. I was afraid
he might make some objection.

Before going into a Horn & Hardart place on Lexington Avenue, I stopped at a stationery shop and got a copy
of *The News*. The triple murders were boldly headlined.
The story was mainly about the death of Mme. Viray, with
a picture of her charming home and one of Van Diegen's
portraits of her. The other deaths had occurred so late that
there was but a brief account and contained nothing that
I didn't already know.

I confess I was somewhat disconcerted, though, at finding a picture of myself captioned: "Well-known Author
who discovered the body of the beautiful Stylist." It was a
terrible picture of me. I don't know where the devil they
ever got it, and so soon.

While I was drawing a cup of coffee from the machine in the Automat, I looked idly about, the way you do. There happened to be quite a lot of people there for that hour, I've no idea why; and I saw the usual collection of humble Tom, Dick and Harriets and a few bums mixed in with well-dressed people scattered all over the place. The Automat, you know, in off hours is really the poor man's club; a place to talk, read the papers or even write letters.

While I was walking about with my coffee cup in my hand, looking for a table as far away from everybody as possible, I noticed a rather pretty, dark girl sitting alone at a table with a bowl of pea soup.

It was the girl, by jove, whom I had seen coming out from the little elevator at Karl Van Diegen's when I was there on Wednesday afternoon. I was sure she was because she had on the same plaid suit made of the Royal Stuart tartan and the same green hat.

I had suspected strongly, you may recall, when I had seen her that day, that the girl had been up in Van Diegen's studio. And if she *had* been up there, she must have had a disagreeable time, I thought, to have left in tears. As she sat there in the Automat, eating her soup, the more I watched her the more I wanted to speak to her. I might possibly find out something that would help solve the mystery of the murders. I don't know exactly why I thought so; probably it was simply because Van Diegen knew the three victims so well, and she perhaps knew Van Diegen. Of course, if she hadn't been crying, that day, if she had emerged from that elevator like anyone else, or even laughing, I should never have entertained the idea of speaking to her. But I decided to try it cautiously.

When I sat down at her table with my tray she didn't appear to notice me, and I began to eat, without looking at her. After a while I laid my paper down where she couldn't help seeing the headlines.

In a few moments I got up. I left my hat on the table, as an indication that I should return. A little way off behind her, out of sight, I stopped to watch her. I saw her snatch up my paper and turn over the front page and begin to read eagerly. I went back to the table with a piece of lemon pie and sat down.

She blushed prettily (she had very little make-up on) and put down the paper quickly.

"Oh, I'm sorry," she said, in a nice, soft voice, "but I just *had* to see what it said about those horrible murders today."

A woman once told me that I had a cute smile. I used it. I forked into my pie and said,

"I beg your pardon, but didn't I see you on Wednesday afternoon coming out of the elevator at Van Diegen's, the photographer's place on East 49th?"

She kept her eyes on me. I smiled again.

"Perhaps you saw me, too, that day," I said.

"No—no, I didn't," she said. And she seemed confused and a bit fearful, too, I thought.

I went on eating my pie for a moment or two, then I asked, "Do you know Mr. Van Diegen?"

She turned and looked at me in the face.

"Who are you?" she demanded.

Well, I gave her my card and told her I was a writer, fairly well-known, and she seemed somewhat reassured, and she said that she had just seen my name in the paper.

Then she asked, "Do you know who I am?"

Of course I didn't. "But whoever you are," I ventured, I was still smiling, "I think you may know something that would help me. Something about Karl Van Diegen."

She took her bag and got up suddenly, and I got up. "I'm afraid I haven't time to talk now, Mr. Gilbert," she said. Then she asked me if Karl Van Diegen was a friend of mine.

"In a way, yes," I said. "And he was a friend also of the three women who were murdered today."

"Yes, I know it," she said.

There was another pause; she stood looking down at the table fingering a spoon.

"Why should you think," she asked me slowly, without looking at me, "just because I was crying, that day, that I know anything?"

"Do you?" I asked.

I thought for a moment she was going to cry. Then she said, slowly, "I don't know much, and what I do know, I'd be afraid to tell." She didn't move away, though, she just stood there, pulling on her gloves. Finally she looked at me and said,

"I'm a professional dancer, Mr. Gilbert. Just now I'm working at the Concha night club on West 57th St. I've got to get over there and dress, right away. But if you'll come in there just before two o'clock, that's when I finish, I may be able to go somewhere and talk to you. I won't promise but I'll think it over. I don't know even that it will help in any way."

Then she gave me a quick lovely smile. "My name is Marcella Northey," she said, and her face grew grave again, and I watched her go out and onto the street. I liked her firm, springy walk.

All this made me more anxious than ever to talk to Van Diegen. As I went out I saw a young man at a table some distance away get up and put on a derby hat. I had noticed him casually while I was talking to Miss Northey, but I thought only that he was good-looking with an athletic figure, and I hadn't been aware of his watching me or her particularly.

As I walked down Lexington Avenue it occurred to me that Capt. Little might have wished to have me followed.

Of course he would; he let me go so easily. So after going a few blocks I stopped to look into a jeweler's window. I looked back, and I saw that the fellow in the derby behind me, across the street, was also looking into a shop window.

Well, it's a queer sensation, being shadowed, especially by the police, and it's not an altogether pleasant one. I was strongly tempted to match my wits with his, and attempt to throw him off the scent. But after all, what did it matter, I thought. I had nothing to hide. So I went on and turned into East 49th St. It was a splendid warm night and I could see stars up in the slit of sky between the rows of dark houses.

I was wondering just how to approach Karl Van Diegen (and wondering, too, why I should think I had to take any particular tone with him), when I saw, in the middle of the block ahead, where Van Diegen's studio was, something that made me stop. A girl in a bright blue coat had just hurriedly crossed to my side of the street. She was carrying a package, a small carton it looked like. She stopped at the curbstone. Ash barrels had been set out all along the sidewalks, and into one of them I saw her empty the contents of her box.

It wasn't only that, though, which aroused my curiosity. It was the fact that the girl immediately recrossed the street to where there was another row of ash barrels, into any one of which she might have emptied her box much more easily. And what interested me even more was that she then went into the doorway of Van Diegen's place. And most suggestive of all was that just then a man came out and stopped and gave a Nazi salute, which she returned, before he went on.

I had recognized her as Karl Van Diegen's assistant, that Miss Frisch. I had never liked her. I waited a moment to think what I should do. Half way down the block behind me I saw the man in the derby who was evidently still following me. He had stopped, too. He was lighting a cigarette.

I had a decidedly unpleasant feeling as I went up to Van Diegen's doorway. Van I had always assumed to be anti-Nazi, and especially so as he was a member of an old aristocratic Prussian Junker family and an intellectual. This Heil Hitler salute in his doorway was detestable. It was sinister.

The ground floor of the building was occupied as a rug shop, with a separate entrance. As the second and third floors were used as business offices, the front door, inside a little square vestibule, was kept locked in the evening. There was an electric bell by which one could ring up Van Diegen's studio and penthouse, and a house telephone with which to communicate with him.

He told me to come up, and on the fourth floor he met me at his door in the hallway. Somehow that night, his tall, round-shouldered figure, with his reddish hair and beard and bluish eyes made him seem, as he had never seemed before, repellent, almost repulsive. I said something about the tragic events of the day and we went on into his studio and he poured me out a glass of whiskey and soda. I didn't touch it.

And isn't it queer how a harmless idiosyncrasy you don't mind and hardly notice when you're on good terms with a person will annoy you like a pebble in your shoe after you've become in the least estranged? Van Diegen's constant wiping the sweat from his forehead with his balled-up handkerchief, got on my nerves so that I had hard work talking to him.

He asked me about Berta Conley's murder, of course, and my part in the discovery of her body, the cyanide and everything, and finally I asked him who he thought was the murderer.

He handkerchiefed his brow again and said in his heavy, ironic manner, "Why, I think you must have killed her, my dear fellow." And he chuckled. "I hear on the radio that you live right next her rooms, and you are a rather romantic novelist, you know. You like excitement."

I thought it wasn't a time for joking and I said so. He said that life was all a joke. I said not for poor Berta and he asked why poor. And again he mopped his sweaty forehead.

I wasn't in the mood for metaphysics, so I said, "Who do you think could have killed Maude Magister?"

Van Diegen crossed his legs and took up a pipe from the table, filled it deliberately and lighted it.

"Perhaps I did," he said. "Don't you remember, my dear fellow, that at Corrijo's dinner I offered to murder her?"

"Did you?" I asked.

"That, my dear fellow," he said, puffing his pipe, "is for the police to decide. But I have reason to believe that she had a lover, other than the noble Señor."

I affected amazement, of course, and asked him what reason.

"Oh, I have friends," he said. "Many friends. Interesting bits of news are brought to me sometimes. I really ought to be a columnist."

I asked him who this lover of Miss Magister's was. He evaded the question and I didn't believe, at the time, that he knew. Afterwards I was sure he didn't. Why he told me as much as he did I couldn't then imagine. It seemed to me, though, to be a red herring he was dragging across his own path to confuse me with a false scent.

"I understand," Van went on in his slow, deliberate way, "that this lover of hers has given Miss Magister considerable trouble. I mean, of course, in keeping him in a discreet background."

"You think this fellow, her lover, killed her?"

"She had some hold on him, perhaps, that he might wish to break."

"Did Señor Corrijo know about him?" I asked.

"Probably not. But perhaps he found out. I'm afraid he wouldn't like it. He has a jealous Spanish nature."

"Why didn't you tell him? Are you sure you didn't?"

Van Diegen laughed. "I don't go round looking for trouble, my dear fellow, I have plenty. And besides I like to watch a game like that from the side lines. I don't care to participate; I merely applaud," he said, "or hiss. But quietly, you know, quietly."

"And Miss Magister didn't know, either, that you knew about this lover of hers?"

"I certainly didn't tell her, my dear fellow. That would spoil the game, too."

"Then why are you telling me, Van?"

"Why not? It doesn't matter now, does it?" he said.

His cold-blooded way of talking about his three friends was hard to bear, but I wanted to get all I could out of him.

I began again. "How about Mme. Viray?" I asked: "Who killed her?"

"Who d'you think, my dear fellow, stole the Señor's ruby ring?"

"I have no idea," I said. I could say nothing of course about the police having found it in Berta Conley's room and I wouldn't have if I could. "Who do *you* think took it?" I asked him.

Van Diegen chuckled. "My dear fellow," he said, "when we find the answer to that question we shall probably be able to know who killed these women." Then he asked me if I recalled our conversation while I was driving him out to Riverdale for the Señor's dinner.

"Yes," I said. "You asserted that everything women ever did was motivated by vanity."

"And perhaps almost everything men do, as well," said Van. "In that little company, my dear fellow, there was present a combination of potent psychological elements. If they had been physical elements instead—hydrogen, oxygen, nitrogen and carbon, for instance, and combined in the right proportions, such as in the case of nitroglycerin—they couldn't have been more dangerous."

"What d'you mean?" I asked.

"Vanity, jealousy, rivalry, ambition, and the primeval feminine passion for precious stones. How could you expect anything but trouble?"

"But those women," I protested, "they were all three so exquisite, so civilized."

Van Diegen chuckled and again he wiped the sweat from his brow. "My dear fellow," he said, "women are not yet civilized—none of them. You know what Kipling said of Judy O'Grady, was it, and the Colonel's lady, sisters under their skins. Women, you see, in primordial days, lived alone and apart in caves while their men were away. They had to boil the pot and tend the brat, while men were learning co-operation by hunting and warfare and games. Men had to create a code for mutual self-protection. They developed a society. But women became individualists, and anarchists. And despite their so-called education they are yet. They are moved by the most obvious reactions to simple stimuli. I ought to know. I have studied thousands, all doing the same things. And, because men have always conferred value on women, women have been forced to seek men's favor. And that inevitably creates jealousy. And jealousy feeds on vanity."

"That's all very well," I said, I was sick of his elephantine humor, "but in what way do these refined, cultivated women—"

He put out his hand to stop me. "Berta Conley was a pretty girl and a clever one, but she was a small town girl at heart. She had ambition—another form of vanity. She might do anything to get ahead. Even marry the Señor Alberto Alvarez Corrijo. Maude Magister was cold and intellectual, yes. But she, too, had her desire to shine in another way. She was the most dangerous of the three. In her beautiful way, she was ruthless. And Hélène Viray, well, her vanity took a more petty form. She did silly things. She wanted to sing, for one thing; and that was silly. She had superficially espoused the cause of Free France, so-called, and she had an idea that, with her seductive beauty, perhaps aiding her, she could play upon the susceptibilities of certain United States Senators in order to induce them to have De Gaulle recognized. That was another silly thing."

I lost my patience then, for I was pretty sure he knew the true nature of Mme. Viray's activities. I got up. Before I left, though, I did a thing I was ashamed of. I hated to accept a favor from him, but I did want some of his pictures of those three beautiful women. I asked him if he would give me some.

"Certainly, my dear fellow," he said. "I shall have some printed for you, with pleasure."

"But you have lots of them," I was foolish enough to say. "How about all those sharp ones, taken from all angles, you know, that I saw here."

Van Diegen looked at me blankly a moment; then he raised his eyebrows. "Sharp ones?" he repeated. "By Karl Van Diegen? It sounds positively indecent."

Van's portraits, you must know, were always taken out of focus, giving a beautiful soft effect.

"Why yes, those sharply focused silver prints," I said. "They looked almost like commercial poses— I supposed they were for reproduction, for publicity, perhaps, weren't they?"

Van Diegen's face showed no trace of feeling, but he said, in his ponderous way, "My dear fellow, are you accusing me of taking pictures like that? And silver prints, too? You may not be aware of the fact, but I am supposed to be an artist. I don't hang my certificates and awards and medals on the walls like a chiropractor, but I think my reputation is well enough established. I don't know what you are talking about."

I went down the elevator that night, puzzled and suspicious. Why should Van have denied having taken those prints?

When I came out onto the street I crossed over to the ash barrel where his assistant, that Frisch girl, had emptied her package. I took out the carton she had thrown in on top.

There was a lot of broken glass underneath, small fragments. I took out a piece and looked at it. The glass was dark coated on one side—a photographic negative. I held it up to the rays of an electric light and made out a piece of an arm and a hand. I tried one after another until at last I found a part of a face. Even though the chin was missing I could see that it was Berta Conley, and I put it into my pocket. Although I found no other faces, on other fragments I found enough details of the gowns to make sure that they were portions of the portraits of Mme. Viray and Maude Magister.

I was examining one of the larger pieces when something made me turn quickly. I saw a man approaching me. He was so near me that he had struck at me before I could more than throw up my arm to ward off the blow. I swung round and gave him a jab in the jaw with all my strength, and then grappled with him. He staggered backward—right into the young man with the derby hat, the chap who had been following me ever since I left the

Automat. I may as well say now, as I found out very soon, that he was a police detective. And let me tell you he was darned good-looking.

"I'll handle him!" he said to me, and he must have been pretty good at jiujitsu, for he wrenched the thug's arm so fiercely that he howled and dropped his blackjack, and a pair of handcuffs was snapped onto his wrists before I knew how it had happened.

The fellow was apparently a German and he was a mean looking customer with a shaved head and little yellow piggish eyes. He refused to say who he was or why he had attacked me. In his pocket the detective found a list of names written in violet ink—good American names, this time—and a letter in German, evidently from the *Weckruf*, the organ of the German-American Bund. To make him more despicable, at least to me, the fellow wore an American Flag button in his lapel.

The handsome young detective who had come to my assistance was a nice chap, I found, one of the new crop of clean, manly, well-trained New York police. I liked him. I liked him a lot.

He told me he'd have to take his prisoner to the 17th Precinct on East 51st St., and if I didn't mind coming with him he'd string along with me and see that I didn't get into any more trouble. Now that I knew he was a detective there was no need of his keeping under cover, he said; and it didn't matter, anyway, since his orders were only to keep me under surveillance.

At the station the surly, silent German who had attacked me—Hans Koltz, was the name he gave—was booked for felonious assault in the first degree, as he had a weapon on him.

Then the detective told me his own name was Robert Catfield. He said he had been on the police force three years, and had only recently been made a second grade detective. When I learned from one of the cops there that he had been cited twice for bravery I could see why the men in the police station called him the Bobcat. He asked me where I intended to go next.

I told him I was going home to my hotel to put on a Tuxedo and that later I wanted to drop in at the Concha night club, on West 57th St. So we walked to Fifth Avenue and took a Southbound No. 4 bus which would pass the rear entrance of the Imperial. On the way he asked me all sorts of questions as to why I should have been attacked; and as I had no idea myself, I told him the whole story of my experiences since I had first seen the photographs of the three beautiful and unfortunate ladies at Van Diegen's studio last Tuesday.

When we got upstairs in the hotel Annex there was still a cop outside Berta Conley's door, but the detectives had already finished their investigation for the time, he said, and were about to leave. In my suite we found the telephone bell ringing. But when one after another of my inquisitive friends had called me up to ask me endless questions about the murder and could they do anything, till I was weary, I asked the hotel operator to cut out my line until morning, unless there was a police message.

While I was dressing in my bedroom, detective Catfield read my Encyclopedia Britannica—the article on potassium cyanide, he said—and then, as there was no particular hurry, we sat quite a while with our drinks—he wouldn't take anything but pineapple juice and lemon—and discussed the murders. We didn't tune in on the radio because it wasn't likely that the police would give out yet anything we didn't already know.

Bob Catfield asked me a thousand questions that evening—about all the women, and all the men. He had been to the Magister flat and to Mme. Viray's and he said he'd like to have a look at Miss Conley's room, next door, but of course that wasn't a part of his job. As I had lived in it a few weeks a year ago, however, while my suite was being repainted and papered, I was able to draw him a fairly accurate plan of the rooms, which he filed in his notebook.

After that he was silent for some time; and I didn't disturb him. Finally he said,

"D'you know what I think, Mr. Gilbert? You're a writer of fiction and you ought to be a pretty fair judge of human nature. If the opinion you had of this Miss Conley is correct, there's no doubt that the ring was planted in her suit case for a purpose."

I was suddenly so relieved and delighted that, if I'd been a girl, I could have kissed him. I knew that Berta never could have stolen that ring.

"I've no doubt," he went on, "that Capt. Little has come to the same conclusion and is working along that line. My idea is that the ring was placed amongst her effects so that it could be found by someone; and it would have been used then as a basis for blackmail, or to force Miss Conley to do something she would have otherwise refused to do. They would threaten to expose her as a thief, you see, and she'd have to do what they said, or else."

"But who would be likely to do a thing like that?" I asked him. "And what would they want her to do?"

He laughed and leaned back with his cigarette. He said he hadn't got to that yet, and he wasn't on the case, anyway.

"But I might answer that question," Bobcat said, "if I could be assigned to make an independent investigation of this girl's murder—or rather of the three murders, as they may be linked up in some way. I have an idea I might break it, if I had a free hand. There are some leads I'd like to follow up, anyway."

"You mean," I said, "that you already have a theory as to who the criminal, or criminals might be?"

He only smiled and smoked his cigarette; but there was a lot of stuff in that quiet smile, I thought.

We went on talking. What puzzled him, he said, was Van Diegen.

"I may be flying wild," he said, "but it seems probable to me that he had you followed and attacked. A few days in the hospital, or even worse might have been desirable for him. For some reason he didn't want anybody to know that he had taken those pictures—what you call the 'sharp' ones. Why not? The only possible reason is that he had made some use of them, or someone else had, that he didn't want to come out."

I said that if Van did send the thug after me, he worked pretty quickly.

"I don't know," said the Bobcat. "Van Diegen already knew that you had seen those photographs. Fräulein Frisch would probably have told him."

"But how could he know that I was going over to that ash barrel and find the broken negatives?" I asked.

"The Fräulein might have seen you stop and watch her, just as I did," the Bobcat said, "or Van Diegen may have watched from his window to see where you went. That didn't matter anyway. That tough was probably going to follow you till he got a chance on a quiet street to blackjack you. He had a chance right there, that's all."

And then we talked about Marcella Northey, wondering if she had any part in the puzzle. The little she had said to me at the Automat was certainly provocative.

It was a relief and a pleasure talking to that young Bobcat, after the hard and heavy detectives I had been with all that evening. He had great charm. His enthusiasm for his work hadn't yet worn off, and I suspected that it never would. His talk was fresh and sharp, it had vitamins in it. Despite the difference in our ages we hit it off splendidly. Only about twenty-six or seven, he was, and the lad was as clever as he was good-looking. How I envied him his heavy, dark, glossy hair!

It was at about 12.30 when we took a taxi to the Concha. With the three deaths still oppressing me I wasn't in much of a mood for gayety, and Bob Catfield was so intelligent and so companionable that I was already calling him Bobcat and I asked him to come into the night club with me. But for some reason he preferred to wait outside somewhere.

There is always something depressing to me in New York night clubs. The architecture and decorations seem so patent, so forced, and assertive somehow, so self-conscious. This place, the Concha, was in that respect like all the rest, not large, but expensively fitted up. A lot of shiny black and chromium, you know, and bright red and mirrors and tiger skins and silly gadgets on the tables.

There was the inevitable collection of bright, determined looking girls there, abounding in curls and bare arms, bare necks but not bare faces, all with their elbows on the table, all smoking, all holding their cigarettes in precisely the same way, up in the air as if they were waiting for Buffalo Bill to shoot off the ash. All the men who weren't drunk seemed bored. There was a tiny dance floor, and a whizz-bang orchestra, with a black drummer making a damn fool of himself. A sign announced that the next floor show would go on at one o'clock.

And then while I was finishing a milk-and-Vichy and wishing again that the Bobcat were there, who d'you think appeared in evening dress and walked past me to a table near that drummer? Karl Van Diegen! He didn't see me, apparently, and I tried to shelter myself behind an orange tree in a big yellow tub.

At one o'clock I didn't have to be so careful to hide, for Van was watching the floor show intently. It was a dull enough entertainment, the same old thing, though the audience applauded wildly and drunkenly every number, especially the sly, suggestive monologues, drawled by a girl I hated on sight.

And then at last I sat up and began to take an interest in the show. It had just been announced that Marcella Northey would dance some Spanish dances and then, there she was, and I saw the girl I had talked to at the Automat a little earlier in the evening. She appeared on the dancing floor in black lace and mantilla and a gigantic back comb and she dropped a deep, sweeping curtsy.

I thought her singing was excellent. She had a rich, full tone with lots of feeling and accent and an abandon such as one rarely finds at such places. I don't know much Spanish, but her accent and temperament seemed authentic. I was quite carried away with her charm and talent, and so was everyone else, apparently, until suddenly she hesitated and faltered and had hard work getting into the rhythm again. She looked frightened and then I saw that it must have been the sight of Van Diegen that had upset her. There was no doubt about it. He was staring at her and her eyes were on him as if fascinated.

She did a dance after that with a man dressed like a marionette in Spanish costume with a lot of strings tied to him, but I could see that Miss Northey could hardly keep it up. She rallied a little for her encore, but all her spirit seemed to be gone and it ended pretty weakly, and she made a quick exit.

I saw Van Diegen get up and he passed me again without seeing me, apparently, and went out the front door. I asked an attendant where the people in the floor show came out and I was directed to a door beside the front entrance. There Van Diegen was standing. Luckily his back was turned, and I went the other way before he could see me, and a little further on I crossed the street.

I wanted to see what Van Diegen was up to, so I took advantage of the cars passing and got back nearly opposite the Concha. There I found my detective escort, the Bobcat. He was lurking behind a taxi keeping a watch on the entrance of the Concha.

"Good technique!" he laughed. "You're doing fine. What's up?"

I told him about Van Diegen and Miss Northey and asked him what I'd better do.

"Give him all the rope he wants," the Bobcat said, "that's primary police tactics. Never break up his game till you find out what he's up to. That's what I'm doing with you, isn't it?" he laughed. "If Van Diegen goes away with the girl, then we've got a line on 'em both, see? and we can follow it up. If he isn't after her, and she goes off alone we can easily pick her up. Say," he said, "the police ought to have a man on this Van Diegen. Maybe they have, at that. I wouldn't know. I wasn't told anything but to keep an eye on you."

Then the Bobcat drew me in closer to a cab and said, in a low voice, "See that chap reading a paper in that yellow taxi parked there a little way down? He's been waiting there some time. He may be tailing Van Diegen. Know what I think? For my money, that bird's a G-man."

After ten minutes or so had passed we saw Van Diegen go back into the Concha. When he came out again, a few minutes later, he crossed the street to our side (we had barely time to dodge out of sight). He got into a waiting taxi and it drove off.

Immediately the yellow taxi behind his—the one with the G-man in it—drove off. It was evidently following Van Diegen.

"But where's your girl?" said the Bobcat. "Time for her to be out, isn't it?"

"Come inside and let's find out," I said. "If you show your badge they'll have to answer you, won't they?"

The manager of the Concha told him that Miss North- ey had left only a few seconds ago. By coming in, we had just missed her. She had told the manager that some man had been following her, and she was afraid of him. The manager had sent someone out to see if the man she de- scribed was hanging about the side entrance, and as soon as it was reported that he had left Miss Northey had gone.

"Which proves," said the Bobcat, "that as a detective, Mr. Gilbert, you're a very good novelist. I should have waited for her outside, if I had to wait all night. But then, I wasn't watching her, I was watching you!"

8

HUGO VLACK

I thought that day, perhaps the most eventful day of my life, was going to end at last when the Bobcat said good-night to me at the front entrance of the Hotel Imperial at 2 A.M. But at the desk a night clerk told me that a man had been waiting in the lobby for me for several hours. I wondered who it could be. The clerk was writing, and he said the man was on the settee at the end of the lobby.

But there was nobody there. The clerk looked up and said he was certainly there a few minutes ago. Then he exclaimed,

"There he is now, going out, there. I guess he was tired of waiting."

I caught the man's arm just before he entered the re-volving door. I had already recognized him as the fellow I had seen watching Berta Conley's window with opera glasses from the street—the same one I had seen standing in the doorway of the Annex. I said to him,

"I beg your pardon, but aren't you Hugo Vlack?"

He looked at me in surprise, and I thought, in a little fear. He was somewhat disheveled, but he had an interest-ing, sensitive face, and longish black hair.

"Who are you?" he asked.

When I had given him my name he looked at me with sunken eyes and he told me in a nervous low voice that he

149

had read in the papers that I was connected in some way with Miss Conley's death. I had found her dead, the papers said; and he asked me if I would be willing to tell him about the tragedy. He had questioned the people in the hotel, he said, but they would give him no information.

Well, this was almost too good to be true, I thought. The police were searching the city for Hugo Vlack, and here I had him—if I could only keep him. I thought quickly. Then I said,

"If you'll come up to my suite, Mr. Vlack, I'll tell you all I know. I live in the Annex, here, you know, and we won't be disturbed."

He hesitated a moment. He looked at me curiously. But I doubt if he knew at that time that he was suspected of the murder, and he finally consented rather reluctantly to accompany me.

We went through the hotel to the 31st St. side and took the elevator. Up on the 7th floor, when we passed Berta Conley's door, there was a cop in uniform on guard in the corridor. The two detectives seemed to have left.

Hugo Vlack stopped and looked at me, and whispered, "Is that her room?"

I yanked his arm and hustled him right into my big front room before the cop had had a chance to identify him. I shut the window, the curtains were blowing out, and Hugo stood in the middle of the room apathetically, looking at—well, at nothing, I imagine. I made him take off his overcoat, and he slumped down into an armchair.

Well, I was in a delicate situation. I didn't know but I was under some suspicion myself and I had to be careful what I did. I knew that Hugo Vlack was suspected; at least he was wanted by the police. Indeed, I was far from being sure that he didn't poison Berta. He had been seen hanging round the hotel shortly before her death, and he was, I knew, in love with Berta and insanely jealous. Berta herself had told me that he was dangerous when aroused. I knew that I ought to telephone Capt. Little immediately and report Vlack's being with me.

But—well, perhaps I had an idea I'd like to do a little detecting myself. I wanted to question Vlack, anyway; and I knew that once he was arrested I wouldn't have much chance to talk to him. I was feeling a little cocky, too, I suppose, at having found Hugo and inducing him to come up to my rooms so cleverly, and I wanted to take advantage of it to hear what he had to say. I wanted to try to find out in my own way, whether or not he might be guilty of Berta's murder. It was a foolish thing to do, though, and it got me into plenty of trouble; and worse than that, as it turned out, it led to another murder.

Anyway, I sat down with Hugo and I told him the little I knew about Berta's death—about the cyanide, I mean, and how I had given the alarm, and how she had been found in her room. And when I had finished, I got up to get some whiskey, for the poor devil looked as if he needed it badly. As I was pouring it out Hugo suddenly exclaimed excitedly,

"I hope to god Berta *was* murdered, Mr. Gilbert!"

And when I looked at him with a shocked stare, he added,

"I mean, of course, I hope she didn't commit suicide, Mr. Gilbert. It said in the paper that Berta killed herself. That would be even worse. It would mean that she was unhappy. Oh, I hope she wasn't unhappy!" And Hugo's face was contorted with pain. He looked terrible.

He wouldn't touch the whiskey. He asked me timidly if I happened to have any milk. And I saw that he was hungry. As I studied him, Hugo Vlack reminded me of the half-starved, hand-to-mouth artists I used to see wandering about the Latin Quarter of Paris, almost as seedy, he was. All he needed to complete the picture was a cane. But he needed a shave, too, and a hair cut a good deal more.

While he ate a can of chicken and a lot of soy crackers and what else I could find for him, I told him how I had met Berta Conley. At my first mention of Señor Corrijo a pained look came into his face, and he started to interrupt me, but he seemed to think better of it, as if he had decided to hear what I was saying about him. But he seemed so excitable that I said nothing about the theft of the Señor's ring. Its having been found in Berta's room was a police matter, anyway, and I knew they wouldn't want the story told, at least not yet a while, and surely not to a suspect.

Before I had finished my narrative Hugo Vlack's head had fallen into his hands, and his shoulders were shaking.

"Oh, that lovely girl!" he kept saying brokenly. "That lovely girl! What'll I do? What'll I do?" And then, after a while, he looked up at me with an agonized expression and he said in a kind of thick voice, "Of course I know who killed Berta."

Well, that was a surprise. Was Hugo trying to protect himself, by a random accusation? I wondered. And my suspicions of him increased. Wasn't it just what a guilty person would do? I thought.

I asked him whom he referred to. And my feeling that he was guilty deepened when he paid no attention to my question. Hugo sat listlessly in his chair in a sort of apathy, holding his chin in his hand and biting his forefinger, with his eyes on the floor. From across the street the night silence was broken occasionally by the roll and sharp wooden click of the balls in Thum's bowling alley, and the clash of falling ninepins.

Finally he looked up and said, "I guess I'm kind of tired, Mr. Gilbert. I haven't done any work for a month and I got out of money. I haven't slept much either. I'm a window draper, you see, but I quit my job to try to save Berta from getting into trouble."

I asked him what he meant.

But he had relapsed into that despairing apathy again, and as he didn't answer, I asked him how long he had known Berta Conley. I wanted to draw him out, you see, and lead him on. I felt sure that something would come of his talk that would give me some hint as to his guilt. It was the psychological method of "free association" I considered, and it would inevitably make him give himself away. So I repeated my question.

"What?" he said. "Oh, how long have I known Berta? Oh, about three years," he said. Then he tried to pull himself together and he said he might try a little whiskey, after all. He drank only a few swallows, but it seemed to do him good.

"Berta thought I was jealous," he said. His voice was low and monotonous. "But I wasn't jealous. I didn't mind if other chaps admired her, so long as she wanted me more than anybody else."

That was another build-up, I felt pretty sure. Hugo was evidently trying to show that he could have no motive for killing Berta. It was just what I would do myself, I thought. But I couldn't forget what Berta had told me about his unbridled jealousy and his violent rages. And it wasn't many hours, either, before I was to find that she hadn't exaggerated them.

But I had to keep him talking; and so I asked him where he had first met Berta Conley.

A faint smile appeared on his face. In a way, the fellow had a kind of charm. "Through a plate glass window," he said, dreamily.

Then he suddenly seized his glass and drank all the whiskey at a gulp, and he began to talk.

"Why, I was working on my own, then," he said, "deco-
rating for small shops; and one night I was dressing a window on West 34th St. They wanted me to keep the curtains
up so as to attract a crowd and get the advertising. But I
don't know," Hugo said, "nobody outside paid much attention to me in the window unless I left some of the models
around nude." And he gave me a wan smile and said that
while that usually got a laugh, he didn't like to do it.

He stopped speaking and for some time he sat just gaz-
ing blankly at me. I didn't want to hurry him, so I waited. Then he seemed to wake again out of his brooding
thoughts, and he said,

"Oh yes—that first time." And he said, "You see, Mr.
Gilbert, why, one night I was arranging a background of
draperies and cords or something, and I saw a pretty young
girl out on the sidewalk watching me. I thought she was
cute. I liked the original way she was dressed, too. Her
clothes were cheap, but she had done something to them,
and she had style. Well, I grinned at her, and she smiled
back at me. It was a kind of a frank smile, a sincere smile.
She wasn't trying to pick me up, she was just interested.
And then, when I went on working, she began to make
motions with her hands. At first I didn't understand just
what she meant. Then I saw that she was showing me how
to arrange the blocks differently, and the screens and rolls
and everything. You see what I mean, Mr. Gilbert?"

I was feeling pretty guilty, by this time, at not notify-
ing the police about him, and it was getting awfully late,
too, but I let him go on because I still felt sure that before
long he'd say something significant.

Hugo showed a little more interest then, and began to
use his hands as he talked.

"Why, you see, she'd signal to me to move a stand, say,
a little more to the left or right, you see, or turn a chair or
table, and things like that; or change the dummies, their

attitudes, or their places, and she'd act it out for me in pantomime, so I'd get the idea. It was funny, it was lots of fun. We got to laughing and talking in a sort of sign language back and forth through the glass. We'd make deaf-and-dumb alphabet letters with our fingers, and like that."

He bit his lip a moment hard; then he said,

"Well, I had thought I knew something about window dressing, but I saw that she was more artistic than I was. She had more style. Everything she suggested that night I could see was right and improved the composition a lot. It had unity and movement and accent. When I had finished she applauded me—she clapped her hands, you know. People were standing round on the sidewalk watching her and laughing. That window made a hit, Mr. Gilbert. I got all sorts of compliments from the people in the shop, next day; but that night, before I could get out onto the sidewalk to speak to her, she was gone." And the poor chap looked sad when he said that that was like Berta, too. You never knew what she'd do, he said.

Again Hugo stopped. He seemed to have lost interest in the story and was thinking of something else. I had to ask him what happened next.

He didn't answer for a minute. I watched him closely. Then he said,

"What? Oh yes. Well, the next Friday night I was working in that same window again, a little specialty shop it was, and along she came. She stopped and waved her hand to me, like a boy might have done, sort of happy and careless, you know, and she looked lovely that night. She had on a gray sweater, I remember, and a gray hat, a cute hat with a yellowish quill. I was darned glad to see her again. I'd been hoping all day she'd show up."

Then Hugo's voice changed and broke. "Oh, she was so gay, Mr. Gilbert. She was so gay she made me happy all over." And he took out his handkerchief again.

It was the way he said it. There was passion in it that almost alarmed me. I got in his tone a glimpse of the intensity of his nature that suddenly made me think of the many murderers who have protested, "I killed her because I loved her so much." There was no doubt about it, in my mind, Hugo Vlack was an explosive nature. He began more and more to fascinate me. I confess I had no great sympathy. He was clearly a psychopathic case, and he appealed to me, as a novelist, because he was a new and moving character. And not only was he himself interesting, but he was bringing Berta to life again for me.

And so I watched him and noted every nervous gesture and tone as he told me how he had taken Berta to supper, that second time, and how she had made him laugh. He told me how, after Berta's father and mother had died, and she had only a younger sister in Philadelphia, and a brother who was no good out West, somewhere, Berta had come to New York to earn her living. She was up against it for a while, he said, and took any job she could get. She was a waitress at Child's, and she was once a shill for a sidewalk peddler. She bought the first gadget, and looked out for the cops. She did all sorts of things, Hugo said, and did everything well, too.

Berta often helped him a lot with his window dressing, Hugo told me. They were like two kids, he said, playing all sorts of pranks together. Sometimes they would pull down the shades to the show window, he said, and then arrange the dummies in all sorts of ridiculous poses, even upside-down; and sometimes he and she would pose stiffly and immovably, like wax figures. Then they'd raise the window curtains for passers-by to see, and then suddenly jump up and make faces at them.

I rather blamed myself now for having pretended to so much sympathy for Hugo Vlack. After all, I felt pretty sure he was a murderer. But how to stop him, and announce that I was going to send for the police I didn't quite know. I really feared that he would blow up. I might be in serious danger. But I was in for it.

"Hugo," I said, "I've got to tell you something."

But he went right on. He was crying, actually crying. And he told me that all that time he had been making love to Berta and trying to induce her to marry him. But Berta refused to accept the $95 diamond ring he bought for her.

And still he kept on, despite my interruptions, and he was telling me about Berta's business career in New York, and how she had steadily gone up till she was making more money than he was, when he was stopped by a persistent ringing of my front door bell.

Hugo was on his feet in an instant, terrified. He begged me not to let anyone in. Perhaps he was afraid of the police; I know I was; but I told him I'd have to answer the bell. He darted into my bedroom and locked the door.

When I went down my hall and opened the door I was immediately blinded by a succession of flash lights, and there was a small crowd of photographers and reporters who had been looking for me all the evening. Before I could prevent it they had all burst in and were shooting questions at me.

I had to submit to being photographed in all sorts of poses, and I told the reporters what I knew about Berta's history—what Hugo Vlack had told and what she had told me herself—how she had been an elevator girl at Gimbel's and had been an aisle model at Altman's, and then how she had worked up and become a designer and stylist and anything I could think of. Then I had to tell something about myself and I had the very devil of a time getting rid of them.

It was almost three in the morning by that time and I hadn't yet got all I wanted out of Hugo. I felt pretty sure that he knew more about Berta's affair, if it was an affair,

with Señor Corrijo, than she had told me. So after Hugo
had come back out of my bedroom, looking paler than
ever, and had quieted down a little, I said, "Then Berta
refused you, did she?" And I said, with some hypocrisy
I'm afraid, "I'm sorry. You could have made her happy,
perhaps, Hugo."

He broke out fiercely, "She loved me! Berta loved me,
I know she did. Only her ambition was greater than her
love. I would have got her in time, if some other man
hadn't come into her life who could help her career more
than I could."

"Who was it, Hugo?" I asked him.

Hugo had a cruel look on his face. It was a fiendish
look. "He was a rich man, damn his soul," he said. "He
was influential, and he had power, damn him! He was what
Berta called 'distinguished,' and romantic and good-looking, too, I suppose she thought. But that wasn't what got
her. He was what Berta called a 'big' man."

Then Hugo jumped up to his feet and he pounded the
table till the milk bottle nearly fell over.

"He's a stinker!" he cried in a voice that was harsh and
wild. "He's a god damned stinker, and he murdered my Berta!"

He had grown so overwrought that it was hard work
pacifying him. I took away the whiskey and finally got the
story out of him that I had been waiting for.

Hugo told me that when Berta had finally dismissed
him—after some extra violent scene of jealousy he had
made, I imagine—he had taken to haunting the places
where she lived, and she had moved from one place to another to escape him. He had written to Berta and written,
and tried to phone her repeatedly but could get no answer.
He had called again and again to be told that she was out.

One day he was hanging about a small hotel uptown
where she was living, he told me, when he saw a big, luxurious Mercedes limousine drive up to the door: Berta came

out of the hotel, beautifully dressed, he said, and got in. Hugo caught a glimpse of a dark, handsome man of about fifty, he thought, inside the car as they drove off. Hugo had the luck to catch a taxi and he pursued the two, he said. This was rather late in the evening. The car stopped at the Concha night club, and Hugo arrived just in time to see Berta and the stranger go inside.

Now here was where his luck helped him. Hugo was of Polish descent and he spoke the language passably. He walked up to the chauffeur and, just on a bare chance from the man's looks, merely, he said, he spoke to him in Polish. The man responded cordially and they continued talking and Hugo succeeded in inducing the chauffeur to take a drink or two with him in a little bar across the street. There he found out that the owner of the car was a wealthy Argentinian.

"Señor Corrijo!" I exclaimed.

Hugo's face was full of grief and hate. "Yes, Corrijo," he said. "That's his name, the dirty stinker!" Then his voice dropped so low that I could hardly hear him. "Do you think Berta suffered, Mr. Gilbert, when she died—much?"

I told him that it was probably all over in a few seconds and she might not have known anything that was happening, cyanide worked so fast.

Hugo wiped his eyes again, and then he told me how he had made an appointment with Corrijo's chauffeur, Pierre, and the two had met in town several times. Hugo tried his best to get the man drunk, he said, to find out more about the Señor. The chauffeur, however, was cautious and told him nothing significant.

"And then, Mr. Gilbert," Hugo said to me, "I did a rotten thing. I didn't care. I don't care now. I simply had to find out what that damned Corrijo was going to do, so as to be able to protect Berta. None of the drinks I gave Pierre would make him talk, and so I asked some fellows about these reefer cigarettes, and they told me where I could get some in a little cigar store up in Harlem."

Hugo waited for a good chance, he told me, on a day that Pierre was off duty, one Sunday, it was, and he got Pierre to come up to his room, and he asked him to try the reefers. Pierre liked them and asked for more. From that time Hugo said he had no trouble in making Pierre talk.

"And what d'you think, Mr. Gilbert," and Hugo's voice grew strident, and he made wild gestures. "I found out that this damned Señor had had all kinds of women at his house out in Riverdale, nice girls, too, and they had had dinner there and I don't know what else, and Pierre has seen none of those girls since. They seemed to disappear—every one of them. What d'you think of that! They were sent to the Argentine, I'm sure. That damned Señor is a fiend! He's a white slaver!"

I tried to pacify Hugo. I told him that the thing was highly improbable. Señor Corrijo, I said, was too well-known, too important a man to dabble in a traffic as despicable as that.

"No, Hugo," I said, "if the Señor is in anything criminal, it's a bigger game than that. This chauffeur Pierre hasn't let you into the real secret yet."

I couldn't convince him. He wasn't listening. He went on and told me that when he had learned about Señor Corrijo he had tried every means in his power to warn Berta and get her out of the Señor's influence. He found out that she had moved to the Hotel Imperial and he had been watching for a chance to speak to her all the week. Then Hugo got up and gesticulated again, walking up and down the room.

"And today, Mr. Gilbert," he said, "that is, yesterday afternoon, I was on 31st St., over there." He went to the window and pointed out. "And I saw Señor Corrijo coming along from Broadway—walking, mind you, the scoundrel

didn't want his car to be seen, d'you see—and he went to
the entrance of the hotel here—the Annex entrance downstairs. I waited and watched for him and in a half an hour
he came out again. I don't know why I didn't kill him right
then. I would have, by god, if I'd known what he had been
up to. I followed him across Broadway and saw him get
into his car that his second chauffeur Leon had waiting for
him down there by the Chinese laundry. And just as sure
as you live, Mr. Gilbert, that damned Corrijo is the one
who put the cyanide into Berta's bottle of water!"

I wasn't so sure about that.

I sat a moment studying Hugo. Then I said, "What
time was this?"

"About two in the afternoon," he said.

"Well," I said, "if we could get that other chauffeur
Leon to corroborate what you say, your testimony would
be important."

Then I got up and said, "Hugo, I'm awfully sorry for
you. You've suffered terribly, I know. I wish I could help
you, but I can't. You've got to give yourself up. I'm going
to telephone the police that you're here." And I went towards the phone in my bedroom.

For the first time Hugo seemed to realize his danger.
He jumped up.

"The police?" he cried. "What do they want me for?"

I told him that he'd been seen hanging around the hotel
for several days before Berta was murdered.

"But my god!" he cried. "They don't think I'd kill her,
do they? Why should I want to kill her? I loved Berta. I
adored her. Why, I was trying to save her." Then he seemed
to crumple up and he lost all control of himself. "Oh my
god!" he exclaimed. "I'm afraid they'll beat me up! They've
got to find someone to pin it onto and they'll give me the
third degree to make me say I did it." And he took a step
towards the door.

"If you try to get away, Hugo," I said, "they'll be pretty sure you did it, and it'll be a lot worse for you."

He was trembling so that I hated to look at him. "But you see, Mr. Gilbert," he whimpered, "if Berta had been shot or stabbed or anything like that, they'd know just when she was killed and I might have an alibi. But nobody knows when that poison was put into Berta's water bottle, do they? It might have been any time during the day." His voice went higher and higher. "I don't know what to do! What'll I say? I couldn't prove I wasn't around here, I *was* around here."

"Did you ever threaten Berta?" I asked him.

"No!" he shouted. "You heard her phoning to me, twice, you said. Did she seem to be afraid of me?"

"Yes," I said, "she did."

"Oh, my god!" he wailed; and he dropped down again into a chair, with his head in his hands. "I never meant anything serious, at all, honestly I didn't, Mr. Gilbert. I only wanted her to meet me so I could tell her what I knew about Corrijo. Are you going to testify that I threatened her?"

"Take it easy, Hugo," I said. "What are you afraid of? If you're innocent you needn't be afraid of anything."

Then I went into my bedroom and rang up Capt. Little. He was delighted to hear that I had Hugo, and he complimented me cordially.

While we waited there in my front room for the police to come for him, Hugo sat disconsolately muttering to himself. After a while he told me, in a desultory way, that Pierre, Señor Corrijo's chauffeur, had come to his room that morning for more reefers. It was Pierre who had told him that Señor Corrijo might come to town that afternoon with his second chauffeur, Leon, and would probably call on Miss Conley.

Why Pierre thought the Señor would call on her, I couldn't make out. But I think that the chauffeur might have got wind, through the Señor's secretary, Dolores Tallia, of the theft of the ring, and perhaps of the Señor's threat to get it back. Pierre seemed to know, anyway, according to Hugo, that the Señor was in an angry mood that morning.

And as Hugo muttered on gloomily, a curious thing came out of his rambling talk. It appeared that the handsome chauffeur, Pierre, was, as Hugo put it, "dead struck" on Miss Magister. Pierre, it seemed, had found Miss Magister's handkerchief in his car when he got back to Riverdale after taking her home from the Señor's dinner that eventful night and he had talked to Hugo of returning it to her as an excuse for seeing her again.

Suddenly Hugo jumped up wildly.

"By God!" he shouted, "I don't care what I promised. They won't beat me up!"

And before I could stop him he had given me a quick, hard shove that sent me down onto the floor, and then he darted out of the room and ran down my hallway. I heard the hall door slam while I was getting to my feet. I ran out into the hotel corridor but he wasn't there. I looked over the balusters down the main stairway, but I didn't see him.

Hugo must have dashed up the back stairs and crossed into the main part of the hotel and gone down the front stairway. The bar keeper in the café told me afterwards that he had seen a man without a hat run through the café out onto Broadway.

9

MARCELLA NORTHEY

I've heard some pretty tough profanity in my life, but the way those two cops who came for Hugo Vlack swore and bawled me out that night surpassed anything in my experience. By letting the only suspect they had escape I had certainly made a fool of myself and of them, too. They reported immediately to Headquarters.

Then at about 4 A.M., Capt. Little rang me up and gave me another tongue-lashing. I told him all I could remember about Vlack and then about my call on Karl Van Diegen, and he asked me not to leave my rooms in the forenoon so that he could get hold of me any time he wished.

The next forenoon at about nine o'clock my telephone bell rang. It was Marcella Northey, the little dancer I had seen the night before at the Concha night club. She was down in the hotel lobby and she said she was awfully frightened, and she wanted to know if she could come up and see me.

The moment I opened my door, Marcella—she was in the same plaid suit and green hat—burst right out, "Oh, Mr. Gilbert! I'm awfully afraid that I may be killed!"

And as we walked down my hall to the front room: she went on, rapidly and excitedly, "You may think I'm silly or something, Mr. Gilbert, but I just don't know what to do, my mother's ill, and she doesn't seem to understand about things here in this country anyway, she's Spanish, you know, and she doesn't speak hardly any English, we've been here less than a year, and I have no one to advise me or help me or anything, and I thought of you." And she sat down on the edge of a chair and looked at me pitifully.

I asked her why anyone should wish to harm her.

"Why, you see, Mr. Gilbert," she said, "I knew those women who were murdered. I knew all three of them."

"Oh, indeed," I said, and I sat down near her. "That's very interesting. I didn't know that you knew them, Miss Northey."

She said quickly, "Why should they have been killed, Mr. Gilbert? Have you any idea?"

I said, "I have an idea that you have an idea, Miss Northey. Why should you be afraid," I asked, "just because you happen to have known them, that you're in danger yourself?"

She seemed to hesitate; then she said, "Well, that's just why I wanted to see you, really. But it's pretty hard to tell. You see, as you had spoken to me at the Automat, you know, and told me who you were, and that you knew Mr. Van Diegen—well, I thought that if I told you what had happened and everything perhaps you might advise me what to do—how to protect myself."

I ordered some orange juice and some sandwiches and cakes sent up, and then Marcella told me her story. Whether or not she was telling the truth, or told me everything, I didn't of course know, at that time, and you may judge for yourself why.

Here was a rather pretty, at any rate a very bright and attractive young girl, who knew almost nobody in New York, and had apparently very little money, telling me about a handsome and courteous and wealthy visitor at the night club where she danced, who had been very friendly and had done many nice things for her, and all that.

Somehow, I couldn't help believing her, though, when she assured me that this sympathetic, middle-aged friend seemed to her so kind and well-bred that she couldn't believe that he would ever take advantage of her inexperience and her confidence to do anything dishonorable. You would have to see Marcella to understand why I was so inclined to believe her. She had a kind of wildrose charm, and a fresh, clean, natural way of speaking.

Well, at all events, I wasn't surprised to learn that this kind distinguished friend of hers was Señor Corrijo—perhaps because they both were Spanish—that is, Marcella was half Spanish, anyway.

Marcella Northey was simple and timid, but she was no fool. She knew something of the world, apparently. She had been on guard with the Señor all along, she said. She had accepted no presents he offered, and she told me that she was careful where she went with him. The Señor did nothing for a month or so to shock her or destroy her faith in him, she said. And when he did ask her a favor it wasn't at all what might have been expected. It was an unusual favor, for an unusual purpose.

Marcella sipped her orange juice a little more calmly, after we had got a little acquainted, and she said,

"I couldn't help liking Señor Corrijo, Mr. Gilbert. I think almost anyone would like him. And for a while I was as happy as anyone could be who had just lost a father—he was Irish, you know, and he was killed fighting with the Spanish loyalists. Or as happy as anyone could ever be who had lost really almost everything and seen the horrible things I have seen."

And then Marcella told me how the Señor took her out to supper occasionally, always to the smartest places. "And sometimes," she said, "out at his house in Riverdale he'd get out some of the dolls in his collection there and we'd have fun playing with them and dressing them and every-thing. He was so kind and sympathetic," Marcella said, "that I felt that we were real friends. Only, under it all—you know how it is, sometimes—I suppose I did wonder why he should be so interested in me. I mean I'm not so awfully pretty, you know, and then I'm so much younger than he is."

She still seemed loath to come out directly with what she wanted to say; so I tried to put her more at her ease by asking her how she had got acquainted with Miss Magister and Berta Conley and Mme. Viray.

She went on sipping her orange juice as if she were hungry, and she said that the Señor, a while ago, had told her that he was going to give a rather exclusive party at his place in Riverdale for some of his friends, and he asked Marcella if she would dance for them.

"He said he would get a gown for me," Marcella said, "and Mother thought that as it was really a costume it would be all right for me to accept it. It was perfectly love-ly and awfully expensive, I guess, a special creation made by Bergdorf-Goodman, you know, and the Señor liked me in it so much that he said he wanted a photograph of me in it.

"That," said Marcella, "was how I first met Mr. Van Diegen. He took dozens and dozens of pictures of me in his studio. He took them from all directions."

I said to myself, there it is again! Why did Van Diegen take so many pictures and in that meticulous way? Mar-cella finished her orange juice. She took a sandwich and almost smiled at me.

"It was a peculiar dance the Señor wanted me to do at the party," she said. "That is, the setting was peculiar. Mr. Gilbert," she said, "did you ever happen to go to that queer cabaret in Paris—they call it the *Café du Néant,* and it's in Montmartre—on the Boulevard Clichy, I think it is—or was?"

"Oh yes," I said. "You go into a sort of dark, spooky crypt-like cellar, and sit down at tables shaped like coffins and drink beer and are served by monks in robes and cowls, all by dim candle light," I said.

"But I don't mean that part of it, Mr. Gilbert," Marcella said, "I mean the transformation they show afterwards."

"Oh yes," I said, "I remember now. They do the trick with electric lights and mirrors, I believe, and very cleverly, too. A girl I went there with once acted as a subject. In the corner there was a long cabinet standing up, like a box—"

"Like a coffin," Marcella said.

"Yes, like a coffin," I said. And then I told how my friend got up from the audience, that night, and walked into it. Then they manipulated the lights and mirrors and things and we saw her body gradually disappear. It was ghastly, just as if she were rotting away before our eyes until there was nothing left of her but a skeleton in the coffin. Then the illusion was reversed, and her body reappeared little by little until she was standing there, smiling. Then she stepped out of the coffin and walked back to her seat.

Marcella told me then that Señor Corrijo had a coffin like that set up at the end of his ball room, only the illusion was done in the opposite way.

"First," she said, "after the lights in the hall were lowered, they saw a skeleton in the coffin. Then my body gradually appeared, as you say, till I was my natural self. Then I stepped out of the coffin and danced a few dances; and then I went back and was turned into a skeleton again. It made a great sensation at the Señor's party," she said.

"Oh, wait a minute," I said. "Just wait."

I had just remembered the talk that had so mystified me at Señor Corrijo's dinner table. What was it that Maude Magister had said? . . . "We shall all have to be put into boxes sooner or later, shan't we? Hens and ladies, too." And then, "And we know just how we'll look, thanks to you—don't we, Señor?" . . .

Marcella asked me what I was thinking about. I said it was nothing; and I asked her who were the guests at the party—what kind of people.

"Why, some South Americans," she said, "but mostly rich German people. They made a lot of noise and I thought they were rather vulgar. I couldn't understand why Señor Corrijo should have them there. But I didn't pay much attention to them because those three wonderful women were at that party.

"Mr. Gilbert, d'you know, I think they were the most beautiful women I have ever seen in my life. I couldn't decide which one I liked the best. Sometimes I thought it was Mme. Viray—she was so adorably graceful and, I don't know, sensuous. Oh, you ought to have seen her dance, Mr. Gilbert! I was ashamed to dance myself after I had watched her. And oh, that wonderful gown Miss Magister had on! I sat and just stared at her. And I said to myself, 'She's a lady. She's an aristocrat, that girl.' Oh, I just loved the proud way she carried her head!"

And then, just as Marcella was beginning to rave about "that darling Miss Conley, too," my doorbell rang, and it was Bob Catfield, the handsome young police detective, more full of pep than ever.

After I had introduced him to Miss Northey, and he had looked at her in a rather interested way, I thought, he told me that he had gone to the Homicide Chief that morning with some ideas he had, and he had asked to make an independent investigation of the three murders. And so he had come to me first to ask a lot more questions.

I explained Marcella's situation to him—he had hardly taken his eyes off her; and then, with a little more self-consciousness, I thought, she went on with her story, and told us about one day when Señor Corrijo had taken her to the Stork Club for supper.

"And while we were there, talking and laughing," Marcella said, "he asked me how I'd like to go to Argentina. He said he could get me an engagement there at a very good salary. I told him, though, I didn't want to leave New York, and he seemed awfully disappointed."

The Bobcat asked her why the Señor was so anxious to have her go. And he moved his chair a little nearer to hers.

"That's just what I wanted to know," she said. "And I told him, just in fun, you know, that it looked as if he wanted to get rid of me. And then Señor Corrijo said that he'd be going to Buenos Aires himself before long, and we could have an awfully good time together down there."

I saw the Bobcat scowling. He went to the couch, took up a pillow and put it in behind her back. She looked up at him queerly, and for a moment she seemed to have forgotten that I was in the room.

Then Marcella told us that she decided to try to find out more about Señor Corrijo before she made up her mind about going to Argentina. She said she thought of the lovely Mme. Viray she had met at the Señor's party, so the next day she phoned to her and Mme. Viray asked her to call.

"She was awfully nice to me," Marcella said. "And oh, she was in the most adorable pink silk negligee. And when I told her what the Señor had proposed she seemed surprised at first, and I even thought she was a little upset by it. But then she seemed to change towards me and she told me very kindly that Buenos Aires was a delightful place and just as lively as New York, and she showed me a lot of photographs of the city and places."

And then Marcella told us that Mme. Viray had advised her strongly to accept the Señor's proposition and go to South America.

"Why?" the Bobcat asked. "Did she give any reason?"

Marcella smiled in a queer way. "I don't think she gave her real reason. She just said I'd like it down there and I'd make a lot of money."

The Bobcat was frowning again. I was amused. I asked Marcella what she thought was Mme. Viray's real reason.

Marcella had on very little make-up and her color rose a little. "Well," she said, "I suppose it will sound conceited, but it was just one woman watching another, you know how it is, but in spite of her being so sweet to me—or perhaps because of it," and Marcella smiled, "somehow, all the time—well, I won't say I think she was jealous, exactly, that would be absurd, of course, but, I don't know, I wondered if she wouldn't be rather glad to get me out of the way."

"Out the way of the Señor," I said, and I laughed.

Marcella smiled and she said, "I could see that Mme. Viray was madly in love with Señor Corrijo. Every time she spoke of him I could see that."

"And so you decided to go to Buenos Aires?" I asked.

"Of course she didn't," said the Bobcat.

"No, I didn't," Marcella said, and she smiled at him.

"Why not?" I asked her.

"Because of what Miss Magister told me, afterward, Mr. Gilbert."

"Oh," I said, "you saw Miss Magister, too?"

And Marcella told us that she had happened to run into Miss Magister at Van Diegen's studio one day while she was there to get some of her photographs he had promised her.

"Miss Magister was awfully nice to me, too," Marcella said, "but in a different way. I mean she made me feel as if I were talking to a Countess, almost, but a very nice Countess. She took me to dinner at Stouffer's that night, Miss Magister did, and the hostesses all seemed to know her, and everybody stared at her and I felt like a poor little country cousin."

The Bobcat muttered something and Marcella said,

"Well, Miss Magister told me that I must certainly refuse the Señor's offer, and *not* go to Buenos Aires. I asked her why, but she only said it might be dangerous and I didn't know what I might get into."

"D'you think it was because she was in love with Señor Corrijo, too?" I asked.

"No, I'm pretty sure she wasn't." Marcella said. "She didn't act like Mme. Viray did, at all."

"I think I know the reason," said the Bobcat. "The British Embassy, I hear, is very much interested in the Magister murder, and they have been wiring the New York Police about it. I understand they've sent a man on from Washington to see about it. Know what I think? This Maude Magister was a British secret service agent."

"Wait a minute," I said. "Don't you mean that she was a Nazi agent? That's what Capt. Little thought, didn't he? They found a lot of incriminating papers at her place, anyway. I saw them myself, maps of New York, with key points for sabotage located, and lists of German names, Nazi agents, probably."

"Take it easy, Mr. Gilbert," said the Bobcat. "Just remember that you're a novelist, not a detective. At that, you must surely have heard of counter-espionage. It looks now that Miss Magister was an English agent pretending to be a German agent. That would account for her dealings with Van Diegen."

Well, I was almost as relieved as I had been when he said that Berta hadn't stolen the Señor's ring. I had admired Maude Magister and I had respected her. I thought her a fine type of true British aristocracy, cold, a little hard perhaps, but loyal to the core. It had been a shock to think she could possibly have been corrupted by German bribes. Of course there was still in my mind what I had heard about her when I was there the night before, but who was I to judge her? If she entertained a man at two or three in the morning in her bedroom she might have a good reason for it. At any rate she was harming nobody but herself.

Marcella said, "Yes, I think she might have been in the secret service, Mr. Catfield, because I thought at the time that she could have told me a lot more about the Señor, and I think she wanted to; but she didn't seem to dare to; she had no right to, I suppose. And that's why I was specially careful when I saw Señor Corrijo after that. And the more he talked to me the less I liked the idea of going to Argentina. I had a feeling that he was leading up to something."

The Bobcat gave me a quick glance and I said that I was afraid I knew what she was afraid of.

"That would be bad enough," Marcella said, and again she was blushing a little, "although the Señor did say that I could take my mother along with me. But I'm afraid it was even worse than you think, Mr. Gilbert. The Señor told me that as I spoke both Spanish and English fluently I could be of great use to him in Buenos Aires. All I'd have to do, he said, was to talk to people the way he wanted me to. And d'you know what he wanted me to do, Mr. Gilbert?"

"I do," said the Bobcat. "Work with the Fifth Column down there and help overthrow the Argentine government, and perhaps that of Uruguay, too, and turn them over to the Nazis, or create some Fascist dictatorship."

"You can imagine how I felt," Marcella said, and her face suddenly seemed older and harder. "No one in the world hates the Nazis as much as I do. I've seen them at work, and I know how horribly ruthless they can be. I've seen them in Germany and in Poland, too."

"Then you broke with the Señor?" I asked her.

"Oh, I tried to. I mean I wanted to, Mr. Gilbert," and Marcella's lips were quivering. "But I didn't dare to," she said. "I don't dare to now." Then she broke down and sobbed, "That's why I came here to see you, Mr. Gilbert. I'm afraid he'll force me to go to Buenos Aires."

The Bobcat looked savage. He went up to her as if he were angry at her, almost. "How can he force you?" he asked her.

And then, as if it took all her courage to tell it, Marcella said kind of brokenly, "Last Monday evening—oh, I do hope you'll believe me!" she said, "he came to the Concha and waited till it was time for me to leave. Then he took me to a restaurant. I hated even to talk to him. But I was afraid to refuse to go. When we sat down at the table he took an envelope out of his pocket. It was a square envelope, rather large. Señor Corrijo was smiling. He ordered something to eat. I don't know what it was. I didn't eat anything. I couldn't. I was fascinated by the sight of that envelope. I didn't know what it could be, but I was afraid."

She looked at me, and then she looked at the Bobcat through great big tears, and he said, "By god!" and she looked so little, and then she said,

"I wish you could see my mother, Mr. Gilbert. She's so sweet; she's so innocent and gentle, she's like a child, and she loves me so, she's so proud of me. Oh, I couldn't bear to have her suffer, Mr. Gilbert; I couldn't bear it!"

"You don't mean that scoundrel tried to get you through your mother?" cried the Bobcat. "Did he threaten to hurt her?"

"Not in the way you think," she said. And then Marcella told us that the Señor finally said, just as suavely as if he were asking her what she'd have for dessert,

"How would you like to have me show this picture, little girl, to your pious old mother? "What would she think of her darling daughter? And how would you like all your friends to see it?"

"And then," Marcella said, "he handed me the photograph."

She leaned forward excitedly and her eyes were full of tears. "Oh, you've *got* to believe me!" she exclaimed. "I can't imagine where that picture came from! Nothing like that ever happened. I never did anything like that in my life—much less let myself be photographed. It stunned me. I can't understand it at all. It was perfectly horrible! But there I was. I recognized myself in the very dress he had given me."

The Bobcat put his hand on her arm, and when she could compose herself a little she gave us to understand that it was a picture of her in a disgraceful and humiliating scene. She saw bottles on a table, she said, with the Señor there too, and another woman, and it looked as if they were drunk, or something like that. And Marcella said she tried to tear up the photograph, but he snatched it away from her and she ran out of the restaurant.

She sat sobbing. "I didn't know what to do," she said. "I didn't dare to do anything, for fear that Señor Corrijo would show that horrid thing to my mother—and I didn't know who else he might show it to."

The Bobcat put his hand on her shoulder again. "Don't worry any more, little girl," he said. "You've got the whole New York police force to protect you. We'll see that that damned brute doesn't keep that photograph very long."

Marcella smiled up at him. It was beautiful. "Well, anyway," she said, "the only thing I could think of then was to appeal to Mr. Van Diegen to help me, he had been so kind. But when I went to see him in his studio Wednesday afternoon he was despicable. He just laughed at me. He's made of iron, that man. And that's why I was crying when I came down the elevator on Wednesday, Mr. Gilbert, and you saw me. I was sick about it and I didn't know what to do. Why, he might have been Hitler himself, he was so brutal."

"That's truer than you think, Miss Northey," the Bobcat said. "Van Diegen is what the Nazis call a gauleiter here; he's a secret commander."

And he told us that he'd just found out that Van Diegen had charge of all Hitler's propaganda in the United States, and had thousands of German sympathizers working for him. The New York police, the Bobcat said, had begun to co-operate with the F.B.I., though, and there'd be something doing pretty soon, he hoped.

Then he took a cigarette and leaned back and crossed his legs.

"Karl Van Diegen," he said, "is hooked up with Señor Alberto Alvarez Corrijo, undoubtedly, in the South American campaign. But, owing to the atrocious methods the noble Señor was employing, Van Diegen wouldn't want his connection known, especially after these three murders in which he might possibly be incriminated. That's why he denied taking those special, 'sharp' photographs, I suppose, Mr. Gilbert, and he got rid of the negatives in that ash barrel where they couldn't be traced back to him."

I didn't understand it yet, but he said I would later, and I said, "Then Señor Corrijo must have been trying to get a hold on Berta Conley, too," I said, "in the same way as he did with Marcella. She told me he wanted her to do him a favor, you know, and she might have to go to Buenos Aires, although she probably thought, poor girl, that she'd go as Señora Corrijo. But I still can't see," I said, "where he got those blackmailing photographs of the women."

"It's very simple," said the Bobcat. "Van Diegen, you see, took a lot of poses of each one. And then—"

He stopped. The telephone was ringing in my bedroom. The operator said, "It's a police call, Mr. Gilbert."

And then I heard the harsh voice of Capt. Little.

"Mr. Gilbert," he said, "I want you to come right out to the Corrijo place in Riverdale just as quick as the lord'll let you, and see if you can identify Hugo Vlack. I think he's the fellow who has just killed Señor Corrijo."

10

SEÑOR CORRIJO

Things began to move swiftly, after that. The Bobcat was on his feet in a jiffy. He said he was going out to Riverdale with me. "I've got something to do out there, anyway," he said, "and now it'll be easier, because I won't have to ask the Señor's permission to snoop around."

"Oh dear!" Marcella said. "Oh, I'm afraid—if you both go away—I'm afraid to go home."

The Bobcat and I had a hurried consultation. He was obviously much worried about her safety, and I was, too. There had been too much violence occurring in the group surrounding Señor Corrijo. His death was ominous.

And so I suggested then that Marcella stay in my apartment till we got back from Riverdale. It seemed the safest place, and she could make herself at home, I said, and she could order up a luncheon from the hotel restaurant if she wanted to.

Downstairs, as the Bobcat and I got off the elevator, Biddy Rumsey was waiting to go up. She gave me a hurried nod and stepped into the car.

The Bobcat eyed her and asked me who she was. He remarked that about the only thing glamorous about her was the perfume she used; and that reminded me of Berta Conley's *Fleurs de Paradis* perfume, and I told him about it.

He said, "Yes?" and asked me where Biddy's room was; and we went out to the street.

The Bobcat had his own sedan with a plaque with a big P.D. on the windshield, and red lights didn't bother us at all. When we got out of the traffic and onto Riverside Drive, he let the car out to 70 or so. He kept his eyes on the road while I told him more about Marcella and about the story Hugo Vlack had told me the night before, and how after he'd escaped I had tried to forget my stupidity in not reporting him to the police by translating the letters and clippings about Mme. Viray.

The Bobcat asked me lots of questions. He seemed to have all the details of the three murders in his head as accurately as I had.

As we flew along I said that the news of Señor Corrijo's murder really was no great shock to me. Hugo Vlack, I said, was undoubtedly unbalanced; that was why Berta Conley had got rid of him. Hugo adored her, though; he was a monomaniac on the subject. He would have talked about Berta to me forever, I said, if I had let him. Hugo was the kind that got hold of an idea and nursed it till it got too big for him and destroyed him.

"You should have seen his face when he spoke of Señor Corrijo," I said. "Hugo Vlack was a gentle chap, he was a poetic soul, ordinarily, but at that moment he had the face of a fiend."

"And yet," the Bobcat said, and he whizzed round a sharp curve, "now that we've found out what that damned Señor was like from Marcella, I don't know that I blame Hugo Vlack so much. I only hope," he said, "that this thing will break up the whole Nazi conspiracy in New York."

I tried to pump him about his theories of the murders, but I got nothing out of him except that he expected to be busy day and night until the case was broken. But what was worrying him most, just now, he said, was Miss Northey's safety; and he hoped she'd be all right.

When we turned in at the Corrijo place in Riverdale there were two patrolmen at the gateway and a lot of cars parked on the drive. In front of the main entrance of the house we saw an ambulance and a big Mercedes car, one of the Señor's, it was.

There was a group of men, detectives, patrolmen, traffic cops, and servants and of course a lot of reporters, some of them chattering women, and an ambulance crew and I don't know who else, scattered about on the lawn and under the big trees.

The murder of Señor Corrijo, coming immediately after that of the three women the day before, had caused a tremendous sensation. More people were arriving all the time, and trying to get in. Many of them, apparently, were the Señor's friends. I heard Spanish spoken, and a lot of German, too.

Señor Corrijo's body was still lying inside his car. I got just a glance at it. He lay crumpled up on the floor with his face hidden, and the body was being photographed. In spite of the despicable things I had just heard about him from Marcella Northey, I felt strongly moved by his death. I recalled his courtly hospitality and his generosity and it seemed impossible, it seemed outrageous that, under his urbane, pleasing manner was the conscienceless and savage cruelty that Hitler seems to have aroused in everyone under his domination.

On the big porch, meanwhile, the Medical Examiner was talking to Capt. Little and a police officer in uniform. The Captain called to me to come up.

"The man who killed Señor Corrijo," he said, "had nothing on him to identify him, but I gathered from what you said, Mr. Gilbert, that he might be the man you had in your rooms last night, Hugo Vlack. He's been shot through the stomach and has internal hemorrhages and probably won't live long. I want you to come in right away and see if he's your man."

I turned to the Bobcat, but he told me he wasn't interested. He had things to do inside the house, he said, and he left me.

I was rather upset by the sight of the Señor, dead there in his car. The whole atmosphere of the place was painful. In the front hall the servants were standing about whispering and staring, and one of the maids was crying. I followed Capt. Little into the same gold salon where the Señor had received us with such elegance when we came out for the dinner with the three ladies, on Thursday evening.

Hugo Vlack was in a coma. He was lying on a great couch that was covered with a cloth-of-gold tapestry—the same couch where I had first talked to Hélène Viray—and a doctor with a stethoscope and a uniformed nurse were bending over him. Hugo's body was bared to the waist and his face was white. His longish black hair was tousled and a heavy strand fell over one eye. Even to my inexperienced eyes he was far gone. Poor Hugo, I was sure, would never speak again.

"He's sinking fast," said the doctor. "There's nothing more we can do now."

Capt. Little jerked his head towards Hugo and gave me an inquiring look. I nodded to identify him.

"D'you know of any way we can find out where he lived, Mr. Gilbert?" I was asked.

I suggested that they try the decoration department of Gimbel's and they might question other window drapers, I said, some of them might know him. And then, as Capt. Little was busy talking to this one and that, I got a member of the Homicide Squad to tell me what had happened.

The Señor, it appeared, had been stabbed with a quarter-inch chisel several times and one stroke had gone clean through the heart. The assault had taken place in front of the house. The second chauffeur employed by the Señor, his name was Leon, I was told, had said that he had brought the big Mercedes car from the garage and was waiting at the portico for Señor Corrijo to come out. He saw a seedy, haggard-looking individual, he said, coming up the drive near the house. Leon said he would have stopped him and spoken to him if the Señor hadn't at that very moment come out of the doorway. The man—Hugo Vlack, that is—darted quickly round behind the car, dodged past Leon who was holding the door open and attacked the Señor savagely as he was stooping over to get inside the car.

"But how was Vlack killed?" I asked.

The chauffeur, Leon, I was told, jumped for an automatic he had in a pocket side of his seat in the car, and he let Vlack have three or four bullets while he was stabbing away at the Señor.

Hugo, I learned, hadn't a cent in his pockets. The police theory was that after he had run out of my place he had gone to his room and got a chisel and had sharpened it to a keen edge. He either took a bus, or else walked out to Riverdale, and then he had probably lurked in the garden somewhere behind the chrysanthemums, hiding till he saw the car being brought round to the front door.

"But why didn't Pierre identify Vlack?" I asked. "He knew him. He's been to Vlack's room several times, anyway."

"He did?" exclaimed the detective. "Why, Pierre was around here with the other servants when we got here and he never said a word to anybody. He saw Vlack taken into the house, too. I don't know but he even helped carry him in."

There was an immediate search made of the house and grounds, and Pierre was eventually found in his room upstairs over the garage, placidly shaving.

He protested that he had no idea who the murderer was. He said he had never seen him before. Pierre thought he was safe in saying that, I suppose, because he couldn't of course have known that Hugo Vlack had told me, only the night before, about his acquaintance with Pierre. And Pierre was undoubtedly afraid that if he acknowledged knowing Hugo, he might be implicated in the crime as an accessory. He was put under arrest and held to be questioned after other details of the murder had been investigated. Leon, the second chauffeur, was also being held.

We were all standing about on the beautiful green lawn in front of the house discussing the affair and dodging the reporters when one of the detectives cried out that the house was afire.

"Look!" he said. "See the smoke coming out of that window there!"

There was a small one-storied ell in the back of the house and from an open window the smoke was pouring out. Immediately there was a dash into the house by a crowd of detectives, policemen, servants and reporters, so many that the hallway was almost blocked and everybody was shouting. Some ran along outside of the house to look in through the window. The photographers were calm as usual, snapping their cameras.

I couldn't get in; I didn't even try. I waited some ten minutes or so, and by that time the smoke had dwindled to a wisp, and everybody was being pushed out of the house, all talking eagerly, by a squad of cops.

Then I saw the Bobcat come out; he was brushing water off his coat sleeve, and he told me that it wasn't much as a fire, because they got it out with hand extinguishers before it could do much damage.

"But not before a lot of valuable evidence had been destroyed, I'm afraid," he said.

I asked him how it had happened and he said, "The Señor, it appears, has, or had, a young Spanish secretary. Her name is Dolores Tallia and she's rather intelligent."

I said that I'd seen her on the night of the dinner, but I didn't care much for her looks.

"She knows her business, though," said the Bobcat. "She evidently scooped up a lot of Corrijo's confidential papers and threw them into the fireplace and set fire to them. But you know how hard it is to make a mass of papers burn. Dolores was in a great hurry, so she evidently ran out to the garage, while we were all absorbed in discussing the affair in front of the house, and got a can of gasoline. She drenched those papers in the fireplace, though, a little too well. Most of them burned up, but she had spilled some of the gas onto the rug and the loose papers and before she knew it the room was on fire, and she just escaped burning to death herself. We're holding her for examination," said the Bobcat.

"Did you save any papers at all?" I asked him.

He took from his pocket a letter on cream-colored note paper such as women use. "The Chief wanted me to show you this and see if you could read it," he said.

The letter was written in the precise, beautiful chirography cultured women use abroad, with every letter perfectly formed. I recognized it at once as undoubtedly Mme. Viray's handwriting. It was identical with that I had seen at her house in the notes I had found in the book. I told the Bobcat so, and then I translated freely:

> "Cher Albert:
> I am afraid that M.M. is onto us *(au courant)*. Do you think she could be working for the British? V.D. says she got the list from him while she was there, but he knows how to get it back. Be careful of that saucy little Yankee, too. She's sharp. Can't you get rid of her somehow?
> Deep love every day,
>
> Hélène."

What she had written was *faire disparaître,* or "make disappear," and in the corner she had written *mille baisers,* "a thousand kisses."

The Bobcat and I walked over to a summer house covered with roses and sat down. I said,

"This letter seems important to me. Taken in connection with what Hugo told about Corrijo's calling on Berta Conley at the Imperial, yesterday, it would tend to help implicate the Señor in her murder, wouldn't it? But now Hugo's testimony is no good; legally it's only hearsay, I suppose. And you can't examine the Señor, either."

"No," he said, "and we won't get much out of his secretary, this Tallia girl, I imagine. Probably she was in love with the Señor, too."

The Bobcat told me that scraps of notes were found indicating a close tie-up with Van Diegen; and there was a letter from the German Consul at Costa Rica, too, indicating the Señor's close co-operation with the Reich's South American propaganda and schemes.

"And there was one more thing," said the Bobcat. "In a closet was a large glass wide-topped bottle with a label marked 'CaCl.' D'you know what that means?"

"Calcium chloride," I said; "what about it?"

The Bobcat told me it was used in bombs sometimes, and it greatly annoyed the bomb experts, he said, because it formed a gas when placed in water, and when the gas reached the air it burst into flame and exploded the bomb. But I wondered why he had such a queer expression on his face and I asked him what he was smiling about.

And then he told me that he had run across something in the Corrijo house that would interest me. "We're just waiting," he said, "till Capt. Little finishes examining the chauffeurs and the Tallia girl to spring it on the newspapers."

It was while we were still talking there in the summer house that we watched Hugo Vlack's body and that of Señor

Corrijo put into the Morgue wagon and taken away. The servants had all been sent to their quarters and policemen guarded every entrance to the house. The reporters and photographers were kept apart in another summer house on the other side of the lawn under the trees until Capt. Little was ready to give them his official communication.

As the murder had been committed outdoors and in view of not only Leon, the chauffeur, but a gardener who had been talking to one of the maids in sight of the car, Leon's story was amply corroborated; and there would have been no need of searching the house perhaps, if the Señor's secretary hadn't tried to destroy his papers. What the police found in the Señor's office, however, was sufficient evidence to warrant a search of the whole estate.

Upstairs in an attic room they discovered a small arsenal of arms and ammunition. They were mostly submachine guns and rifles in cases. It was one of these wooden cases, undoubtedly, that, as you may recall, I had seen carried past the garage while I was sitting in the loggia that dramatic Thursday night, after the dinner. There was a well-fitted chemical laboratory, too, down in the basement where it is possible that bombs were manufactured. None, however, were found there.

I was allowed to attend the examination in the dining room and I saw Dolores Tallia, the tall slender black-haired secretary of the Señor's, brought in. And when she was given a seat she seemed to me genuinely affected by his death. It wasn't, however, only because she dabbed her eyes with her handkerchief occasionally. What seemed to prove it more convincingly was that the girl resolutely refused to answer a single question put to her.

"I shall not answer," she kept saying.

Capt. Little told her that she could be put in prison for destroying evidence; but she simply looked straight at him without a change of expression. They asked her about the laboratory and workshop, what it was used for; they asked her if she knew Karl Van Diegen, and if the Señor had any political affiliation with him; they asked her if the Señor was in communication with the German Consulate, or with Berlin officials.

"I shall not answer," she said; and I couldn't help admiring her courage and devotion as she left the room with her head up and her eyes flashing.

Outside in the marble corridor I heard someone exclaiming, "Yes sir. Yes sir, I certainly will," and a detective shoved in a little, short, roly-poly man, with a mop of hair as black as ink, and he was still saying, "Yes sir, yes sir." He had a round ball of a head and round eyes, and he looked stupid enough.

"Yes sir," he said. "Yes sir, I certainly will."

It was Señor Corrijo's second chauffeur, Leon Strazzi his name was, and there was no unwillingness about *him*. He was evidently trying to ingratiate himself with the police. They couldn't stop his talk and it filled the room when he answered the questions.

"Yes sir," he said, "yes sir, I certainly did drive Señor Corrijo to West 31st St. Yes sir, I certainly did."

"Yes sir, I stopped my car between Sixth Avenue and Broadway, yes sir. Yes sir, that's right, that's just where I stopped, just exactly. Yes sir, right in front of a Chinese laundry, yes sir, I certainly did."

Capt. Little asked him what time it was then.

"Why, I got there about two o'clock, sir. Yes sir, that was the time I got there, it certainly was, yes sir. Yes sir, in the afternoon. Yes sir, it certainly was. That's the time, two o'clock, yes sir.

"Yes sir," he said, "the Señor got out and walked towards Broadway, he certainly did. What time did he get back to the car? In about twenty minutes, yes sir, about twenty minutes, yes sir."

This, I saw, corroborated not only Hugo's story, but
that of the elevator boy in the Annex of the Imperial who
had seen a dark gentlemanly person going out the street
door.

Leon then said, with still more yes sirs, that he had
then driven the Señor to First Avenue, near East 58th St.,
yes sir, near Mme. Viray's house. The Señor had got out
and had been gone only a few minutes.

I said to the Bobcat that I thought Mme. Viray was
probably out in her car at that time, as it was parked in
front of her house later; and I wondered where she had
gone, just before her death.

To me, Leon's testimony tended to substantiate what
Mrs. Splicer, the woman who lived opposite Mme. Viray,
had told the detective about seeing a dark man with a
moustache at about 2.30 that afternoon. Leon asserted
that the Señor had worn a dark suit and a dark hat, he certainly had. And, if Mme. Viray *had* returned at that time,
it would have been possible for Señor Corrijo to enter the
house, administer the cyanide and get back to his car in a
few minutes. And you remember that Mrs. Splicer hadn't
been able to say whether or not the dark man had gone
into the house.

Leon was asked where he went after that. Did he drive
to Miss Magister's apartment on East 46th St.?

"Yes sir. Yes sir, I certainly did," Leon declared, nod-
ding until I thought his head would come off. "Yes sir."

"How long did you stay there?" a detective asked. Leon
thought it was only six minutes or six and a half, possibly
seven, yes sir. Then the Señor came back into the car? "Yes
sir, he certainly did. Yes sir."

I wondered what Maude Magister was doing at that
hour? Was she out of her apartment, or was she in there,
dead? If we could find that out the mystery might be
solved, I thought. Or it might not. With all his yes sirs,

Leon might be lying. He might be trying to protect Pierre, his fellow chauffeur.

It was near four o'clock, Leon said, when the Señor had him drive back home to Riverdale. It seemed evident to me that Señor Corrijo must have been out on a quest for his stolen ring. Nothing, however, was said about that at this investigation.

Leon was asked if Señor Corrijo seemed particularly excited when he came back from his visits to the homes of two ladies.

Leon gave a tremendous "Ha ha! Ha ha! Seller Corrijo excited?" as if it was the biggest joke he had ever heard. "No sir, he certainly was not, no sir. Nobody never seen Señor Corrijo excited, they certainly did not. The Señor never lose his temper, no sir. He never like nobody who lose his temper, no sir, he certainly did not, no sir. Señor Corrijo was a big gentleman, he keep his temper. Yes sir, he sometimes get angry, but not get excited, no sir. He was very good man, Señor Corrijo, he was good to all people work for him, yes sir, he certainly was." And then we heard Leon outside, and way down the corridor still saying "Yes sir, yes sir!"

And then the head chauffeur, Pierre, was brought in; and he was a bird of a different feather.

I didn't like Pierre, and yet I had to admit that there was something fascinating about him, a kind of romantic, olive-skinned motion-picture look that might attract some women. His eyes were sleepy and seductive. And I remembered that even the cold, intellectual Maude Magister had called him "horribly good-looking."

Capt. Little snapped question after question at him, and Pierre ran his hand back over his sleek black hair continually as he told of driving Miss Magister home after the dinner, that Thursday night. He admitted that she had asked him for a cigarette, and he had given her one.

The Captain aimed his long forefinger at the chauffeur. "Was that cigarette a marijuana, what they call a 'reefer'?" he demanded.

Pierre at first denied it. But after he was told that reefers had been found in his room over the garage he sulkily admitted that "it might have been." He admitted, too, finally, that he had obtained them from Hugo Vlack. With further pressing he told that Miss Magister had asked him what brand the cigarette was, and he had told her it was a special kind he had made for himself. Miss Magister seemed to like them, he said, and he gave her three or four more, maybe a half dozen.

Then the Captain asked him if Miss Magister acted any differently after smoking that reefer.

"Well, yes," Pierre said. "She got kind of 'high' in the car and she was singing. When we got to her house in East 46th St.," he said, "she wanted me to come in. She was laughing and acting funny on the sidewalk. Talking pretty loud."

"Did you go up to her flat?" he was asked.

At first Pierre said no. Then, after more urging and threatening, he said that he did go up, "just for a minute," and they had a drink together. "And then," Pierre said, "all of a sudden Miss Magister changed completely and she swore at me and kicked me out. Told me to go home and forget it."

Capt. Little asked him if he had ever seen Miss Magister after that.

Pierre was firm in his denial, and nothing could move him.

The Captain asked me to repeat to him what Hugo Vlack had told me in my room at the Imperial the night before. Pierre listened, but only shrugged his shoulders. It was true, he said, that he had told Hugo that he had found a handkerchief of Miss Magister's in the car after he had

got home, that night, but he had had no intention of returning it to her, he said, and he hadn't told Hugo that he
was going to. He said he'd rather keep the handkerchief;
it smelled nice.

"Well, what did you do yesterday afternoon?" Capt.
Little asked him.

Pierre said that after leaving Hugo Vlack's room in the
morning he had gone to several shops along Broadway
looking at shirts and neckties, and after a luncheon at
Child's he had gone to a movie.

He was asked what theater he went to.

"I don't know the name of it," Pierre said. "On Seventh
Avenue near Times Square, it was, I think."

"What picture did you see?" the Captain asked him.

"I don't know what it was," said Pierre. "I came in
when it was half through. All I know is it was lousy—
something about a fellow making love to a dame," and
everybody laughed except Capt. Little. "I went to sleep,"
Pierre said, "and I didn't wake up till after five o'clock,
and then I went out."

"Pierre, have you a light overcoat and light felt hat?"
Little asked.

Pierre shrugged and said he hadn't worn any overcoat
on Friday.

"Little won't get anything out of that chap," said the
Bobcat to me. "It would take a damned good cross-exam-
iner to trip him up. He knows just how much to admit,
and where to stop. I don't like his looks."

The Captain turned his questions to the subject of Van
Diegen.

Pierre admitted that he had driven the Señor there
occasionally, but he said that neither the Señor nor he had
ever carried any packages to Van Diegen's or back from
there. I took it that the Captain was thinking of bombs
and explosives.

"That's all for the present!" snapped Capt. Little, angrily.

We all left the room—detectives, policemen and everybody—and I suspected that Pierre would be handled without gloves by the detectives in the station house.

"Now for the pay-off," said the Bobcat. "I've shown Capt. Little what I've found here, and he's going to put on a grandstand play for the reporters. I don't care," the Bobcat said, "because, while it solves one mystery, it doesn't get us anywhere at all in breaking the murders. Still, it's going to be good."

The Bobcat and I walked to the doorway and stood there on the wide portico looking out over the grounds. It was a charming place, I said.

"Yes sir," said the Bobcat, "yes sir, it certainly is. Yes sir."

I saw Capt. Little over by the summer house under the trees. He was surrounded by a crowd of eagerly questioning reporters and photographers, and I asked the Bobcat what he was telling them.

The Bobcat laughed. "The Chief doesn't mind a little publicity, when it's good," he said. "And so when I made my little discovery here I suggested that he dramatize it some. The papers will eat it up. He'll tell them all first about finding that outrageous photograph in Mme. Viray's house, the picture of the three ladies, and also about the one Marcella described or rather didn't dare to describe.

"Then he'll explain how the lordly Señor used these damnably suggestive photographs to blackmail women into becoming Nazi agents in Argentina. Then, of course, they'll want to know just how Señor Corrijo ever got those photographs, if the women didn't pose for them—which they undoubtedly did not—and then— Oh look! Here they come!" he said, and the Bobcat drew me aside.

Capt. Little limped up to the porch and into the house, followed by an excited, chattering crowd of reporters and photographers talking and laughing and pushing. They streamed through the vaulted marble corridor and we followed them round a corner into the beautiful ballroom where Señor Corrijo had showed us his collection of rings and dolls on the night of that never-to-be-forgotten dinner. It seemed almost a desecration to have that noble hall filled with the excited chattering of that little news-hungry rabble.

And there Capt. Little went immediately to the central arched panel between two pilasters, in the wall opposite the windows. He turned a small rosette in the moulding and inserted a key into a hidden keyhole. The crowd of curious newspaper folk closed in and surrounded him.

"And this," said Capt. Little in a loud voice, "is how Señor Corrijo got those ineffable photographs." He threw open a concealed door which completely filled the panel.

For a moment there wasn't a sound in the ballroom. Then the silence was broken by a loud burst of voices, a babel of exclamations and questions, and the women reporters' shrill, excited cries, and the photographers' flash lights began to explode one after another.

It was like opening Bluebeard's secret chamber. There, each one standing upright in a sort of coffin-shaped frame, covered with cellophane, all expensively gowned, were seven lovely ladies in their transparent boxes. They looked as if they were frozen in blocks of ice. And those seven wax figures were so realistically and exquisitely made that the ladies seemed actually alive.

I finally succeeded in worming my way in through the crowd and got a nearer view. And then, of those seven wax figures I recognized three. I gasped. Each of the three beautiful ladies I had met at the Señor's dinner was there, and each one was wearing, apparently, the same exquisite gown that she had worn that night.

It was too much for me. I couldn't believe it. I didn't know what to think. All sorts of queer contradictory feelings were confused in me. They were alive, but they were dead. They were dead, but they were alive. They were looking at me. They had come back from the dead, more beautiful than ever. It was marvelous. It was hideous. It was maddening.

The Bobcat pulled my arm.

"Look at the one at the end, there," he said, bitterly.

And then I noticed, beyond three young ladies I didn't know, the dainty, pathetic figure of Marcella Northey.

"The Señor died just in time," said the Bobcat grimly.

Señor Corrijo's dolls . . . Ladies in boxes . . . I was glad he was dead. The noble Señor would never play his infamous game with his lovely dolls again.

11

MRS. E. BALL

That Saturday, when the Bobcat and I jumped out of his car to snatch a hurried lunch at a drug store on Upper Broadway, I was still too depressed by the two deaths at Señor Corrijo's to care much for food. And I sat on that stool at the soda counter considerably puzzled, too, by what I had seen at Riverdale.

The Bobcat said, "Why, this is the way the Señor worked it, Mr. Gilbert. Look: He picks a girl whom he thinks he can use in his conspiracy in Argentina, and has her photographed by Van Diegen in a gown he has given her. He has a duplicate of that gown made at the same time. From Van Diegen's many 'sharp' photographs—the ones you saw at his studio, you know, taken from every point of view—any good model manufacturer could make a very realistic wax image of the girl. The Señor then dresses this wax portrait figure in the extra gown. Then, all he has to do is to pose that figure in any infamous way he wants to, and have Van Diegen make a photograph, slightly blurred, perhaps, so that you couldn't tell it from life."

I sipped my coffee slowly. "I see," I said. "So that's why the Señor had those motion pictures taken at his dinner when we were all there on Thursday evening."

"Exactly," said the Bobcat. "It was certainly a thorough and artistic job. With all those motion pictures to study he would be able to get natural and characteristic poses for his wax figure."

Then I asked the Bobcat how he discovered where the figures were kept.

"Oh, I knew they'd be in the Señor's house," the Bobcat said, and he bit into another sandwich. "You said he collected dolls, you know, and those wax figures were really dolls, you know, life size. I had an idea that besides using them for blackmail the Señor might have some abnormal mania about them, a sort of complex. If so, he'd be sure to keep the figures somewhere near him so he could take them out and look at them whenever he wanted to." And the Bobcat said that the noble Señor was probably posing them for another photograph when I saw him with them in his dining room window yesterday noon.

"I suppose you went all over the house, then," I said, "tapping the walls to see if they sounded hollow?"

The Bobcat laughed. "No, I was lucky enough to run across a plan of the house in the Señor's office before it was set afire. I noticed some spaces like closets along the wall of the ballroom opposite the windows. When I went into the ballroom, though, there were no signs of them, so I was pretty sure they were hidden behind those arched panels between the pilasters."

I asked him how he had got the keys to the closets.

"Oh," he laughed, "I threw a good scare into the Tallia girl, the Señor's secretary, and she handed them over as if she were giving up the crown jewels."

I began to eat again. "But, as you said out there," I said, "finding those wax figures doesn't really help much in solving the mystery of the murders, does it?"

"That's why," he said, "I'm going to have another look at Miss Magister's flat the very next thing I do."

We got up and he put his hand on my shoulder and smiled at me.

"You know, Mr. Gilbert, you're still technically under surveillance, and so I'm afraid you'll have to accompany me."

I laughed and said that I could have got away last night, if I'd wanted to.

"Not a chance," said the Bobcat. "There was a man on guard at the 32nd St. entrance to the Hotel Imperial all night long. The 31st St. entrance is closed at midnight, you know, and the Broadway door of the bar at about 3 A.M., but there was a man at each place when they opened up this morning."

"Which didn't prevent," I said, "Hugo Vlack from getting away."

The Bobcat frowned, then smiled. "That was just one of those things," he said. "They happen once in about a thousand times. Our man spent the whole night sitting in an armchair in the lobby watching, but he had to go downstairs for five minutes—and of course that was exactly the time you were talking to Vlack there, before you both went upstairs." And, the Bobcat said, he was afraid that fellow wouldn't get promoted this year.

When we got to Miss Magister's flat we found a uniformed cop in her dining room. He was tilted back in a chair with his feet on the table, reading the sporting pages of a newspaper. He told the Bobcat that Detective Dan Leary, who was in charge of the Magister case, was out with another man, interviewing people on the block to find out if anyone besides the letter-carrier had seen any callers at the front door, downstairs, the afternoon before.

The Bobcat said he was going to make another search of the living room—he didn't tell me why—and he said he preferred to be alone. I sat down in the dining room and picked up a part of the *Herald-Tribune* the cop there had thrown aside. I skimmed through the story of the three murders, I found nothing new. Van Diegen's photographs of the three women victims were featured on the page.

I sat there awhile thinking how strange life was—that, of all the frumps and cowcats in New York who never would be missed, it was these three lovely ladies who had to be murdered. It would be a long time, I thought, before I met a woman with the charm of any one of them. . . . The cop was still studying the ponies.

The Bobcat came back into the dining room, and he looked rather pleased. He asked the cop to go to the kitchen and draw him a glass of water and be sure to let it run till it was cold.

As soon as the cop was out of the room the Bobcat came nearer to me and held out his hand.

"Look at this," he said.

I saw a small brilliant such as are used nowadays in the manufacture of women's costume jewelry.

"Why, it's just like those stones Detective Leary found in the front room where Miss Magister was murdered," I said. "I was here, you know, when he showed them to Capt. Little. He found them on the floor, Leary said."

"Yes," and the Bobcat nodded. "And Leary evidently thought they all came out of the clip Miss Magister was wearing. But he evidently didn't count the holes in Miss Magister's clip where stones had been. Well, I did. There were nine stones missing in the clip, I've found out; but Leary found ten stones on the floor. And now I've just found one more. It was hidden under the base board of the wall."

Then the Bobcat smiled at me and asked, "Does that suggest anything to you, Mr. Gilbert?"

It did, but I didn't want to acknowledge it; so I said No.

The Bobcat gave me a rather keen look, and laughed; but he didn't press the subject.

"When I go down to the Morgue tonight," he said, "I hope to prove that two and two are four."

He drank the glass of water the cop brought in and then he went out into the kitchen closet and brought back the glass jar I had seen the night before when I was there with Capt. Little, and he had several small bottles, as well. He said he was sending them to the Police Laboratory. Then he asked the cop there if he could get Maude Magister's cook, Mrs. Ball.

The cop said, "I'm afraid you won't get much out of that old dame, Mr. Catfield. Dan Leary had to give her up cold," and he tapped his forehead and said she belonged in a cage, that woman.

The Bobcat and I went into the front living room. All traces of the struggle and tragedy there had now been cleaned up, and the big pastel portrait of Maude Magister looked down at us with a subtle smile.

In ten minutes or so a thin, bony female of about sixty or so, with two big moles on her cheek, was brought in by the policeman and she was dressed in dingy black with a heavy black veil stringing down from a small rusty crepe bonnet.

When I saw her straggly gray hair and her roving little whitish-blue eyes I thought she looked like a rag-picker on a cold day, and I wondered why the fastidious, exquisite Maude Magister had ever employed such a creature as housekeeper and cook. It didn't seem to me that I'd ever care to taste anything she ever cooked. I sat in a blue armchair by the secretary and smoked and listened to the Bobcat interviewing her.

At the very first question she stopped him to correct him. He had addressed her as Mrs. Ball.

"Mrs. *E.* Ball, if you please," she said, sternly.

The Bobcat apologized for not knowing about the E; and then he pointed a lead pencil at her and said, "Well then, Mrs. E. Ball, have you any idea who killed Miss Magister?"

"I have no idea and I think so," she declared, "but I know what I think so. I know it."

The Bobcat looked at me as if he hadn't heard aright.

"Who did it, then, if you know, or think you do?" he asked.

"It's not for me to accuse," she said stiffly. "I might accuse an imagination and there would be no two ways about it."

"What on earth do you mean, Mrs. Ball?" the Bobcat asked.

"Mrs. *E.* Ball," she corrected.

"Oh, of course," said the Bobcat. He was getting annoyed and impatient. And he repeated his question,

Mrs. E. Ball said very slowly, "What I have seen I do not know. And what I know I have not seen. There's not a doubt in my mind about it." And she nodded gravely.

"Well, what *have* you seen, Mrs. E. Ball?"

She was clutching the arms of her chair tightly, and her eyes wandered up to the portrait on the wall, "Nothin' in this world would induce me to tell," she said, "but things will they make me. I am a poor woman, an' all I have is most of all." And she nodded again.

The Bobcat threw up his hands and rose. "Well, all right, Mrs. E. Ball. You win." And he said to me, "There's no use talking to her, not in that language, I'm afraid."

"Indeed it is!" she exclaimed. "An' what's more, the shoe fits! If a grand handsome man had an atonement with her, should I speak it out?"

"What handsome man?" the Bobcat asked and he folded his arms and stood glaring at her. The cop was standing up leaning against the mantel, chewing something.

That word "atonement" made me think of how many times, when I was young, I had heard ministers in church explain, as if it was their own original, new thought, that atonement really meant at-one-ment. wondered what was in the old woman's mind.

"Wait a minute," I said. I thought I saw a streak of sense in the woman's baffling talk. I remembered that Van Diegen had insinuated that Miss Magister had a lover. And hadn't two witnesses been found last night who had seen a man in her apartment in, the middle of the night?

"Mrs. Ball," I said, "I mean Mrs. E. Ball, pardon me, was this handsome man her lover, or was everything all right?"

She turned to me and looked at me as if she hadn't seen me before.

"They had an atonement, one and each one," she said, "and here it was. And the goin's-on was open to love, if love that be, with a rat the likes of him. 'Twas a midnight room for midnight business."

I said to the Bobcat. "You see, some man did come here to see Miss Magister; he came at night, and Mrs. E. Ball didn't like it." Then I turned to her and asked her with all the sympathy I could why he was a rat.

She leaned forward to listen to me as if she were deaf. And now she put her hand to the side of her mouth and whispered,

"The very King's colors he turned tail on. A rat he is, and black be his guts. A turn tail he was, and she abridged him! A glorious lady she was indeed in the flesh, as I say it; why did she not announce him? She was a rat, too, for all the sweet face of her an' didn't I cuddle her, a baby? Rat she was, they was two birds in the one bush, she an' him, an' she shamed the King's color thereby, so she did, an' bitter was the pill. But she had to go."

"I give it up," said the Bobcat, and the policeman shook his head and laughed immoderately. But I said,

"Why, don't you see? This chap, Maude's lover, is evidently a deserter from the British Army, and Mrs. E. Ball thinks that Maude should have notified the authorities and have him taken." I appealed to her. "Isn't that so, Mrs. E. Ball?"

She nodded her head and clenched her fists, and I asked her who this fellow was. The Bobcat watched me as if fascinated. The cop stopped chewing.

"If my corporil with his stripe didn't save the very life of him," she said, "what would he have had to give her with, I ask you. It was the other war, mark you." She shook a skinny finger at me. "This war is no war at all, at all; 'tis an abominative manslaughterin', and my son Willy, he knew well 'twas his own Major, the same one, uniform or no uniform. And of his memory there is no mistake."

"I get it," said the Bobcat. "The handsome chap's a British Major. Well, that's something, anyway."

"Yes," I said, "and her son was a corporal in his regiment and saved his life in the first World War." Then I asked the old woman what the Major's name was.

"He's handsomer than you be, Mr. What's-your-name," she cackled. "I'd like to kiss the livin' face of him, I would that, an' me a widder in weeds. That's my sin, god help me. What did ye say?"

"What's his name, Mrs. E. Ball?" I repeated. And then as she wouldn't answer, and just grinned at me, I tried another tack. "Perhaps you don't know his name," I said. "But I know it. It's Everett. Major Everett. Now isn't it?"

"Iverett, Iverett, Iverett, Iverett!" she sang, up and down the scale. "An why should it be Iverett when he's a Godwil just as easy as the cat jumps; an' Archie Godwil to boot, to be primp about it."

Then her voice changed to a lower tone. "I seen 'em talkin' behind the door, the two of them; more than once I seen 'em, an' passin' papers with lines on 'em, an' good green money, at that, I did, didn't I?"

"How about that, Gilbert?" the Bobcat asked eagerly. "Sounds like those maps they found here." Then he said to Mrs. E. Ball, "She gave him money, did she?"

"An' what's money, where that come from," she ex-claimed. "If he wanted to pay her, that's one way to the woods, ain't it?"

I said, "You're wrong, Bobcat. *He* gave *her* money— didn't he, Mrs. E. Ball?"

She grinned at me and said, "'Tis plain as a pancake ye're a gentleman o' brains, an' that's what meets the eye. But my son Willy, he's smarter nor you, Mr. What's-your-name. He'd know it if he was here, god bless him. Be ye British?"

"What did he give her money for?" I asked her.

"Do I know?" she sang. "No idea, not the littlest, as sure as you fall off a log I tell ye!" And then she almost yelled, "An' what's more I don't know it! Then let nature take its course."

I asked her then what the handsome Major did here in New York.

"If I had the knife," she said, darkly, "I'd work it on him like she got that same. Him an' his butterflies! Is that a task for a Major in the King's troop?" The old woman flung out her hands. "What's that for a soldier? Butter-flies! Poisonin' of 'em, an' stickin' pins!"

"Good!" cried the Bobcat. "That accounts for that case of drawers in the kitchen closet. It belonged to Miss Ma-gister's lover, the Major. But I don't like that word poison. What d'you mean by that, Mrs. E. Ball?" he asked.

She sat silently, working her fingers in her lap. The cop who had watched, spellbound, all this while, sat down on a small settee and began chewing again.

I then asked Mrs. E. Ball if she thought the Major had killed Miss Magister.

She startled us with a kind of shriek. "Awk!" she cried. "What would a rat mischief, who'd turn tail to the King hisself! I seen the knife. I seen her dead. A rat he is an' a grand handsome man he is, dirty be his soul."

"Did they ever have any quarrels?" the Bobcat asked.

"Who are ye askin'?" she demanded sharply.

"Mrs. E. Ball," said the Bobcat.

"Then take trouble for your pains," she said. "Would I speak ill of the dead?" She looked up at the portrait and crossed herself. "'Tis bad luck to ye, an' cold over your head when your grave's stepped on. She was a lady, that she was, an' she was hard to suit since a baby. But he was hard, too, and between husband and wife happen tears as often as kisses, do I know it? An' as frequent, yes, an' sharp words an' blows into the bargain an' that's what makes a mountain out of a marriage bed, heaven help us."

The Bobcat looked at me in amazement. "By jove!" he exclaimed, "Maude Magister was Major Godwil's wife!"

"Yes, an' you," she said, "who be so sharp, how did ye know that?"

I said, "Mrs. E. Ball, we want very much to find this Major Godwil. If he's a deserter perhaps we can get the British authorities to have him arrested. Where does he live?"

"No sir," she said. "You can't pull no wool into me, I won't have it."

Then the Bobcat said, he had caught onto my method, "Oh, I remember now. He lives in Harlem, doesn't he?"

"That I couldn't say," she said, with sudden dignity. "I don't believe it, I never believed it, an' I never shall believe it. 'Tis in the graveyard I wisht he lived, deep down near the Pit, to burn the black soul of him."

I was getting exhausted and I said carelessly that the Major could live on Park Avenue for all I cared.

She jumped and pointed at me and cackled, "An' why not? Ain't Park Avenue good enough for him, with a big high man at the door in a coat with silver and gold all over him?"

"What number?" I asked.

And she surprised us by saying, "There's an eight and a seven and a five to it. You can add it up for yourself."

"Bingo!" cried the Bobcat, and he pounded the arm of his chair. "875 Park Avenue." And he said he felt as if he'd won a thousand-mile steeplechase.

Then he told the old lady very politely that that would be all, and he asked the policeman there to take her home.

For a moment the old woman sat looking up at the portrait of Miss Magister. And, for a moment, as she dabbed her eyes with a dirty handkerchief, I thought I caught a glimpse of something that once might have been rather fine, hidden deep down under in the cracked old creature's tortured soul.

And then, as she stumbled down the stairs with the cop, we heard her muttering to herself brokenly, and sobbing.

We found out that afternoon that Major Archer Godwil did indeed live at 875 Park Avenue. The clerk in the office of the magnificent Moldavia Apartments told us, however, that the Major was away. By some police magic, though, we were taken up to the 21st floor, and the Major's room was opened for us.

I was fascinated by the swift and systematic way the Bobcat went through that room, and the bathroom and closet, searching drawers and suit cases and boxes, hardly disturbing the position of a single thing.

He found a list of names and addresses written in violet ink. He found a map of New York with red circles marked at all the electric power houses and telephone stations. There were maps too of the Argentine Republic, also marked with red circles, and maps of Brazil and Uruguay. He found no letters, however, and nothing else the Bobcat seemed to consider significant, until, as we were about to leave, he suddenly turned back and went to a shelf in the corner. He took down a cigar box. He opened it and whistled. In it was a package of greenbacks—over a thousand dollars, he found.

On our way down to the street the Bobcat said, "If this Major Godwil is a deserter, as the old lady seemed to imply, I should say, by what I found in his room, that he's a turncoat, as well. A deserter you see, would be just the kind of man the Nazis would want to use. With his rank he'd have valuable knowledge of British organization and Army methods, and he'd probably be sore at his government and ready to help—especially as these Nazis seem to be pretty generous with their money.

"And at the same time," he said, "if Maude Magister, his wife, were in the British Intelligence service, he might be able through her, but without her suspecting it, to secure valuable information as to British counter-espionage activities."

I said, though, that I thought Maude Magister had plenty of brains; and it seemed to me that if he were a Nazi agent she'd be pretty sure to suspect it.

"Maybe the Major wanted to get rid of her because she did suspect it," said the Bobcat. "To protect himself."

In the Bobcat's car I reminded him of what the old woman had said about the Major's giving his wife "good green money." The Major seemed to have plenty of it, I said. "But if he's the treacherous character he seems to be," I said, "a renegade and Nazi spy, I wonder why he'd be so generous to his wife, whom he doesn't even live with."

"Blackmail, perhaps," the Bobcat said, as we sped down Park Avenue. "To keep his wife from informing the British authorities about him. He could be deported, you know, as an undesirable alien, if he's not naturalized. Perhaps too, he's sick of paying her hush money, and wanted to have a free hand. That would be another reason for his wanting to do away with her."

We had got down to near West 59th St., discussing it, when we heard a terrific explosion. It was followed by another and another.

"Good heavens!" I exclaimed. "Are the Germans over New York already? Certainly sounds like bombs, all right."

At 49th St. we saw people running. We heard the clang of bells and fire engines' sirens screaming. Police radio cars were charging down the street. We stopped and saw smoke curling up out of the ruins of a house near Lexington Avenue. The whole upper part had been destroyed and the street was littered with debris, and a crowd was being pushed back by policemen. We heard the clang of a police emergency car.

"Isn't that near Van Diegen's place?" the Bobcat asked.

"My god," I exclaimed, "it *is* Van Diegen's place—what there is left of it."

The Bobcat stopped the car and hopped out. He went over and spoke to a police sergeant, and then ran on towards the wrecked house.

In a moment a stout, jolly patrolman came up to the car and stood there, talking to me. Evidently he had been told to keep an eye on me. And he told me that it was some German's place that had been blown up, and it looked like it wasn't only the R.A.F. that was chucking bombs nowadays; but with all these strikes and highjacking and holdups and everything there were so many kinds of gangsters you didn't know which was the worst.

When the Bobcat came back to me in the car he said,

"They tell me that someone must have tipped Van Diegen off before the police could get to his place for a raid," he said, and he drove off.

"The F.B.I.," he said, "has been after Van Diegen for some time, I hear, but they haven't been able to get anything on him in the way of subversive action. But the G-men had evidently discovered or suspected that Van Diegen's place was a sort of store house for bombs and ammunition." And the Bobcat said that his idea was that the bombs were made out at Riverdale in the Señor Corrijo's basement laboratory.

We swung round the ramp of the Grand Central Station and I asked him who blew up Van Diegen's place.

"Why, Van Diegen must have done it himself," said the Bobcat. "He evidently found out about the proposed raid too late to get the bombs away, and he was afraid he'd be caught red-handed. So he probably set 'em all off with a time fuse so as to get rid of all the evidence."

"Did they get Van Diegen?" I asked.

"No, he managed to give 'em the slip, somehow." And the Bobcat looked at his watch anxiously as he turned west into 31st Street, and he said that now he'd have to hurry to fix up that cute little mouse at my hotel somehow so that she'd be safe before he did about a million things he had on hand today.

At the rear entrance of the Hotel Imperial he took off his hat and slicked his hair back and began to smile. But upstairs, when I opened my door and called out, "Here we are, Marcella! Here's the handsome cop who's going to protect you!" we didn't hear a sound.

She wasn't in the front room. I looked in my bedroom and in the bathroom, and I even opened the doors of the closets.

Marcella Northey wasn't anywhere in the apartment.

12

MAJOR GODWIL

On Sunday I was tired out, physically and emotionally. I was so affected by the whole sad sequence of fatalities, in fact, that it was all I could do to dress and go to Berta Conley's funeral. I dreaded it as probably a melancholy little affair with a few dispirited mourners. And it seemed to me that it was a hundred years since Berta had died, though in point of fact it was only two days ago.

And until I walked into that undertaker's chapel, too, I had thought of Berta, I don't know why, as being more or less alone in New York—an ambitious and talented girl working her way up to success.

I had sent a lot of roses, and I rather expected to see them there, somewhere near the casket, perhaps. but I found the chapel was piled so high with flowers that you could hardly see the back wall.

Many of the people there, I supposed, were strangers who had read of "The Beauty Murders" in the papers and were morbidly curious to see one of the victims. But most of those filling the seats were apparently Berta Conley's associates and acquaintances in the fashion business. You might have thought it was some social affair of gossip and gayety. Everyone was whispering and looking about to see who was there, and you almost wondered where Berta was, in that smartly dressed crowd.

And when I went forward and looked down amongst the masses of flowers, there she was, all in white, with her hands folded over her breast. Poor Berta was quiet now, her eyes were closed. And Maude Magister's ironic words at that dramatic dinner came back to me again with a hideous humor. "We shall all have to be put into boxes sooner or later, shan't we?—hens and women too." . . .

Berta Conley in a Funeral Home. . . . Maude Magister at the Little Church Around the Corner. . . . Hélène Viray at St. Patrick's Cathedral. . . . And so they lay, all three, that Sunday afternoon, those lovely ladies in their boxes . . . to be prayed over, and taken away. . . .

I took a farewell look at Berta. And then I heard a heart-broken sobbing and I turned and on a front seat beside Biddy Rumsey, who was weeping copiously, I saw a small, blonde freckled girl who looked like a thin, washed-out copy of Berta, and I found out later it was Berta's sister Alice.

And later that afternoon at the Hotel Martinique, where I went to see her, Alice Conley talked and cried for hours about Berta. Berta was so frank, she said, she couldn't keep anything hidden; it seemed to destroy her self-respect, somehow. Sooner or later Berta always told everything, Alice said. She had a sort of passion for confession. Berta always said she wanted the truth, good or bad, to come out, she said, and she was willing to take the consequences. That was her kind of courage. . . .

I felt sorry for Alice, but somehow as she talked and cried and talked about her sister my mind kept drifting all the time to the little cabaret dancer who had disappeared from my rooms the day before. I had thought about Marcella Northey all day, even at the funeral, in fact, and wondered what had happened to her. I was really terribly worried.

It wasn't till six o'clock that Sunday evening that the Bobcat appeared at my door, looking weary and pale and a bit disheveled, and I asked him immediately about Marcella.

He dropped into a chair in my front room.

"Well, she'll pull through," he said. "She was pretty badly hurt and they were afraid of internal injuries, but she's resting easily now at Bellevue Hospital."

I was shocked. I couldn't imagine what could have happened.

And then he told me that as soon as he had left the Imperial, the evening before, Saturday evening, he had run into a radio police car and they had told him that early in the afternoon a patrol over on East River Drive had heard a woman screaming and they found a sedan that had stopped and there was a fight going on inside. The police got there just in time to save Marcella from being clubbed to death with revolver butts by two men in the car. And while they were attending to Marcella, who was almost unconscious, the Bobcat said, the thugs escaped.

I asked him who the men were who had attacked Marcella, and how she had ever got into that car.

The Bobcat seemed a good deal affected, for him. He had evidently blamed himself, too, for not having taken sufficient precautions, and he sat looking down at the floor.

"Well," he said, "I didn't want to tire the little girl there in the hospital, but as near as I could make out, while she was waiting in your room here for us to come back, you know, somebody phoned up from the lobby of the hotel and said I wanted her to go to her mother's, and told her that you and I would meet her there. She went down to the hotel lobby and some guy there showed her a police badge—or what looked like one—and said he had a car waiting for her."

"It looks like Van Diegen's work," I said.

"Sure," said the Bobcat. "He evidently thought that Marcella knew too much about his trick photography and the South American game with Señor Corrijo and had her followed. The men in the car spoke German, anyway, she said, and that aroused Marcella's suspicions. And when she saw that they were going over towards the East River, instead of going north to Columbia Heights where she lives, she was sure that something was wrong and she began to scream for help, and they began to beat her up. And the poor little girl is lucky to be alive."

The Bobcat was still looking down at the floor. It would teach him a lesson, he said, that he'd remember all his life. He looked tired and worn. He asked me for a glass of milk, and he ate some cheese, too; and then he sort of looked around the room and asked me if I had anything to smoke. Then he yawned and remarked casually that he guessed he'd broken the case.

"You mean you've solved the Conley murder?" I asked. "Already?"

"All three murders," he said. Then he yawned again and got up and said he'd worked all night long and he wanted to know if I'd lend him a razor.

He came back from the bathroom looking fresher, and he told me that he had been down to the Morgue and had examined all the clothes and things there belonging to the three murdered women. He had been to the police laboratory too; and he had even gone through Berta Conley's rooms in the Imperial here, he said, while I was asleep next door, at 4 A.M., and I don't know where he hadn't been.

While I was making some coffee for him, the telephone bell rang and a cultivated masculine voice wanted to know if Mr. Catfield was in my room. The Bobcat grabbed the receiver and told somebody to come up. And then he explained to me that he had had a man stationed at the Moldavia Apartments on Park Avenue waiting for Major Godwil to return; and if the Major got back in time today, he was to be requested to come to see Police Detective Catfield at six o'clock at Suite 761 in the Hotel Imperial.

I went to the door to find two gentlemen. One of them was a handsome, military looking fellow of forty-odd. He was quite distinguished, straight and well set up, with graying hair brushed back and a thin line of moustache that had evidently been colored. He bowed.

I told him that Mr. Catfield was here, if he would come in, and after I had given him my name, he said,

"I am Major Godwil, sir, at your service"; and he turned to his companion, and introduced him as Counsellor Sir George Grayson, of the British Embassy in Washington; and I shook hands with a short, bald, anxious-looking red-faced man with his face full of lines.

In the front room, the nervous little Sir George cleared his throat and said stiffly,

"All this, you must understand, gentlemen, is strictly off the record. This interview is highly regular, considering the nature of Major Godwil's duties and my own." And he said, "I have been instructed by the Ambassador to use all care, discretion and precaution in keeping the affair as quiet as possible. He does not wish to imply any commitments, guarantees or precedents." And the Bobcat and I had to listen to a lot more diplomatic verbiage like that before the Counsellor announced that Major Godwil was willing to help in any way possible to solve the mystery of his wife's, the late Miss Magister's, tragic demise.

The Major had a strained and suffering look on his face and he told us that he was a British secret service agent. He accepted a cigar and expressed himself as being deeply indebted to the Ambassador for having intervened in his behalf, and permitted him to speak.

"Because as you probably know, gentlemen," he said, "I am really nothing better than a spy; and spies are seldom recognized or protected by their governments. That," he said, "would, of course, nullify their effectiveness. And so, if they get into trouble they usually have to shift for themselves."

Sir George made a sweeping gesture with his rubber-framed glasses and said, impressively,

"Major Godwil, you may be interested to know, gentlemen, has the Victoria Cross. His case, I may say, is exceptionally privileged. And besides, a question of murder is involved which is intimately related to his work in the Intelligence."

We all had drinks and then Major Godwil explained that he and his wife had been working together to combat German plots in the United States and South America. He had posed as a deserter from the British Army, he said, and had been so posted in English papers in order to encourage overtures from Hitler's agents and gain their confidence. For the same reason the Major said, he and his wife had kept their marriage secret, when they came to the United States, and they had worked independently, seeing each other only surreptitiously and at rare intervals. She, as Miss Magister, had been worming herself into the confidence of the agents of the Argentine conspiracy, while he was working with the German-American Bund.

The Bobcat asked the Major first about the butterflies in Miss Magister's flat.

The Major was silent a moment. I saw a shadow cross his face. Then he said, "You'll pardon me, I trust, gentlemen. I find it a bit hard to—to adjust myself, you know— to what has happened." And then he said, abstractedly, "Oh yes, the butterflies." And he told us that he was by way of being an entomologist of sorts and that it worked in very well with his programme.

"I went about," he said, "collecting butterflies in the vicinity of the country camps of the Bund, d'you see; and that was how I made connection with the leaders. When they found out that I was a deserter—I was a prisoner in Germany during the First World War, you know, and that made things simpler—it was easy enough. The Nazis seem unable to comprehend how anyone can possibly fail to agree with their outrageous doctrines and methods."

The Bobcat asked him how he killed his butterflies.

"With cyanide of potassium," the Major said. "I used that glass jar you may have seen in my wife's flat. I left the collection there as I had no room for the butterflies in my quarters at the Moldavia."

The Bobcat's next question was as to whether or not the Major had helped support Miss Magister. Did he give her money? he asked.

"That was the one jolly part of the whole rotten business," the Major said, and his faint smile was ironic. "The Nazis have kindly, though of course unwittingly, helped finance the British Intelligence service. And they pay, I may say, very well. Why, in my quarters at the Moldavia I now have over a thousand dollars in specie given me by the Nazi secret service."

The Bobcat glanced quickly at me, and then asked the Major what he did with the Nazi money.

The Major deposited his cigar ash very carefully in a tray, and Sir George looked at his watch.

"I was supposed, as a Nazi agent," said Major Godwil, "to corrupt Irish republicans and disaffected Britons here in the United States, and pass bribes here and there, help on propaganda work, that sort of thing. All that takes money, you know, but I spent as little as possible for their work and diverted as much as possible for use in sabotage of the Nazi plans. Of course checks are no good for brib-ery, and hence the greenbacks which you discovered, Mr.

Catfield, yesterday afternoon in my room." And he really smiled, now, at the Bobcat.

Sir George, the methodical Counsellor, made a gesture with his rubber-framed glasses and said, "The Major, you will understand, gentlemen, is naturally unable to give any specific information regarding his special work. But I am authorized to let you know that he has been working in close connection with your Federal Bureau of Investigation and was able to furnish evidence leading to the attempted seizure, unfortunately forestalled yesterday, of bombs and ammunition stored by Nazi sympathizers in the studio of Mr. Karl Van Diegen."

The Bobcat made a few inquiries about the Nazi plot and Señor Corrijo's connection with it, and Major Godwil said, a little cautiously,

"I imagine you are acquainted with the main lines of it, Mr. Catfield. But I might tell you that my wife learned only this week of Mme. Viray's participation in the conspiracy, and as Mme. Viray was posing as a friend of Free France you may imagine that my wife was pretty indignant and was very anxious to outwit the lady."

And then the Bobcat asked with an effect of real sympathy, if Major Godwil had any idea who was responsible for his wife's death.

The Major waited a moment, as if trying to speak without emotion, and then he said, and I saw his face harden, "I have a very strong suspicion, Mr. Catfield. My wife informed me recently that she had succeeded in securing from Karl Van Diegen's papers in his studio, an important list of names."

The Bobcat asked if it was written in violet ink.

"Yes," said the Major, "it was."

The Bobcat then asked what those names were, and the Major told him that they were the names of private parties owning airplanes kept at various air ports and dromes and private grounds in the United States and that his opinion was that when and if the time should come for overt action on the part of a Fifth Column here, the plan was that all these planes would be seized and flown to some base and organized to fight the Federal forces.

And then the Major said in a hard voice, "I have met Karl Van Diegen fairly often in my work and I happen to know that he has discovered the loss of this list and believes my wife to have got possession of it. And I know something of Karl Van Diegen's character also, and his methods. I believe that he would use any means, fair or foul, to get the document back and to revenge himself upon the person who had abstracted it. He had many tools he could use for persecution—or worse."

Sir George shook his glasses at us again and said, "But this suspicion, you must understand, gentlemen, is only a personal surmise on the part of Major Godwil and has no official connection with his work."

"Official or not," the Major said, "it seems very likely that there was some conflict between Van Diegen and my wife. I believe he visited her and threatened her and perhaps used force. Maude had a strong will and a high pride, and her hatred for Hitler and his brood of devils is no mere sentiment. She herself has suffered at their hands. I mean that her brother, a very clever and lovable young subaltern in the Guards, was made a prisoner in the last war, and was horribly tortured and starved. In point of fact, he died while interned, from the effect of exposure. I myself was captured at Vimy, later, and my wife knew from my experiences how damnably cruel the Germans were then—and what they are doing now is undoubtedly ten times worse. My wife, too, has told me that she has had trouble all along in her dealings with Van Diegen. She has had hard work preventing him from getting his hands on her, physically, I mean. Many of his women clients have had the same experience. Perhaps something like that happened, and she attempted to defend herself, and he killed her."

Sir George sat there frowning, and he seemed to think the Major had said too much, and he said that he thought the New York police would be able to discover the murderer.

"How about this Mrs. Ball?" the Bobcat asked, "the woman your wife employed as housekeeper. She is certainly mentally affected in some way. Isn't it possible that in some moment of increased dementia—a psychosis, I think they call it—she might have—"

He didn't finish because the Major interrupted him with an emphatic "No, no, Mr. Catfield, that's impossible.

"Mrs. Ball," he said, "was a servant in my wife's family, the Garths, for years and years. In fact she was my wife's nurse when she was a baby. I am positive that she was heart and soul devoted to my wife. Until a year or so ago, you see," the Major said, "Mrs. Ball was quite sane, and she was a great help and comfort to my wife." And then he explained that when Mrs. Ball's son Willy, who was rather wild, was convicted of some minor offense, stealing perhaps, and had to serve a term in jail, the anxiety and disgrace of it set Mrs. Ball to brooding over what was, to her honest soul, a calamity, and she suffered so intensely that her reason became affected.

Major Godwil stopped a moment to finish his drink and then he said, "My wife understood her rambling talk sufficiently, and as the poor soul could still do her work well enough and the two got on well together, and from pity, too, my wife couldn't bear to send her away to a sanitarium."

The Counsellor looked at his watch again and the Bobcat said that, even although Mrs. Ball was in nowise implicated in the crime, she perhaps knew who was guilty, if anyone could get it out of her.

"No doubt Mrs. Ball thinks I did it," said the Major in all seriousness. "She thinks of me as a deserter, you know, a traitor to the King, a renegade and a thoroughly despicable character, capable of any crime in the calendar. It was one of my wife's greatest sorrows that she couldn't reassure her old nurse of my true situation, but obviously that was inexpedient. It was a terrible strain on poor Mrs. Ball's loyalty and devotion to condone my wife's continued relations with me when I risked going to see her, which was always late at night."

There was a silence in the room for a moment. Major Godwil seemed to be lost in his thoughts and I saw that shadow pass again over his face. Sir George was nervous and evidently impatient. I sat and watched them and the Bobcat, who was apparently thinking how to put his next question, sat with his chin in his hand looking at the Major. Finally he said,

"Major Godwil, I don't wish to add to your distress in any way in this sad affair, but I shall have to ask you if you were on good terms with your wife at the time of her death."

The Major looked puzzled for a moment. He looked at Sir George, who frowned. Then he said, "Do you mean that—is it possible that I could be suspected of—" Then in a changed voice he said, "The answer, Mr. Catfield, is yes. I loved my wife as well as—" and he didn't seem to be able to go on.

He got up and went to the window and turned his back on us. He stood there a moment, and then I saw him stiffen as a soldier does when he salutes; and then he turned round to us and said, with great dignity,

"I have seen many of my friends die in agony on the battlefield, Mr. Catfield. I have seen them tortured in concentration camps. I have seen my friends despised as spies and go to a shameful death. But when a woman—and when that woman is—is my wife—" He paused to get possession of himself. "Yes," he said, simply, "I loved her, Mr. Catfield. Dearly. And I believe she loved me." Then he reached in his pocket and drew out a folded paper and handed it to the Bobcat. "Perhaps this will answer your question better than I am able to do," he said, and he sat down with his head in his hands.

It was Maude Magister's will, signed a week before. Evidently realizing that she was engaged in a hazardous career, she had left everything to "my beloved husband Major Archer Godwil," and gave an address in Surrey, England. And Major Godwil told us that at the same time he had made a similar will in her favor.

There was another rather painful silence, and then Major Godwil, who, like a true Englishman, seemed to feel a bit uncomfortable at having been led to betraying sentiment, told us, while Sir George looked at his watch again, that it was his wife's indignation at her brother's suffering, and a desire for revenge that had led her, when the present war broke out, to offer her services to the British Intelligence Office. And it was while they both were working there, the Major said, that they had met and married.

Sir George Grayson then got up decisively. He told us that he had an important appointment in half an hour, and then had to take a plane back to Washington. Then he hesitated, and said apologetically that he should like a few words with Major Godwil, if we would forgive him. Official business, he said.

As the Major went down my hall to the door with him, the Bobcat said to me quickly and quietly,

"Keep Godwil here if you possibly can. I want to get him to talking about Miss Magister. I want to know what sort of woman she was, you know. It fits right in with my

investigation, and if I get what I want it will be the last
link in the chain."

Then we heard my front door close and Major Godwil
came back, and took up his hat. I begged him not to go
yet, and I offered him another drink, and the Bobcat said,

"Major Godwil," and I could see he was trying to be
very friendly, "I never had the pleasure of meeting your
wife, Miss Magister, unfortunately, but from what I hear
from Mr. Gilbert she must have been a most delightful
woman. I know that it must be a painful subject, Major,
but if you wouldn't mind too much telling me a little more
about her, there might be something that would give me a
clue to work on."

And the Bobcat smiled charmingly and said that a doctor, you know, often had to know about a patient's an-
tecedents before he could diagnose wisely.

The Major sat down slowly. He sipped his whiskey. I
got the idea that he rather liked us both and he liked the
room, and that he was tired and lonely.

"It's been so long," he said in a low voice, "since I've
been able to talk freely about my wife, even to acknowledge that she was my wife, that it's a relief, in a way, you
know, to be able to speak of her without extreme caution.
She was an extraordinary woman," he said, "an original
character." And then he relapsed into silence.

"You were telling us," the Bobcat said, quietly, "about
how you happened to marry her."

A faint smile showed on the Major's sad face, and we
waited again.

"Oh yes," he said, "it did come about rather queerly,
you know," he said; then he thanked me and said, yes, he
would have another cigar, and he lighted it.

Then he said, "And curiously enough, our courtship
and marriage are really the only things there are to tell,
of a personal nature, that is. Of course, as Sir George

told you, I can hardly go into the details of our official work since then. As soon as we were married, you see, the war broke out and we became completely absorbed in our work in the Intelligence, and we had no time for private matters. As a matter of fact we were separated by it almost immediately, anyway. But our pre-marital affair—well, at all events, it may give you an idea of what she was like, perhaps, if you'd really care to hear."

We assured him, both of us did, of our interest, and he went on. I listened as a novelist, I suppose, to a character study, but the Bobcat was all detective and followed every word closely.

"My wife was always extremely proud," the Major said, "and she had reason to be. She belonged to a proud old Westmoreland family. Although the Garths were untitled they had owned their lands since the Norman Conquest, I believe, and they were so influential in the county that they rather looked down upon the mere patented nobility.

"I was in the Decoding Department—what you called the Black Chamber here in the States, during the last war. Miss Garth, Maude Garth, she was then, was assigned to my office. When I first talked to her, I give you my word I don't know which struck me most, her beauty or her brains. We were thrown together a good deal, and I saw a lot of her in our work; but it never occurred to me that she would ever care particularly for me. I was much older than she, and I had nothing but my army pay, you know. In fact she seemed to be much more interested, at the time, in a young architect chap she was going about with all the time. He was very well off, and of a very good family, and they made a handsome couple."

The Major's face had lighted up a little, and he was really a rather stunning old chap himself, I thought, and he must have a lot of charm hidden under his sadness. He had stopped a little self-consciously and he said he didn't know why all this should interest us. But the Bobcat urged him earnestly to continue.

"Well, then," the Major said, "one day after we'd shut up shop, I was in my office, and I was puzzling over a rather difficult Japanese diplomatic cipher message, I remember, that we'd just picked up secretly. I thought everybody had gone home. Miss Garth knocked on my door and told me that she'd like to speak to me about a confidential matter.

"Well, I was always glad to see her, of course, delighted. She sat down and looked at me in a rather odd way, I thought, as if she were trying to summon her courage for something, and I wondered what the devil was up now. Then she lifted her head in that proud way she has—she had—and she said, 'Captain Godwil,'—I was a Captain then, you know—'I'm going to ask you a question that I want you to answer with absolute frankness. I don't want you to evade it,' she said, 'or try to spare my feelings, or anything like that.'

"And then she came out with it. She asked me if there was any possibility that I would ever ask her to marry me.

"Well, my word, you know," the Major said, while we listened, breathless, "I was fairly bowled over, you know. Lovely girl like that—you should have seen Maude at twenty, before this bloody war had tired her out—and she jolly well meant it all, too, by jove. She wasn't spoofing; the girl was in dead earnest, by jove, she was pale. And I knew that it must have cost her no end of a sacrifice of her pride, a Garth, you know, and all that, to ask me that question. The odd part of it was that she didn't seem bold at all. She simply wanted to know, you know; the way you'd want to know whether a man was going to buy your house, you know, or your horse."

We had to smile at that, the Bobcat and I; and I asked the Major what answer he had made to her.

The Major said, "Why, before I could get my breath to answer her, she told me that the rich young architect she'd been going about with—Eric Lash, his name was—had asked her to marry him. 'He's a good match,' she said, 'and Eric and I'll get on all right enough; and if you have no idea of ever marrying me I shall accept him. But if there's any chance at all, even the remotest chance,' she said, 'that you may ever feel that way towards me, then I shall say no to Eric.' And she told me that she had promised him to give him his answer that night.

"Well," the Major said, with a queer expression on his face, "you can imagine what I said. If I'd ever had any idea that she'd have me. I'd have proposed to her long before then. I couldn't believe my luck. It was as if somebody had offered me a gold mine."

I said, "And so you married her, Major? What a delightful romance."

"Wait a minute," the Major said. "Well, my back was nearly slapped off at my club and everywhere I went. I'd won the proud, aristocratic beautiful Maude Garth, you know, and I was happier than I ever, thought I'd be in this world or the next. The banns were published and we got ready to be married in St. Martin's-in-the-Fields, and Maude's family came up to London for the show. The day came, and I waited in the chancel for her with my best man and the organ kept playing and playing and playing and the bride didn't come."

The Major smoked awhile thoughtfully and we waited without a word.

"Well," said the Major, finally, "I was all at sea. Maude and I had never had the slightest disagreement, you see, and we were sweethearting right up to the very day. I didn't know what the devil to do, and everybody, of course, thought there must be some scandal. And at last, when I

had motored break-neck to Garth Manor, near Windermere, it is, there she was, by jove, more beautiful than
ever, and she said she was delighted to see me."

The Bobcat said, "I don't understand. Why had she run
away from the wedding?"

"That's what I asked her," the Major said. "And she
simply laughed and said she thought I didn't really want
to marry her, and I was going through with it just because
I didn't want to let her down."

"But you did marry her," I said.

The Major had that queer faint smile again on his lips.
"Not until she had puss-in-the-cornered me like that three
separate times," he said. "I would propose all over again,
and she'd accept me, and then leave me waiting at the
church. Once at Windermere, and once again in London.
And then I got furious and I took the bit in my teeth. I
have a lot of pride myself, you know, but I've got a will,
too, and when I want a thing I get it or damn well know
why. I ran her up to Scotland in my car on some pretense,
one day, and I married her practically by main force."

I had been smiling at the story, but the Bobcat had an
intent look and he was frowning.

"I get it," he said, slowly. "She felt she had lost her
self-respect by making that advance to you, didn't she?
And the only way she could regain it was to make you propose to her three times."

"Yes," said the Major. "It was just as if, say, in a burst
of unbridled generosity she had given me five pounds. She
felt so poor, then, that she made me pay her back fifteen."

He rose, then. He said that perhaps he had been a bit
garrulous, and he was afraid that what he had told wouldn't
help much in discovering the criminal.

"On the contrary," said the Bobcat, "you've told me
just what I wanted to know about Miss Magister." When
we were alone again the Bobcat said to me gravely,

"That chap Godwil is a good soldier, Mr. Gilbert. He's gone through hell with his head up. But I'm afraid he's in for something still worse before long."

I didn't know what he meant, but he wouldn't explain. I would find out later, he said. And then he said that Capt. Little was coming at 9.30 that evening and they would examine a new witness.

"In my room here, d'you mean?" I asked.

"Why not?" said the Bobcat and he grinned. "We can keep an eye on you, you know, and not have to follow you round to funerals and things." And he said it was handy to Miss Conley's rooms, too, and besides, his new witness happened to live at the Imperial, he said.

We had dinner, that evening, at the McAlpin Roof restaurant, but the Bobcat was absent-minded. Every time I spoke to him he scowled, and he ate hardly anything. He'd shoot a question at me, occasionally, about Berta or the Señor, or something; but most of the time he was studying his notebook or writing things down in it.

And at nine o'clock that night we hurried back to the Imperial Hotel.

13

THE BOBCAT

The Bobcat and I were just in time to find Capt. Little and Detective Pearson waiting to take the Annex elevator up to my room. They both clapped the Bobcat on the back jovially. Both knew, of course, what he had been doing and Capt. Little seemed highly pleased that the confidence he had placed in the young detective had been so well rewarded.

At 9.30 there was a ring at my doorbell, and I admitted Mr. Gross, the District Attorney. He was in top hat and evening dress with a camellia in his buttonhole and a little extra wax, apparently, on the ends of his black moustache. He came in as if he were the best man at a wedding, and said good-evening elegantly to the three detectives, then pulled up the knees of his trousers and sat down in my favorite chair, and passed round a handful of dark, fat cigars.

"Well, boys," he said, "I understand you've done a swell job, and in a hurry, too, I'll say. I hope," he said, he was smiling broadly, "you're giving me a good juicy, sensational society trial for me to show off at in the court room."

Capt. Little said, dryly, "There'll be no trial, Mr. Gross, I'm afraid."

The D.A. pounded the arms of his chair. "What!" he exclaimed. "You mean I don't get a chance at this triple-killing show? No press? No kudos? How's that?"

Capt. Little said, "Why, Mr. Gross, after Catfield, here," and he waved indulgently to the Bobcat, "had told me his theories of the case and pointed out a few things he had come across, I authorized him to conduct an independent investigation. And he's the man who put the puzzle together. So it's really up to him to explain."

The Bobcat was sitting on the edge of my library table, his eyes on the District Attorney.

"Well, in the first place, Mr. Gross," he began, "there's an important psychological aspect to this case. That is, the relations of these three beautiful women with Señor Corrijo.

"There's no doubt," he said, "that the French woman, Mme. Viray, was in love with him. Dahlia, her colored maid, believed so, and we found letters in the Señor's office at his residence which indicated very strongly that she was the Señor's mistress."

"But how about Maude Magister?" asked the District Attorney. "She doesn't seem to have been exactly that type."

"No sir," the Bobcat said. "She was a British secret agent engaged in counter-espionage, and working with her husband, Major Godwil. Her will, which he showed me, testified plainly to her love and loyalty to him. It seems probable, therefore, that she was merely pretending an affection for Señor Corrijo, in order to gain his confidence and obtain information about his Nazi and Fascist activities in Argentina.

"The case of Berta Conley," the Bobcat continued, "is more doubtful. She seems to have been talented and ambitious. And not being aware of the Señor's true character she would conceivably have liked to marry him for his money, his position and his influence. At any rate, that's the opinion of her sister, Alice Conley, in whom Berta apparently always confided."

The Bobcat then stood up with his hands in his pockets.

"Somehow," he said, "I couldn't imagine Señor Corrijo, just to avenge the theft of a ring, however valuable, doing away with three women, two of whom must have of course been innocent."

"That's how I felt," said Capt. Little; and Detective Pearson nodded too and pursed his lips.

The D.A. looked amused and watched the young detective.

"But the Señor might have known which one was the thief," the Bobcat said, "and he may have even wanted to kill her."

"Well," said the D.A., "did he, or didn't he? And which one was it?"

The Bobcat smiled good-naturedly. "The murder of Mme. Viray," he said, "was a comparatively simple problem. We are pretty sure that Señor Corrijo called at her house—perhaps to question her about the loss of his ring—at about three P.M. on Friday. But we eliminated him as the criminal, because of the testimony of the negro husband of Mme. Viray's cook—a fellow named Sam Jones. He said he had seen Mme. Viray attacked in her living room by a man with a light felt hat, light overcoat and light hair. At about the same time, or probably a little earlier, a man named Dibling, the janitor of a house across the street, saw a person at Mme. Viray's front door. Dibling's description was about the same as that of the negro's, and Dibling said that the person's hair seemed tousled.

"But please note, Mr. Gross," and the Bobcat shook his finger, "that neither of these two witnesses was able to see the person's legs and feet. Dibling's view, I ascertained, was cut off by the buttress of the front steps, and the negro Sam's by the back of the couch in Mme. Viray's living room. Her caller, therefore, might have been a woman."

The District Attorney raised his eyebrows and smiled.

"Miss Magister," said the Bobcat, "sometimes wore rather severe, almost mannish clothes."

The District Attorney brushed some cigar ash off his black trousers. "You think that Miss Magister was a murderess?" he asked.

"Judge for yourself, Mr. Gross," the Bobcat said, a bit sharply. "Miss Magister had a light raglan and a light felt hat, and her hair was light, and being worn rather short with a lot of curls in the back, it might be considered, some way off, as 'tousled.' Anyway, I examined her clothes at the Morgue. Now, get this, Mr. Gross," the Bobcat said. "The negro, Sam Jones, said that at the time of the murder the sun was coming in through the living room windows and shone on the murderer."

We were all watching the Bobcat, now, as if it were a trial in court, and the District Attorney's expression of amused incredulity had given way to a look of a little more interest.

"Sam Jones," said the Bobcat, "said that the murderer's coat showed a faint stain on the shoulder. Now you probably know that stains on garments, such as aniline inks, for instance, are sometimes removed so that they are practically invisible in the shade, but still may show a faint trace in direct sunlight."

"That's right," said Detective Pearson, "and the spots come back after cleaning, sometimes, when the garment is worn."

The Bobcat said, "Miss Magister's raglan was examined by Dan Leary in the shade, probably, and the spot didn't show. This morning, however, by sunlight a spot was faintly visible, on the shoulder of the coat."

Then the Bobcat pulled a chair up near the D.A. and sat down.

"But I found further proof, Mr. Gross, to connect Maude Magister with the crime. I suspected that the glass jar on her kitchen closet shelf had been used at some time for killing butterflies. As they sometimes do this with cyanide of potassium, I guessed that there might be other evidences and I examined a small collection of bottles under the kitchen sink. At the police laboratory one of these bottles showed positive traces of having contained cyanide."

Capt. Little then asked the Bobcat if he would reconstruct the murder as he saw it.

"Well, it was like this, I imagine," said the Bobcat and he got up again and spoke with expressive gestures. "Miss Magister," he said, "has the solution she has made, in a bottle. She has a medicine dropper. All right. She sets out for Mme. Viray's house. She wouldn't be likely to fill the dropper until the last minute, and after that she would probably keep it hidden in the pocket of her raglan while she talked to Mme. Viray. All right. On the front steps of Mme. Viray's house, she quickly fills the dropper with cyanide."

"How would she dispose of the bottle?" asked the D.A.

"Well," said the Bobcat, "there is a short flight of stone steps leading up to the front door of the Viray house. Buttresses on each side of the steps. At the top of each buttress is an ornamental concrete urn, used at some time probably to contain flowers, but now they're partly full of dirt and stuff. In one of these urns I found a small, empty bottle."

"D'you mean to say," said the District Attorney, "that any sane woman would have left evidence of her crime in such an easily discovered spot as that?" He scowled at the young detective.

"No sir," said the Bobcat. "No sane woman. And just there is the significant point, Mr. Gross. Maude Magister's natural sense of precaution was inhibited that day, as I shall explain later. Anyway, the bottle I found was tested and proved not only to have contained cyanide solution, but it also plainly showed Miss Magister's finger-prints. Also the right hand pocket of her raglan, where she had probably concealed the medicine dropper after filling it, also reacted to tests for cyanide."

Capt. Little grinned and said, "That's a pretty strong chain of circumstantial evidence already, Mr. Gross, but Mr. Catfield hasn't yet told you how he clinched it."

The Bobcat sat down on the table again and lighted a cigarette.

"You remember, Mr. Gross," he said, "that at the time of the murder Mme. Viray's small reception room off the front hallway was being papered. There were little scraps of paper all over the floor and some were tracked out into the hall. They had been scraped off the walls after the paper had been soaked, I suppose, and were more or less sticky. Upon examining Miss Magister's shoes at the Morgue I found a tiny scrap of that same wall paper. It had been worn off of the sole, but a bit of it was sticking to the shank of the shoe—in between the sole and the heel, that is, where it doesn't touch the ground."

We all watched the District Attorney. He threw back his head and blew a beautiful smoke ring. Then he asked skeptically, but amused too, why Miss Magister should want to kill this Mme. Viray.

Capt. Little put out his hand. "Why, you see, Mr. Gross, the Magister girl had been working for months, evidently, making up to this Señor Corrijo, in order to get information about the South American plot he was concocting; and I suppose she couldn't bear to have the Viray woman block her game just when she was winning."

The District Attorney was following it closely now, and he wanted to know how they knew that Miss Magister was afraid of the French woman's interference.

"We've got it two ways," said the Bobcat. "A note in French was found in Señor Corrijo's office, and it said that *'M. M. is onto us,'* or words to that effect, and *'Do you think she could be working for the British?'* And this afternoon Miss Magister's husband, Major Godwil, told me that his wife had found out recently that Mme. Viray was working hand-in-hand with Señor Corrijo in his Nazi-Fascist plot in Argentina."

"Yes," said the D.A., doubtfully, leaning back and looking up at the ceiling, "but still, cold-blooded murder like that, you know—the secret service hardly goes in for that sort of thing, does it?"

The Bobcat leaned forward with his hands on his knees. "Reefers, Mr. Gross. That's the answer. Maude Magister smoked reefers."

The D.A. scowled. "Reefers! A lady like Miss Magister?"

"She apparently smoked them innocently," said Capt. Little.

"What d'you mean?" asked the D.A. "How, innocently?"

"Mr. Gross," the Bobcat said, "Maude Magister had been given a lot of marijuana cigarettes, or reefers, on Thursday night by the Señor's chauffeur, Pierre, when he drove her home from that dinner out at Riverdale. Evidently she had no idea what they were, nor how dangerous they were, because she asked the chauffeur what brand they were, and he evaded the question. He told us that after smoking the first one in the car she acted queer. She must have liked them, because on Friday she evidently smoked the other cigarettes he gave her."

"Why evidently?" the D.A. demanded.

"Because there were spots of lipstick red on the butts we found in her living room. The spots were very small, but a microscopic examination showed the pigment to be the same as that on Maude Magister's lips."

"Yeah," said Capt. Little, and he ran his hand back through his coarse white hair, nervously, "Dan Leary, the man I had there on the job, missed that trick."

I was amused, recalling that when I was at the Magister fiat with him, Friday night, the Captain himself had advanced the theory that the butts of the reefers found there had been smoked by some amorous caller who had stabbed her.

"Anyway," said the Bobcat, "smoking those reefers evidently sent her into a mental state where she lost all sense of compunction or responsibility. She acted as she never would have, normally."

Capt. Little turned to the D.A. and said, "You must know the effects of smoking marijuanas, Mr. Gross."

And the Bobcat said, "No, perhaps he doesn't, because nobody can predict what smoking marijuana will do to you. It doesn't have the same reaction on everybody. When you get to 'floating' as the addicts call it, the stuff can make you jump out of the window, or become outrageously happy, or drive you to fiendish cruelty."

"In other words," the Captain put in, "Maude Magister killed Mme. Viray while temporarily insane."

The Bobcat answered thoughtfully, "Insane, yes, perhaps; but it was a special kind of insanity. I mean she probably had no illusions and fantastic, unreal creations and beliefs such as you see in most insane patients—those who believe they are Napoleon Bonaparte, for instance, or that their head is a cannon ball, and that sort of thing, or the pink elephants of delirium tremens. Her mania, I think, took the form of an immense exaggeration of her normal ideas."

I ventured to suggest that this mental aberration might be like the effect of hashish, which is to magnify time and space, so that it seems to take years to drink a glass of water, and an ordinary room seems miles long.

"Something like that," said the Bobcat, "only it was her emotions that were exaggerated, and to a tremendous and irresistible degree."

"Wait a minute," said the District Attorney, "isn't all this a bit academic?"

The Bobcat said quickly, "You seemed to question the probability, Mr. Gross, of 'a lady like Miss Magister,' as you called her, committing such a crime. I am merely trying to establish a probable motive."

"All right, all right," said the D.A., and he looked up at the clock.

"Well," said the Bobcat, "if you realize what was in Miss Magister's mind, all ready to be exaggerated in this way by the effects of marijuana, you can't wonder at her homicidal mania. Here was a woman," he said, "whose brother had been tortured and killed by the Nazis. She had a husband who had suffered only a little less at their hands. She had seen the diabolical savagery of the whole Hitler regime all over Europe. And now she discovers that a beautiful French woman, who, Miss Magister had probably thought, lived only for flattery and pleasure, double-crossing the Free French movement here in the United States and conspiring with Señor Corrijo to overthrow and enslave the South American republics, and also abetting the Señor in blackmailing innocent American girls so as to use them in his fiendish work.

"Now," the Bobcat asked, "wouldn't that inflame the indignation of any ordinary woman of high moral character who had devoted her life to a fight for the world's freedom? But Miss Magister wasn't an ordinary woman, Mr. Gross. She had an inordinate pride and an indomitable determination."

And to illustrate this the Bobcat told how she had proposed marriage to her husband, Major Godwil, and then, to redeem her self-respect had compelled him to propose three times to her before she would marry him.

"And if she were capable of such originality and will when normal," the Bobcat asked, "what wouldn't she be capable of when her indignation and her determination were multiplied in her mind by that damnable drug which is known to cause excesses even in the most timid and harmless victims? She was indubitably driven to a frenzy; and assassination, in her overwrought state, was a perfectly justifiable and logical action. She was a modern Charlotte Corday."

For a moment nobody spoke in the room. I was thinking of that gallant English officer who was sacrificing his honor and his good name for his country. . . . Only that forenoon he had sat there where the District Attorney was now. And Capt. Little echoed my thoughts.

"Well," he said, "I hope I don't have to tell Major Godwil that his wife was a murderess."

The District Attorney, during the Bobcat's little lecture, had sat twisting the ends of his black moustache and looking superior and a bit impatient. Now he said, sententiously,

"Your explanation of Miss Magister's mental state is interesting, Mr. Catfield, and I see your point as to motive. But, after all, it's mere speculation, isn't it? I hadn't heard that you were a psychiatrist," he added condescendingly, "and I doubt if your psychoanalysis would have much legal weight. However, the essential point is that Miss Magister killed Mme. Viray, and I think you've proved that conclusively."

And then he looked up at the clock on my wall and asked the Bobcat with an ironic smile, if he thought that, in this homicidal mania Miss Magister had killed Miss Conley, as well.

The Bobcat asked to be excused a moment, and he went into my bedroom and phoned to somebody, and I heard him say, "Yes, come right up now!" And while I was pouring more drinks my hall doorbell rang.

It was Mrs. Rumsey, and Biddy was mopping her eyes with her handkerchief and wailing, Oh, what were they going to do with her, and she was so frightened, and would she have to go to jail?

The Bobcat pushed a chair at her and explained to us that something I had said to him about Mrs. Rumsey's perfume last night had given him the idea that she might possibly know something about Berta Conley's death. Then too, a chambermaid in the hotel had told him, he said, that Mrs. Rumsey had been crying in her room almost continually ever since the tragedy. He had searched Mrs. Rumsey's room, he said, while she was out, and had found a small vial of perfume that he suspected to be the same *Fleurs de Paradis* which Miss Conley had used. And then he said,

"It was about one o'clock, wasn't it, Mrs. Rumsey, when you went into Miss Conley's room on Friday, the day of her death?"

Biddy dabbed her eyes and looked down at her lap.

"And you had and used a duplicate key to her room, didn't you?"

"Why, you see," Biddy said, in a frightened voice, "when I lived in those rooms, two years ago, I had it made at Macy's because I wanted an extra one without the brass tag on it. But I've never used it since I moved out, really I haven't, not till last Friday."

"You wanted to get some of Miss Conley's perfume, didn't you?" the Bobcat asked.

"Oh, I only wanted to borrow a little, just a teeny, weeny little bit," Biddy said. "It was only a drop, really."

"Never mind the exact amount," Capt. Little growled.

"But really, it was only a drop, honestly it was," Biddy protested. "You see, I was awfully fond of that perfume. They say on the radio it's so exotic and mysterious, you know, and I was going to a bridge party and Bertie wasn't in when I knocked, but I knew she wouldn't mind at all my having just a teeny, weeny little bit, we were just like sisters, you know."

"Never mind that sister business," the Captain barked. "What happened?"

"Well," said Biddy, and she looked to him as if he were incredibly stupid, "I had just put some into a little bottle, just a teeny, weeny bit, you know, just a drop or two, really, and suddenly I heard someone putting a key into her door. Oh, I was so frightened. I thought it was Bertie coming in, and I didn't know what to do."

"Why not?" said Capt. Little, "if you were just like sisters and everything and she wouldn't mind?" And we all smiled.

"Oh, but I was afraid it might be the chambermaid bringing clean towels," said Biddy, "and so I ran into the closet and shut the door. But when I had stayed there a little while I was afraid I'd suffocate, so I opened the door just a little bit— Oh, just a teeny, weeny, little crack and I looked out."

"Well," Detective Pearson whined, "what did you see?"

Biddy turned round and looked at him with her big round eyes. "Why, I didn't see anything," she said, "except Berta's room, of course."

"I'm glad it was still there," said the District Attorney, and he looked at his wrist watch.

"You mean you didn't see anyone there?" said the Bobcat.

"No, I didn't see anyone," Biddy said, "but I heard someone moving in Bertie's bedroom, I don't know what she was doing, and then I heard somebody doing something in the bathroom, and I thought it must be the chambermaid bringing clean towels, you know they do, sometimes—"

"Never mind the towels," said Capt. Little. "Did you see anybody, or didn't you?"

"Why, yes, I did," said Biddy, still looking as if she couldn't understand his stupidity. "I peeked out through that little teeny crack of the door, just like I told you."

Somebody asked her who was there in the room.

"I don't know. I couldn't see anything but her legs and feet."

"Why not?" the Captain fairly shouted at her.

Biddy jumped and looked at him. "Why, because I couldn't."

"See here, Catfield," said the D.A., looking up at my clock again, "I haven't got all night to listen to her. I've got a date. Can't you make this woman talk?"

And with the Bobcat's questioning it came out that Biddy's view from the closet was cut off by the table cover which came down to within a foot or two from the floor, and on the other side of the table Berta Conley's easel cut off Biddy's view of the upper part of the person in the room.

"A woman, was it?" the District Attorney asked.

"Why, yes, of course," Biddy said. "She was at the little table near the door and she was doing something; I don't know what she was doing."

"Was that the table the water bottle was on?" asked the D.A.

"Yes sir, that's where it was," Biddy said. "She seemed to be doing something, this person, whoever she was, and then she went out and shut the door before I could see anything more, and then I knew it wasn't Bertie, probably, but I was awfully frightened and I ran out as fast as I could."

"Then you couldn't identify the woman?" Capt. Little asked.

"You mean tell who she was?" Biddy asked, soberly. "No. No sir, but I know she couldn't have been a chambermaid," Biddy said, "on account of her shoes and stockings."

The Captain asked her what the stockings were like.

"Why, very sheer black mesh stockings, they were, and almost nobody wears black stockings nowadays, you know. They were awfully fine silk and the meshes were so big you saw the skin right through, like netting, and I don't see how she could ever have got them on without tearing them."

Capt. Little asked what kind of shoes the mysterious visitor wore.

"Oh, they were black and white," Biddy said, "that woven straw, you know, and patent leather, they were awfully expensive shoes."

Then Biddy turned to the handsome Bobcat and her eyes streamed again. "Oh, Mr. Catfield, if I had only known what that woman was doing—putting that poison in that water bottle. Think of it! I might have saved dear Bertie's life!" and Biddy began to weep so sentimentally that the Bobcat asked me to take her out.

The District Attorney was saying, when I got back into the room, "But how do you know this woman wasn't lying? She had a chance to put the cyanide in the bottle herself, didn't she?"

"She had a chance," said Capt. Little, "but she didn't have a motive, I should say."

"And a woman who'd sneak in like that," drawled Detective Pearson, "just for a teeny, weeny little drop of perfume, would hardly be the type to go in for poisoning, would she?"

The Bobcat said, "The key to the Conley murder, Mr. Gross, is the Señor's ruby ring. Berta, of course, might have stolen it. It seems incompatible, though, with her character as described by her friends."

"Of course the ring was planted in her room," said Capt. Little, "by someone who wanted her to be accused of having stolen it."

"It was planted there," said the Bobcat, "by the person who poisoned the water. The poisoner knew that the room would be searched by the police after her death. Now, we found that on Friday afternoon at about five o'clock, Berta Conley telephoned to Señor Corrijo. He was out. That led me to suspect that after he had called on her here at the Imperial at two o'clock, she may have discovered the ring in her room somewhere and wished to tell him about it and return it. When she couldn't get him on the phone she hid the ring for safe keeping in her shoe. She was hurrying to get away, and she intended to return the ring as soon as she was safe."

"Is all this merely your opinion?" the D.A. asked.

"My evidence, Mr. Gross, I intend to submit before I have finished," said the Bobcat.

The D.A. asked what was the motive was for the poisoning.

"Jealousy," said the Bobcat. "All three women were, in a way, rivals for Señor Corrijo's favor, each, however, for a different reason. Only one of them was really in love with him, but Berta Conley was getting along altogether too well with him. We have considerable evidence as to that. Here's one bit."

The Bobcat took out his notebook again. "In a letter I read from, a little while ago—found in Señor Corrijo's office, at his house, you remember—there was one line I didn't read. It said, *Be careful of that saucy little Yankee, too. She's sharp. Can't you get rid of her somehow?'* And that letter, Mr. Gross, was signed 'Hélène.' So that's where the shoes and stockings Mrs. Rumsey saw on that person in Berta's room walk into the picture. Mrs. Rumsey described perfectly those worn that Friday by Hélène Viray."

"Yes," said the D.A., "but as evidence all you seem to have is the word of a self-confessed petty thief."

"I beg pardon," said the Bobcat, "Berta Conley's lost key to her room was found in Mme. Viray's bag."

The D.A. raised his black eyebrows. "How did Mme. Viray get that key?"

"She must have got it out at Corrijo's after the dinner on Thursday evening." was the Bobcat's answer.

"That's possible," I said, "she had several opportunities to pick up Berta's bag when Berta wasn't holding it—in the dark room while we were looking at the movies, or while we were looking at the dolls, or up in the ladies' room where they left their wraps. It was a small blue silk evening bag and it wouldn't take but a moment to open it and take out the key."

"Mr. Gross," said the Bobcat, "my theory is that Mme. Viray became frightened at what she'd done—stealing that ring, I mean—because of the Señor's anger and his threat, and she decided then to plant the ring in Berta Conley's room and poison her. In that way she'd get rid of the ring and a rival at the same time. But whatever her exact motive was we have absolute proof of her guilt. On the bottle of cyanide Berta Conley had in her bathroom closet we found Mme. Viray's finger-prints."

Mr. Gross turned to Capt. Little with a slight sneering smile, and asked him why he hadn't discovered Mme. Viray's guilt in his investigation.

The Bobcat made a friendly gesture to his Chief and said, "Of course if Capt. Little had found out about the prints he could have broken the case just as well as I did, Mr. Gross. But I was ahead of him."

"Yes," said Little, somewhat huffed, "I didn't get that report on the prints till Saturday noon, you see, because I was tied up with the murder out at Riverdale."

"And that's why I hustled all night to get ahead of him," the Bobcat laughed, "and I certainly did some jumping around."

I was foolish enough to say that it didn't seem possible that so exquisite a woman, so cultured as Mme. Viray, could commit so vile a crime. And you should have heard the way the D.A. and the two older detectives laughed at me. Capt. Little told me that the girl with the sweetest face and most innocent air he had ever seen had been convicted of working the badger game and Detective Pearson boasted of having known plenty of female crooks and murderesses lovely enough to have got into the Ziegfeld Follies.

The D.A. sat tapping the fingertips of one hand against those of the other. "Very pretty pattern for the murders, so far," he said. "Very pretty. A kills B, and B kills C. Now you're going to prove that C killed A, I suppose. Then let's hear who killed Miss Magister."

The Bobcat gave a little laugh. He looked handsome and he looked subtle. He took an envelope from his pocket and emptied the contents into his opened palm. Then he showed his hand to the D.A. like a stage magician preparing for his best trick.

"These little glass stones, Mr. Gross," he said, "were found on the floor of Miss Magister's living room after her death. She was wearing one of these costume jewelry clips; and as some stones were missing it was taken for granted by Detective Dan Leary, I suppose, that these stones on the floor were all scraped out of Miss Magister's clip during the struggle she had. Will you kindly count them, Mr. Gross?"

"There are ten," said Mr. Gross.

The Bobcat took another package from his pocket, opened it, and handed it to the D.A., telling him that it was the clip Miss Magister was wearing when she was killed.

"You will notice," said the Bobcat, "that some stones are missing. Will you please count the holes where they were?"

"Only nine," said Mr. Gross. "Then the extra stone must have come from some other clip."

"And also another stone which I found in the crack under the baseboard in Miss Magister's room where she was killed," the Bobcat said. "And here it is," he said, and he took it out of another envelope. "You will see, also, that this stone and one of the others are both too large, anyway, to fit into Miss Magister's clip."

The D.A. tried to fit them into the empty sockets and saw for himself that they wouldn't go. And he wanted to know where the clip was that they did fit into.

The Bobcat took a last package from his pocket, opened it and showed us a clip of a quite different pattern. Three stones were missing, but the D.A. found that the two large stones fitted the empty sockets.

"Well, where did you find this clip?" the D.A. asked.

"I found it," said the Bobcat, "amongst the clothing and other effects in the airplane grip which Miss Berta Conley had packed before her intended escape. And it proves beyond a doubt that she was in Miss Magister's room at the time of the murder. The one missing stone must have dropped from her clip somewhere else."

I couldn't help exclaiming, "But Berta Conley simply *couldn't* have killed Maude Magister! It's inconceivable, from what I knew of her."

Pearson drawled, "You knew her for almost four days, didn't you, Mr. Gilbert?"

"I haven't yet accused anyone of murdering Maude Magister, Mr. Gilbert," said the Bobcat. "I'm merely describing the evidence I've found. And I think you can guess why Berta would be calling on Maude Magister that day, Mr. Gilbert?"

"You mean to get that caricature Berta had made of Señor Corrijo?" I asked. "Yes, I remember she told me she'd have to get it back somehow. Berta said she was afraid Maude might show it to Señor Corrijo and get her in bad."

"And besides," said the Bobcat, "Berta also probably wanted to warn Maude, her friend, that the Señor was on the rampage."

"Then why the devil were two women of that type fighting?" the D.A. asked.

"You've forgotten the reefers again, Mr. Gross," said the Bobcat. "That fight must have occurred around four o'clock in the afternoon. Maude Magister, you must remember, had already been rendered insane enough by the marijuana cigarettes to murder Mme. Viray. She was undoubtedly still under that influence and in that abnormal state she was evidently infuriated by Berta Conley's attempt to secure the caricature of the Señor. There was a sharp knife on her table which she had for a paper cutter. She must have attacked Berta."

It gave me a feeling of sickness. Berta Conley, so pretty, so gay . . . Maude Magister, cold and aristocratic . . . in so disgraceful, so monstrous a scene. I managed to say,

"Then you think Berta murdered her?"

The Bobcat said, "Did you ever see a fight with a knife?"

"Only in the movies," I said.

"Well, they're usually authentic in details," said the Bobcat. "Men who fight with knives in earnest don't hold them the way they do in old fashioned pictures or in melodrama or the opera. They hold them with the thumb to the haft of the knife as you'd hold a sword. There's no drawing back to stab, they simply push in the point. But if an insensate woman snatched up a knife to attack another, it's ten to one that she'd grab it just as she'd grab an ice pick, and stab downward. That's probably the way Maude Magister held her knife."

"Yes," the District Attorney interrupted, impatiently, "but that's all speculation, isn't it? You can't build a case on a theory alone, you know."

The Bobcat smiled. "How about a confession then, Mr. Gross? Would that satisfy you?"

"A confession from the killer—from Berta Conley?" the D.A. said, and he was frowning. "What are you talking about, Catfield?"

Capt. Little winked at Detective Pearson, but I was mystified.

"I'm talking," said the Bobcat, "about the dumbwaiter in the Conley rooms here, just next door. When the hotel took over this building, which was an apartment house, you know, the dumbwaiters in the different apartments were put out of commission and the doors closed. Some of the dumbwaiter doors though will still open. Sergeant Pearson here did a pretty good job when he searched the Conley suite, but he overlooked one thing."

Pearson's face was getting red. "Yes," he whined, "I saw that wire all right, it was fastened to a nail down inside the dumbwaiter shaft pretty far down, and the wire hung down way out of sight, and it looked just like the end of some disused electric wire that had been connected with the bells on the different floors. If I'd only pulled it up—"

"Yes, if you only had," laughed the Bobcat, "you'd have found that it was new wire. It was the same kind of blue-and-white insulated wire that Miss Conley used to make those little animals and men with. You saw them in her room, Mr. Gilbert. And you all know that Berta Conley used a dictaphone for her fashion articles."

"Go on!" said Mr. Gross. He seemed to have forgotten his social engagement.

"Well, I pulled up that wire, that's all," the Bobcat said quietly, "and it had a dictaphone record fastened to the end of it. Berta must have dictated her confession to the recording machine and then attached it to a long wire and hung it down inside the disused dumbwaiter shaft. She probably drove a nail down as low as she could reach to fasten the end of the wire to. Would you like to hear that record played, Mr. Gross? It isn't a very humorous record."

And the Bobcat left us and walked down the hall and out the door. The D.A. turned to Capt. Little.

"D'you mean to tell me," he said, "that a girl who had just killed her friend, stabbed her to death after a fight, and was hurrying to escape, would stop and dictate her confession and hide it as elaborately as he says? It's fantastic."

"Mr. Gross," I said, "I think I can explain it, perhaps. I was the last one to see Berta Conley alive, you know, only an hour or so before her death. She was half crazy with fear and horror. But that girl had a passion for the truth, Mr. Gross. I know by what her sister Alice said that if she had even committed murder she would have to confess it sooner or later. No doubt she was afraid to give herself up and stand trial; that's why she was running away; yet she must have wanted the truth to come out.

"But you must realize too, Mr. Gross," I said, "that the poor girl was hysterically afraid of being killed. She had been all worked up by the prophecy of that gypsy at the Corrijo dinner. He said, you know, that all three of those women there would die within the week. When I last saw her I told her that Mme. Viray had been killed. That was the first one. She knew that Maude Magister had been killed because she saw her die. That was the second one. Berta then would be the third of that trio and she was afraid that her turn would come at any moment. It looks as if she didn't dare to wait and send her letter of confession when she had got away to some safe place. She was probably afraid that she might be killed before she'd have a chance to write it. So she made the record and hid it where it could be found after she had got away."

The Bobcat came back with a black rubber cylinder and two cops were with him, carrying the dictaphone on its stand.

And while we sat in the room, amazed and stirred, we heard the voice of Berta Conley brought back to life. It was a suffering, distraught voice that brought tears to my eyes. And this is what we heard:

"I've got to get away. I'm afraid they'll arrest me for murder. I'm going to leave this record here and when I'm away safe somewhere I'll write to the police and tell them where to find it. I've got to tell. I must! I don't want anyone else to be accused. Señor Corrijo came to my room and he was awful and he searched all my things for his ring. But I never stole it! I went to Maude's flat to warn her about him, and I wanted to get that caricature too. I was afraid it would make him still more furious at me if he ever saw it. Maude was in an awful state. I thought she was drunk, or insane or something. She was awful. She wouldn't listen to me. She was awful. She kept screaming, 'I finished that Helêne! I finished that cat, all right! She won't spoil all my work!' Then I saw my caricature on the table. I tried to get it. I picked it up. Maude swore at me. She snatched up the knife and she screamed that she'd kill me. She tried to stab me, and I was frightened. It's the truth! I swear to god it's the truth. I was awfully frightened. I ran behind the table. The table tipped over. She came at me and I caught her wrist so she couldn't use the knife. I was afraid she'd kill me. We fought all over the room. It was awful. I tried to run away but I couldn't get away from her. I was awfully frightened. Finally while we were struggling together I was trying to push her away and she slipped on the rug. I fell onto her. She was holding the knife. I didn't have the knife. I was holding her wrist so she couldn't stab me. When she slipped we both fell over together. We fell over an armchair. I was on top of her. We fell over so hard that the knife stuck into her and she screamed. It stabbed right into her breast. But she was holding the knife. I wasn't holding it. They'll think I murdered her, but I didn't. I didn't, at all. I wasn't holding the knife. She stabbed herself. Now I'm afraid I'll be the next one to be killed. I'm the third one. Someone put the ring into my empty suit case. I found it. But I never stole that ring. I'm afraid. I'm afraid I'll be the third one. I'm going to run away."

And then there was a harsh scraping sound, and that was all.

There was a moment's silence, and it seemed as if Berta's agonized voice was still in the room magnetizing us. Then there were a few muttered exclamations and the men in my room rose from their chairs, the District Attorney and the three detectives. The D.A. went over and shook the Bobcat's hand.

But I couldn't speak. I was thinking, "She didn't murder her. Berta was innocent."

To those men it was just another homicide case, I suppose. Very interesting. Very clever work, they said. I couldn't speak. I thought, poor Berta!

The District Attorney put on his silk hat and glanced into the mirror. "Well," he said, "what are you up to next, Mr. Bobcat?"

"I think I'll run over to the Bellevue Hospital," said the Bobcat, "and see how that little dancer's getting along."

That night, after they had all gone, I sat for a long time thinking it over. . . . Then I got up and went to my bedroom closet and brought out the three wax dolls I had taken home from the Doll Show four days ago. It seemed ages ago. I took them out of their boxes and I laid them on the table of my living room, before packing them up to send to my little niece in California. . . . I looked at them. . . .

The beautiful French doll with the black hair, I would tell her, was named Hélène.

The name of the lovely English blonde doll was Maude.

And the pretty American doll with the soft, light brown hair, her name was Berta.

I put them into their boxes, and they were sent away. I never saw them again.

"Little ladies," Berta had called them.

Ladies in Boxes. . . .

About the Author

Gelett Burgess (1866-1951)

Burgess was best known for his nonsense verses (including 'The Purple Cow') and children's books, but he also wrote the occasional mystery story. *The Master of Mysteries* (1912), for example, featured Astro, a fake psychic who solved crimes through surreptitious investigation.

Death at
Windward Hill

Murder in the
French Room

HELEN JOAN HULTMAN

SALLY WOOD

MURDER
OF A
NOVELIST

DEATH
IN LORD
BYRON'S
ROOM

Also Available

CoachwhipBooks.com (print)
Coachwhip.com (epub)

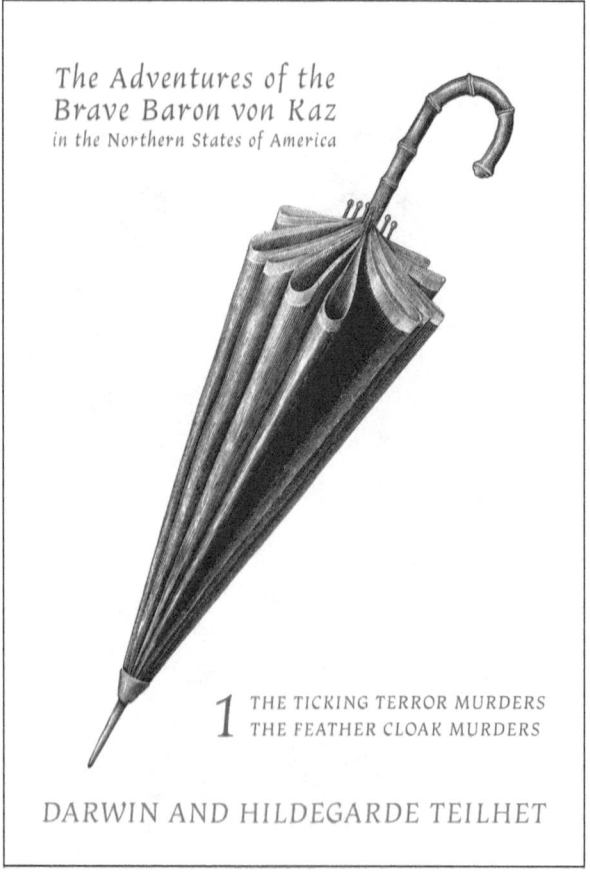

The Adventures of the
Brave Baron von Kaz
in the Northern States of America

1 THE TICKING TERROR MURDERS
THE FEATHER CLOAK MURDERS

DARWIN AND HILDEGARDE TEILHET

Also Available

CoachwhipBooks.com (print)
Coachwhip.com (epub)

LOUIS F. BOOTH

THE BANK VAULT MYSTERY
BROKERS' END

ALSO AVAILABLE

CoachwhipBooks.com (print)
Coachwhip.com (epub)

THE SERGEANT HARTY MYSTERIES

JOEL Y. DANE

MURDER CUM LAUDE

1

THE CABANA MURDERS